FAKING LOVE
A KIMBELL TEXAS SWEET ROMANCE
BOOK THREE

ANGEL S. VANE

BONZAIMOON BOOKS

BONZAI
MOON

BonzaiMoon Books LLC
Houston, Texas
www.bonzaimoonbooks.com

CHAPTER 1

ILEY

I RUB A SWEATING PALM DOWN MY FACE AND CHECK MY watch.

Again.

There's still plenty of time.

I don't need to panic.

The dense forest-lined streets of the county road pass by in a blur as I push my truck past seventy, gripping the steering wheel tighter and navigating a series of turns I could make with my eyes closed.

There's no point in rehearsing what I plan to say at the most important meeting of my life—an interview with Heather Grimley, love guru and one of the top social media influencers with over fifty million followers on all her platforms combined. It's impossible to predict what Heather will want to know as she decides on the futuristic dating app to feature on her vlog for Valentine's Day next year.

It's no mystery why I made her short list.

What started as a joke in the fire station between me and my fellow firefighters—Darren Manning, Ronan O'Reilly, Luke Diamond, and Nate Bell—has blossomed into a locally popular but not yet profitable dating app named Ladies Love Country Boys.

The premise was simple.

Help country boys expand their dating pool outside of their small towns. Back then, we were Kimbell's most eligible bachelors and had dated most of the women in our hometown of 3,089 people.

I chuckle under my breath.

Not much has changed in the years since.

We're still the town's most eligible bachelors, minus Ronan, who got taken off the market when he fell in love with a hot fitness trainer from Round Rock. Some kind of way, I'm the only one who has gotten the reputation of being a playboy, which, if you ask me, is insulting. A playboy insinuates that I'm heartless, cold, and uncaring, using women like tissues and then tossing them out like yesterday's cold, gnawed-on, gristly chicken fried steak.

That's not me.

Not by a long-shot.

I date a lot because I find women to be the most fascinating creatures on the planet. Each one is beautiful and impressive in unique ways. Ways I can't help but want to discover. If I find real love in the process, then it's a win-win.

Except, I haven't. Not even somewhat close. Not by a long shot.

That brings me to the second reason I pulled the trigger on making the joke a reality—the secret to true love. I have a long list of ex-girlfriends who believed I was their soulmate while I struggled to feel anything that deep in return.

How could they be so sure when I wasn't?

Since my intuition couldn't be trusted, I needed a more objective way of figuring out when I'd found the woman for me.

Thus, my side hustle was born.

I used my knack for coding and computer programming to create an artificial intelligence algorithm that scoured all the research on true love. In a matter of months, the program figured out what would've taken me years to discern—the key to finding your soulmate. A set of consistent characteristics identified from the thousands of research papers written on the subject over the past fifty years emerged. This became my proprietary and patented method for matching daters on the app.

The sound of tires screeching roars in my ears as I take a right turn onto a secluded, tree-lined, unmarked road. Another quick glance at my watch, and I know I'm cutting it close. Too close. Heather Grimley is demanding and exacting, with high expectations because of the high rewards any mention by her will bring.

Joining our video conference late would be a sign of disrespect and no doubt get my dating app crossed off her list. I flatten the gas pedal and barrel toward the guard shack, decorated with a three-foot wide wreath adorned with bright bulbs, glittery ribbon, and multi-color twinkling lights.

Luckily, the guard recognizes my truck and opens the gate with a slight nod. In minutes, I blaze past the mile entrance to the estate and burn rubber along the curved driveway. I bring my pickup to a stop in front of the ten-thousand square foot, massive Victorian-style mansion constructed of light stucco and hill country limestone.

Jumping out, I slam the door and race up the steps, turning the knobs to push open the dark cherry double doors that are always unlocked. The house is quiet as I rush along the maze of hallways.

Darren's voice bellows as I slow my steps and approach the open doors of the media room. My best friend and former NFL defensive superstar doesn't miss a beat. While live streaming on ESPN, providing analyst commentary on the upcoming playoffs, he deftly taps his watch at me.

As if I don't realize how close I am to dialing in late to the video conference with Heather. I can't remember the last time I was this nervous to talk to a woman if I ever have been. But I never had this much riding on a conversation. One call can catapult me into the stratosphere. Botching it isn't an option.

I side-step into the room, sticking close to the wall, careful not to video-bomb Darren on his feed for Sportscenter. I make my way into a smaller enclave turret equipped for videoconferencing. Shutting the door behind me, I take a deep breath and glance at the clock.

Two minutes to spare.

I ease into the Italian leather chair. The scenic backdrop of towering pine and oak trees peeks through five narrow windows along the curved wall. White sparkling lights adorn the trunks of the trees, and multi-colored lights hang along the branches. I'm only half way done helping Darren decorate his monstrosity of a house for the holidays. You'd think the guy would hire a service to do the work, but I get tricked into helping him DIY it every year.

Fumbling for my phone, I access the email and type in the video conference number. An eighty-inch screen descends from the ceiling. A red light glows from the webcam tucked into the recess of the wall.

My nerves are fried. My knee bounces uncontrollably underneath the desk as I force myself to take deep breaths. I can do this.

Heather Grimley's face appears on the screen. Pecan-colored chin-length hair frames a narrow face dotted with freckles. Her eyes are dark and shrewd despite her pleasant, plastered smile. She's wearing an ugly Christmas sweater about two sizes too small that stretch across her ample chest.

"Mr. Alexander, it's a pleasure to meet you," Heather says, widening her smile without showing any teeth.

"Please call me Wiley," I say, then run a hand through my hair, disguising my attempt to wipe the sweat beading along my hairline. "How are you, Ms. Grimley?"

"Now, it's my turn." Heather's eyes dance. "Call me, Heather."

"Okay," I say, then lick my lips. "Heather."

"You should have given me some warning. In all my team's research on your dating app, they never mentioned how sexy the app's creator was. Definitely elevates you on my list. Whenever I can put intelligent eye candy on display, I get an enormous boost in views and likes." Her gaze is more like a clinical assessment than a woman looking at a man she finds attractive. I don't mind. I'm not being cocky when I say I'm used to it.

"Happy to oblige. I'm willing to do anything to convince you to pick the Ladies Love Country Boys app for your feature."

Heather raises an eyebrow, then flicks a hand through her hair. "Now that's the type of commitment I love to hear. Let's get to it, shall we?"

"Yes, ma'am."

Over the next thirty minutes, Heather batters me with various questions ranging from the mission statement of my business, target audience, and market research to specific numbers on demographics, subscription volumes, profitability, and the AI that drives the entire app.

My underarms are a pool of sweat by the time she finishes.

"Very good, Mr. Alexander," Heather says. "Normally, I'd consult with my team first, but I'm very confident in allowing you to proceed to the next phase of our selection process."

I'm surprised. I seemed to have passed the test.

The first one, at least.

"What's the next phase?"

"Technical evaluation," Heather says.

"Technical evaluation," I repeat, rising in my chair. "What would that involve?"

"The focus of my Valentine's Day vlog is to highlight the best dating app that uses the most cutting edge technology to give daters a leg up on finding the loves of their lives. I can't showcase an app that is no different from the typical "swipe right" dating apps on the market. But I'm not a techie. So, I hired a team of artificial intelligence experts to evaluate each app and rate them based on the level of reliance on futuristic technologies. How comfortable are you that your app will pass that test?" She asks with a slight challenge in her tone.

Makes sense that she'd want to weed out any scammers.

"Very comfortable. My app is based on over fifty years of research on love and relationships gathered through data mining. I coded a program that combined deep learning and predictive analytics to be the foundation of how the app matches the daters."

"And that's the love match score, which is reflected as a percentage?"

"That's right."

"My notes show you have a near one hundred percent success rate of couples that received higher than a ninety percent love match score."

"Early on, I noticed many of those matches unsubscribing from the app. So, I automated an exit survey to reach out to those people to find out why. Turns out, they left the app because they had found their love match. Most were in happy relationships, either married or headed there."

Heather leans back in her chair, arms crossed over her chest. I can read the skepticism in her eyes as she goes quiet for a long moment.

"Surveys can be faked, Wiley. Plus, people lie. Maybe they didn't want to hurt your feelings, so they pretended the reason was that they'd found love. Why should I trust those results?" Heather's eyes narrow as she waits for me to respond.

I rub my sweating palms against my jeans.

I need to come up with a compelling comeback.

Quick.

But my mind is blank.

She's not wrong.

I haven't done anything to validate the accuracy of the exit survey responses. Maybe I should have. But there hasn't been time between my job as a fire fighter and all my efforts to get the app to generate more money.

I feign thoughtful contemplation of her question as I stare up at the ceiling for some kind of divine inspiration. Something to convince her not to cross me off her list right now.

A thin sheen of sweat covers my entire body. It feels like the room is crumbling around me. My heart pounds wildly as the kernel of an idea takes shape. One that is perfectly designed to get me out of this predicament but full of disaster if I can't pull it off in the long run. I don't have any other choice.

Heather won't wait much longer for an answer.

"You shouldn't," I say, sounding calm and confident. "You should talk to people who've found love on my dating app, and the best place to start is … with me."

"With you?" Heather's voice hits a soprano note.

"I created the app to find the love of *my* life," I say, the lie tumbling from my lips with ease. "The fact that others are also seeing success is the cherry on top."

Heather's eyebrows raise, and her eyes come alive with excitement. "You used the app?"

"That's right."

"And it worked for you?" Heather presses.

My mouth goes dry. "Like a charm."

"You found the love of your life?" Heather asks, leaning closer to the camera.

"Not only did I find her," I say, unwilling to let her revived interest in my app die, and add, "I asked her to marry me."

Heather gasps.

I give her a sexy grin and ignore the burning in my gut. "I'd be honored to introduce you to my fiancée. We are one of the many couples connected through my dating app, and the reason I know my app is the real deal."

Heather clasps her hands. "Now, this is the story my followers will go crazy about. A devastatingly handsome man in search of love takes matters into his own hands by creating an AI-based dating app to find his one true love."

I inhale a sharp breath. "Yeah, that's right."

"I still need to get my tech guys to confirm that the app uses artificial intelligence, but this story is too good to pass up," Heather says, beaming with another wide smile that still doesn't show her teeth, which I find disconcerting. "Wiley, this feature is yours."

"Heather, I can't thank you enough."

"Don't thank me yet. I want to meet you and your fiancée in person. I can come to Tomball the third week of December?"

"Kimbell," I say, then clear my throat. "Tomball is a few dozen miles east of here."

Heather consults her notes as if to verify where I know I live.

"Right. Okay, I see it here. Kimbell, Texas. Can you make the 20th work?"

"Absolutely. And we can't wait to meet you," I say, then watch as the video conference ends. The screen goes black, and I face plant onto the desk.

I jump as Darren's words boom through the room. "You've screwed up now."

"Tell me about it," I mutter.

CHAPTER 2

Z^{AIRE}

Z AIRE

~

"NO! WAIT, YOU CAN'T GO IN THERE."

I hear my assistant Simona Ivanov's frantic cries as Mrs. Williamson bursts through the door to my office. Her pale face is flushed a bright pink as she unwraps the scarf around her neck and stops in front of my desk. Her flaming red hair is twisted into a tight bun behind her head.

"Is she always this rude?" LaQuandelier "Quan" Payne, my hairdresser, leans down to whisper in my ear. Every Monday, Quan shows up at the Kincaid Real Estate offices to wash and style my hair for the week. It's our regular session to glam me up while giving us a chance to catch up on the latest town gossip.

I shush her, then turn my attention to Mrs. Williamson and a spooked Simona standing a few feet behind her.

"It's okay, Simona. Will you get Mrs. Williamson a beverage?"

There's nothing she could've done to stop the Kimbell Planner of Community Events from barging in.

Simona takes a deep breath, then says, "Of course," as she scampers out of the room.

"To what do I owe the pleasure, Mrs. Williamson?" I wonder how much my bank account will take a hit from this latest visit. The woman is notorious for her aggressive tactics to secure funding for all the events she plans in Kimbell, especially since the town's activities are well beyond the means of the city coffers.

The woman sits in the chair across from my desk and gives me the once over. "Have I told you that your new look is beautiful?" Mrs. Williamson says, giving me a bright smile. She's trying to butter me up.

"Told you!" Quan says. "After five years of me telling you the truth and nothing but, you'd think you'd listen by now. This hair style is fire!" Quan winks then turns her attention back to my hair.

She's not wrong.

I stare at her through the five-foot floor mirror on wheels that Quan never leaves home without. One second, Quan is lifting her hands like a triumphant prized fighter. The next, she's shimmying, then twerking, before placing her hands on her curvaceous hips. Quan is petite and plump, with three-inch metallic gold fake nails accented with faux diamond studs, huge gold hoop earrings in each of the three holes of her ears, and a honey brown, twenty-four-inch human hair weave sewn into her head. She could've walked straight off the set of one of those urban movies focused around a black-owned beauty salon.

We couldn't be more different, but in some twist of reality, Quan was the friend I needed when I needed one the most. Five years ago, I slumped down in her salon chair and demanded that she cut off my shoulder-length hair.

Quan didn't flinch.

And she didn't try to talk me out of it.

She simply asked, "Chop cut or fade?"

I went with the fade and never looked back.

Until she convinced me a few months ago to grow my hair. I'm now rocking a TWA. That's a teeny, weeny afro, on which Quan is executing surgical precision to separate and define tiny sections of the curls until they look like glossy, little loops all over my head. When I'm in the mood, I let Quan blow out my curls and flat-iron them into a cute pixie cut. But I'm not in the mood to deal with my hair this week. I'm going for low maintenance.

I give Mrs. Williamson a smile. "That's very kind of you to say. Thank you."

"Well, I can see you're busy, so I won't take up too much of your time," Mrs. Williamson begins. "I've heard you'll be out of town for most of the holiday season in Paris at your sister Persia's wedding."

The muscles in my neck constrict as I force a pleasant look on my face. "Yes, that's right."

"So, you won't be in town for the annual Jingle Bell Festival or the Kimbell Caroling on Christmas Night?" Mrs. Williamson asks, concern creeping into her voice.

"Not this year. I'll fly out to Paris on December 20 and won't be back until the New Year. Persia insisted on having a Christmas Day wedding."

Quan interrupts, "Mrs. Dub, why are you so worried about where Zaire's going to be for the holidays?"

Mrs. Williamson blanches, then eases out of her leather coat. "Well, all of our traditional holiday events depend on the generous donations of local businesses."

"Not to worry, Mrs. Williamson. As usual, Kincaid Real Estate and Kincaid Construction will fund a third of the budget for each. And I was planning on talking to you about supplying furniture for the Hospital's Santa Claus Day in Bell Park from my new venture, Kincaid Furnishings." I hope that this will satisfy Mrs. Williamson.

And it does.

Her face lights up brighter than the eight-foot Christmas tree in the corner of my office.

"I'm always so impressed with you! I should have known you'd ensure everything was taken care of before you left town," Mrs. Williamson says. "You remind me so much of our founding mother, Kimberly Bell. You have an amazing business mind combined with such a generous, giving heart. It's such a shame what happened to you all those years ago. You, more than anyone, deserve to find a good man who'll love you to pieces."

Pinching the bridge of my nose, I cringe and resist the urge to roll my eyes. If I was a man, no conversation about my professional success would ever end with an indictment of my relationship status or lack there of. But as a woman, it's like all my accomplishments are lessened because I haven't achieved what others believe is the ultimate goal— having a good man on my arm.

It's ridiculous, and I'm beyond sick of it.

"But she has one." Simona beams as she hands Mrs. Williamson a cup of steaming cinnamon hot chocolate. "She's just not flaunting him around town."

Quan shoves my arm. I don't need to look at her to feel the hot sear of her glare. Simona sits next to Mrs. Williamson, oblivious that she's blatantly forgotten that I'd sworn her to secrecy about my mystery man.

"He surprised her with a trip to St. Barts last week for Thanksgiving," Simona continues.

"Why didn't you tell me you had a new bae?" Quan glares at me.

I stifle a scream, thinking of my Thanksgiving spent on the beach … alone.

My family agreed to let me skip out on the family gathering in Atlanta at my sister Sydney's home when I told them I was celebrating the holidays with the new man in my life. I had whiplash from how quickly their tunes changed.

Simona overheard my conversation and added her own elation for my new relationship.

Did I mention that this new relationship is fake?

The one with an imaginary man that doesn't exist.

It was a move made in desperation. A Hail Mary attempt to thwart another awkward matchmaking attempt by my family. A big fat fraud that I made up on the spot when I realized there was no way I could suffer through Thanksgiving dinner with them pestering me about moving on and finding a new man to love.

I never meant for anyone else to know about my little white lie. Not Simona and not Quan, who can't keep a secret to save her own life.

I take a deep breath, then say, "Well, it's new—"

Simona interrupts, "I think keeping him a secret for a while is good. We can meet him when Zaire is comfortable that he's a keeper. After what happened five years ago, can you blame her?"

"Absolutely not," Mrs. Williamson nods in agreement, a look of pity etched across her face. "Our founding mother, Kimberly Bell, was in a similar situation."

"She was?" Quan asks, seeming interested in the history and folklore of Kimbell for the first time.

"It's rumored that after spending five years alone after her husband's untimely death, Kimberly Bell embarked on an elicit, secret affair with the town gigolo. It was well known that he was head over heels in love with her, but because of the difference in their statuses, she could never marry him. Still, all accounts are consistent that he made her very happy and was a wonderful companion in her life."

"Is your secret man someone from Kimbell?" Quan prods.

Simona responds before I can get any words out of my mouth. "She refuses to say, although I'm pretty sure Harlow-Rose knows who he is."

As a matter of fact, my bestie is the only person who knows that my mystery man is imaginary.

"Well, there's nothing wrong with keeping your relationship away from prying eyes for a while," Mrs. Williamson blows on the liquid in her mug, then takes large gulping sips of the cocoa.

"I hate to burst your bubble, but you won't be able to keep him a secret for much longer. I'm sure your family will expect him to be on your arm at Persia's wedding in a few weeks." Quan whips the satin cape from my neck with magician-like flair.

And with those fateful words, my entire world implodes.

What have I done?

Of course, she's right.

There's no way I can show up at the wedding without this fake boyfriend.

Why didn't I think this through?

A headache claws at the edges of my head as I fight panic.

What am I going to do?

There's a knock on the door, yanking me out of my inward spiral of doom.

I glance up to see Troy Renault, my brother-in-law twice removed, meaning the brother of Sydney's husband and Chief Operating Officer of Kincaid Furnishings, lean inside.

Troy's sultry, deep baritone fills the air. "Zaire, I need to talk to you ... alone."

CHAPTER 3

W ILEY

"HAVE YOU LOST YOUR MIND?" DARREN ASKS, GRIPPING ME by the neck and lifting me like a rag doll from the leather chair. I wiggle from his grasp and stalk over toward the windows.

A nervous laugh slips through my lips as the warm rays of the winter sun battle to soothe the panic clawing at my muscles. "Relax. I have everything under control," I say.

Lies followed by more lies.

Darren scowls, skepticism laced in the glare he's giving me.

He sees through my fake confidence.

"So, you know how you'll conjure up a fiancée in three weeks to introduce to that love guru?" Darren leans against the edge of the curved mahogany desk.

"Not yet …" I frown, then swing a fist into the air as the gravity of my situation hits me like an avalanche.

"What did I tell you yesterday about these so-called social media influencers?" Darren sits on top of the desk. "Didn't I warn you how they're always trying to find the most salacious angle to a story? It's always your best move to stick to the truth and nothing but the truth. Even if you do that, there's still the chance that your words could be twisted and used against you. Manipulated into a narrative you can't control and must scramble to change."

"I was desperate. Heather wasn't buying that my app was a success based on the exit surveys. She brought up some good weaknesses in relying on them. I needed something bigger to convince her." The words tumble from my mouth as I try to defend what I've done. "And it worked. I got the feature."

"But what story is that going to be?" Darren challenges. "Will she highlight the success of your dating app? Or will she dig deeper and realize she's sitting on an explosive story that could generate millions of hits? You know the one about an AI dating app developer who lied about finding the love of his life on the app so he could trick unsuspecting single people into pouring hundreds of dollars into his pocket?"

"Ohhhhh." I slump to the floor.

"You and I know that's not what happened, but can't you see how this will look?" Darren hammers into me, not letting up. "It could bankrupt your company. Destroy everything you've built. Ruin your reputation. Make you a pariah."

His words are like bullets ripping through my body. My company is still in the bloody red, not turning a profit, despite the increase in subscribers. This feature on Heather Grimley's vlog was supposed to help me change that, not make it worse.

"Alright! I get it! I messed up …" I yell, shaking under the harsh realities of the potential consequences of my lie. "There's got to be something I can do to fix this."

"Well, coming clean to Heather isn't an option," Darren says, shaking his head.

Darren knows first-hand how confronting a social media influencer can turn your life into a dumpster fire, even if temporarily. My life's work could go up in smoke because of one poorly thought-out decision. I can't let that happen.

"For this, we need whiskey," I announce, scrambling up to my feet.

Ten minutes later, I'm sitting at the table that seats twelve in Darren's dining room, sloshing a tumbler of twenty-thousand-dollar whiskey in my hand.

Darren takes a sip from his glass, then fixes his eyes on me. "From what I can figure, our best option is to pay an actress to play the role of your fiancée. We'll get Lance to draw up an NDA for her to sign, then you can create a fake profile for her on your app. Rig it to show that y'all were a match. Back date it to whatever date so it can look like y'all connected months ago."

"What's an NDA?"

Darren looks at me like I'm an idiot. "Non-disclosure agreement. The actress would need to be legally bound not to turn on you later and reveal that the relationship was a fraud."

Misery snakes through me. I raise the glass and allow the smooth liquor to ease down my throat. It isn't a bad idea on the surface, but Heather plans to have AI experts assess the app.

"One major problem with that plan," I start. Darren slumps in his chair, waiting for me to drop the bomb. "My automation uses predictive analytics and machine learning."

"Not so technical," Darren interrupts. "I'm a former jock, remember?"

"Dude, that wasn't technical at all," I say, and it's my turn to look at him like he's an idiot. That gives me a brief smug satisfaction. I'm surprised that the mainstream understanding of AI has bypassed him. "Fine. In simpler terms, that means what I designed changes every time someone uses the app. It refines my proprietary method for matching profiles at a rate much faster than I could recreate."

Darren still looks confused.

"Bottom line, I don't know what to put in a fake profile that would guarantee the app would match it to my profile." I gulp the rest of the whiskey and slam the glass on the table. "Not only that, the profile will have to be a ninety percent love match or higher. That's the threshold with the near hundred percent success rate, which would be necessary to convince Heather that the app is effective."

Darren leans over and refills his glass, then mine. "So, you'll have to back up your claim of finding the love of your life through the app with a profile that is at least a ninety percent match to yours?"

"For it to be believable, yes," I say glumly.

"And you haven't had any matches so far?"

"I don't know," I admit.

"What do you mean, you don't know?"

"I have a profile, but I've never activated it to see if there were any matches. I'm not struggling in the dating department," I remind him.

"But you are struggling in the quality of relationships department," Darren retorts.

"Okay, pot, nice to meet you. I'm kettle." I rake my hands through my hair.

"Touché." Darren lifts his phone, snaps a pic, and then turns it toward me.

My blond strands are sticking up on my head like I've been electrocuted. My blue eyes are wild with panic, and my face looks paler than I've ever seen.

"I'll add this to my blackmail collection," Darren jokes, but it doesn't bring a hint of a smile to my face.

I can't laugh or joke right now because I'm thoroughly screwed.

Darren strums his fingers on the table as his eyes search the recessed ceiling of the room for answers to my problem. I glance up, hoping to get a glimpse of inspiration, but feel nothing.

My life is a few weeks from being ruined.

"So let's run your profile now," Darren says, slapping a hand on the table. "The answer could be in one of the thousands of women already on the app."

"Good point." I pick up my phone and access the developer tools of the app. Quick typing on the screen through several forms, and my profile is hidden but activated. I wait a few minutes as the program cycles through all the women on the app.

"Why is it taking so long?" Darren asks, snatching the phone from my hand. He frowns, then says, "Oh. This is not good."

"No ninety percent love matches?" I ask.

"How about no matches ... at all," Darren says, turning the phone toward me. He takes a sip of his whiskey.

I scan the screen, confirming that my profile has been assessed against every woman in the app.

"The highest match is only thirty-two percent," I say, dumbfounded.

Whiskey spews from Darren's mouth as he stares at me. "Thirty-two? That's what the number means?"

I nod. "Thousands of women on the app, and the highest connection I have with any of them is in the toilet. No one below eighty percent is shown as an option for matching. It's why I have the highest marriage rate of all the dating apps in the U.S. based on the exit surveys and follow-ups."

"But not effective at finding one for you."

"I wasn't looking for a love match. That's why I kept my profile private and inactivated," I say, shrugging. "There are too many beautiful women in the world for me to think about settling down with one. Between fire fighting and running the dating app, I'm in no position to give a relationship the time and attention it needs."

"So why have a profile at all?" Darren asks.

It's a good question.

I was never an ugly duckling or computer geek who was ignored by girls. When I was young, I realized people were drawn to my looks. That worked out fine for my extroverted personality. I loved being around people, playing the class clown, and getting as much attention as possible.

I've never had to struggle to find dates.

Yet, the idea of finding the elusive soul mate had always stuck with me. Maybe it was due to watching the revolving door of men my mother gave her heart to without getting the love she deserved back. And seeing too much of myself in all those men as I backed away from dozens of relationships over the years.

Who knows?

But that doesn't explain why I bothered to create a profile for myself.

"I don't know," I say in response to Darren's question.

He raises an eyebrow, then wipes the spray of whiskey droplets from the table, seemingly satisfied with my answer.

"Well, I'm sure Amanda, don't call me Mandy, Tucker, would love to fill in for the role of your fake fiancée." Darren can barely get the words out as he bursts into laughter.

"That's not funny, and you know it!" I point my finger in his face. "Don't forget, I have the scar to prove that psycho girl and I should never be in a relationship again."

"Alright, alright. I know that was a low blow." Darren sits back in his chair and says, "Listen, there are around two thousand active football players in the NFL."

"What?" I frown.

"Stay with me," Darren says, raising his hands. "Getting to the NFL is like finding a needle in a haystack. I should know. But the NFL ensures it has ample hay with over two million kids playing in youth football leagues. Two million kids dream of playing professional football, but the NFL wants that elusive needle. That unique special talent that will be a beast on the field and line the owners' pockets with billions of profits. Only 0.1 percent of those kids will play in the NFL."

"I don't get how this matters for my situation." I scratch my eyebrow.

"You need more hay and fast if you have any chance of finding that ninety percent match."

"So, you're saying if I can get more women to join the app—a lot more over the next few days—I could have a shot at finding one with a higher connection rate," I say as Darren's point pierces through the fog in my head. "Some kind of promotion that could drive up interest ..." A huge grin spreads across my face. "Does this mean what I think it does?"

I leap from my seat, crossing the room to wrap Darren in a bear hug.

"Yeah, yeah," Darren says, shaking his head. "I'll do a promo spot for your app. Don't be disappointed if it doesn't bring in the numbers you expect."

"Are you crazy?" I ask, feeling like a glimmer of light is at the end of this tunnel. "You're still wildly popular. If I can get a fraction of your social media followers to join the app, it could be the boost I need to find my match." I don't think about how I would convince that woman to pretend to be my fiancée in less than three weeks.

One problem at a time.

Darren pushes me away. "I'm not doing a profile. You can imply I did, but I'm not doing one, you hear me?"

I chuckle under my breath. "Of course, you're not. We both know you've already found the love of your life. You're too scared to tell her—"

The force of Darren's shove sends me careening into the back wall.

"I'll let that go ... for now," I say, then drape an arm around him. "Let's see how fast we can get a video crew here ..."

CHAPTER 4

Z AIRE

~

"WHAT IS IT?" I STAND AND WALK TO THE WINDOW, putting as much distance as possible between Troy and me. Heat burns across my skin. I force back the bile rising in my throat. I thought I was ready to see him again, but I was wrong.

Troy leans against my closed office door, full of the cocky, confident swagger that makes women drool. The caramel-hued, green-eyed brother was the epitome of what one would consider "a catch."

I'll admit I've caught him without trying and want nothing more than to throw him back.

I'm reminded of Sydney's pitch to get me to hire her brother-in-law.

"He's a Wharton grad. He's worked for two of the top furniture makers in North Carolina, and I swear he's had a crush on you since my wedding," Sydney said.

My mouth gaped open as I stared at my sister in disbelief. "That was almost five years ago, Syd."

"Honey, you made a lasting impression. You're horrible at picking men for yourself, so you should trust me this time," Sydney said, a hint of sympathy in her eyes.

"No." I shuddered at the thought. I'd been on a merry-go-round of dating over the past few years. The process left me exhausted and convinced that maybe finding real love wasn't in the cards for me.

Turns out guys aren't that interested in a type A, driven businesswoman who became a millionaire at twenty-five and hates being bored. Doesn't help that I work ridiculous hours from taking on more and more challenging businesses to keep life interesting. Or maybe, if I'm being honest, to hide the fact that sometimes I feel ... lonely.

That's despite having a whole gaggle of friends, close ones at that.

"Well, hire him because he's highly qualified," Sydney continued. "He's the missing piece. You need him for your new venture to take off at warp speed, and you know it."

At least she was right about that part.

Hiring Troy was a good move for my business.

There were only a few instances of his real feelings for me rising to the surface, but nothing I couldn't manage ... until last week.

Troy's gaze lingers on me. I cross my arms over my chest and glare back at him.

"You know I have a strict no bad news before ten a.m. policy, so if that's why you're here, you better turn around and come back in ..." I glance at my watch, then curse under my breath.

"I'm aware, and I timed my visit perfectly." Troy saunters over to my desk and leans against the edge, closing the distance between us. He runs a hand over his wavy curls as he gives me a sad smile. "I know you're a rip the band-aid off kinda person, so here goes."

I stiffen, realizing that this conversation is all business and not personal.

That scares me.

I launched Kincaid Furnishings online on Black Friday. The sales reports over the weekend have far exceeded all of Troy's projections and my stretch goals. The company is an overnight success thanks to strategic marketing through pop-up shops in affluent areas months before the e-commerce site went live. The shops teased our custom-made furniture to an elite clientele who want furniture tailored to meet their unique personalities.

But I also knew that sometimes people don't always know what they want. You have to show them the art of the possible, which is why I had a cutting-edge website designed that leverages artificial intelligence. The recommendation search engine combines interests gathered about the customer from their searches on the site with predictive analytics. The AI provides suggestions of complimentary products that push the envelope and show them how to take the expected to the "wow" level.

I'm proud to say it worked like a charm. We have a mountain of sales to prove it. On Cyber Monday, the biggest online shopping day of the year, the last thing I want is to have my COO in my office being the bearer of bad news.

Troy clears his throat. "The website crashed."

His words settle like an atomic bomb detonating in the room.

I gasp, then lean forward to grip the back of my desk chair. "That's not possible," I whisper, searching his face for some sign that this is a cruel joke.

"We've lost all the orders from the weekend. The tech team has been trying to fix things for the past few hours but can't get any traction. We've already started the business recovery plan and contacted the third-party IT service to come out and troubleshoot with us. Everyone is working as hard as they can to get the site back up and recover the weekend sales from our back-up servers."

"The entire weekend's sales? Gone?" The shrill sound of my voice is foreign to my ears. I shake my head in disbelief as numbness infects my body. "The website is down on Cyber Monday?"

"It couldn't handle the number of hits we were getting, and it crashed."

All the work over the past few years to launch the business online is now obliterated in a single day.

This cannot be happening.

My worst nightmare come to life.

"We were prepared for this and ready to enact a contingency plan based on the level of hits over the weekend." Troy places his hand on my shoulder to steady me. "The plan didn't work. It's like the website self-destructed. The team can't find all the elements to piece it back together. No one has ever seen anything like it." He says, compassion replacing the cockiness that's usually in his voice.

"Self-destructed?" I yank the chair from the desk and slump onto it. Dragging a hand down my face, I fight the wave of panic. I can typically handle any kind of business crisis. Brand reputation taking a hit in the eyes of public perception? I have multiple plans to turn that around. Product failures? I have the contacts and resources to rectify those mistakes. Shifts in the market demand? I can pivot with the best of them.

But a technical issue?

I don't have a clue where to begin.

How can a website self-destruct from too many hits?

"I don't understand how that's possible," I say, forcing the words from my mouth.

Troy nods his head. "Neither do I. I've never dealt with anything like it. But like I said, we've already called a top company in website recovery to assist. Hopefully, they can help us get the website back up today."

"And if they can't?"

"You know much better than I what that will mean," Troy says, concern etched in his dark brows.

"I want regular updates. Every hour or quicker," I say.

Troy nods, then heads to the door. "I'm sorry about this, Zaire."

"Yeah. So am I," I say.

As the door shuts behind him, I yank open my desk drawer and grab my Dior purse. Fumbling inside, I grab my personal cell phone and scroll through the contacts until I get to the Ws.

It's a long shot, but I think the only person who can fix this disaster is the person who created the e-commerce website for me. The person I shouldn't have given a chance to take part in one of the most important aspects of my company. Who knew I would succumb to the aqua-eyes and comedic charisma like every other woman in this town?

But it had been more than that.

He was the person I'd shared my vision with who seemed to get it and could help me make it come to life. That he was willing to do the heavy lifting for a quid pro quo arrangement had made trusting him with the task less risky. If it wasn't a success, I wouldn't have lost anything but a few hours of professional mentoring to help him with his fledgling start-up business.

It was supposed to be a win-win.

Until the e-commerce site self-destructed on the year's most important online shopping day.

"Wiley, I hope you can fix this," I mutter under my breath as I press the call button.

CHAPTER 5

ILEY

"Hey, Beautiful." I nudge the front door with my foot as I balance the six-foot Virginia Pine tree on my shoulder. The heady scent of pine wafts in the air as I maneuver into the narrow foyer dominated by a side table adorned with a winter wonderland scene. Miniature houses, cars, and people are meticulously constructed on top of fluffy white cotton representing snow that we rarely see in the Hill Country.

"Wiley!" I hear Ma call my name before she emerges from the kitchen around the corner. Her blonde hair is piled into a high messy bun coated in a dusting of flour. She rubs her hands against her red apron, smearing cookie dough over the "Baking Spirits Bright" words on the front. "Come, give your Ma a hug."

Easing the tree onto the floor in the adjoining living room, I turn and cross the room in two steps, embracing my petite, plump mother in my arms. At five feet tall, she barely comes to my chest. I kiss the top of her head, then pull back.

"What are you baking? Smells wonderful in here." I peek into the kitchen.

"Found this recipe for pecan snowball cookies. I thought this would be a good snack for the grandkids while we make gingerbread houses. But only if I can perfect the recipe." Ma wraps her arm around my waist and leads me into the kitchen. The week before Christmas, it's a tradition for my older sister, Hayley, and her four kids to come to Kimbell to make gingerbread houses. Once the houses are built and decorated, Ma hides gifts inside and then takes them to Hayley's home in Houston on Christmas Day, pretending that Santa and his elves added the treats inside to the delight of my nieces and nephews.

"Taste this." Ma shoves one of the fluffy powdered sugar balls toward me. I take a bite and feel like I've bitten into heaven.

"This is amazing," I mumble between chews. "Perfect, Ma."

Her smile spreads across her face as she beckons for me to sit down at the small table. I'm not surprised that the kitchen and the entire house are littered with Christmas decorations. There's not a spot that doesn't have lights or ornaments or wreaths or candy canes. Each year, I think Ma can't add more, but she proves me wrong.

"You know what would be more perfect?" Ma asks.

I scratch my forehead, then grab another pecan snowball. No point in me saying anything. I know where this conversation is going. The same place our conversations have gone since my thirtieth birthday a few months ago. She's going to barrel full steam ahead into the subject, whether or not I like it. Ma eases down in the chair across from me. She looks at me with wide, doe-like eyes that obliterate the exasperation threatening to overcome me.

"You should take one of those sweet girls that you've dated in the past on a second date. I was on the phone with Mrs. Barnes, and she mentioned how the ladies around town are fit to be tied because you haven't been on a proper date in almost six months," Ma chides, placing a soft hand on mine.

"How do they know all of this?"

"There's a secret tracker of your dating activity, Wiley. It's on some Kimbell social media group page for women only. Knowing the relationship status of Kimbell's most eligible bachelor is very important in this town," Ma says. "They call me to check in and to validate some of the information is accurate.

"So, you're in cahoots with them?" My voice grows louder. I'd heard rumors about this social media group but thought the tracking of my dating activity had been exaggerated. Guess I was wrong.

She gives me a sheepish shrug, then says, "There are some good women on the tracking sheet, like that new nurse Avril and Liesel, who I've heard is a great nanny."

I stuff the cookie in my mouth before I tell her why her two examples are the last two women I'd ever date again. Avril's husband refuses to give her a divorce, and Liesel is the worst nanny on the planet. She abandoned Ronan's kids without a second thought on her first day as their nanny. Not that either of those is the reason I didn't go out with them again. Or any of the other women, for that matter.

"I don't understand why my favorite, most handsome son has slowed down dating at the very time when he should look to settle down."

"Ma, I'm your only son, and you shouldn't help this group keep track of who I'm dating. Stop feeding them information about me, okay?"

"Fine," Ma says.

She and I both know she has no intention of stopping her antics. At least not until I'm in a relationship again. Finding a woman to be my fake fiancée would help me kill two birds with one stone. She'll be my plus one for the interview with Heather and also get Ma off my back about settling down.

"But I don't want you to end up one of those bachelors for life." Ma sounds as if that would be a fate worse than death. "This is an emergency in my book. Especially since you spent Thanksgiving all alone. Hayley and I were so worried about you."

I drag a hand down my face. Between Ma and Hayley, who is fifteen years older than me, I've always felt like I was growing up with two moms. Double the trouble when those two make me the focus of their attention. I say, "There's nothing to worry about. We talked about this months ago. I told you I was taking a break from my personal life to focus on my dating app business. I need it to turn a profit. Once I do, then I'll focus on love again."

"You can tell that lie to anybody else, but don't tell it to me. Ever since that horrible Amanda—"

"Please don't mention her." I raise a hand. I'm in no mood to think about my last ex-girlfriend and how she wreaked havoc on my life. Trimming the Christmas tree with Ma is supposed to be a fun night. A way to take my mind off the blunder I made with Heather Grimley earlier. I can only hope the video Darren and I recorded to boost sign-ups to the Ladies Love Country Boys app will be the key to finding someone who's a ninety percent love match with me. Until then, I need a distraction. But this isn't the distraction I had in mind.

"I hope you realize that one rotten apple doesn't spoil the bunch. I promise your life will be much better when you fall in love and settle down with a good woman. If there's anything I can do to help, you just say the word. I can't tell you how many lovely young ladies come to my line at the grocery store asking about you," Ma says, tipping her head toward me with pride. "Your grandma left you a gorgeous diamond engagement ring in her will. It would be a shame for it to go to waste."

"Trust me, it won't," I say. That ring will come in handy to convince everyone that my fake relationship is real. But first, I gotta keep my fingers crossed that I'll get a match soon. Three weeks will be here faster than I know it. "Are you ready to get this tree decorated?"

Ma claps her hands with glee. "I was at the local craft store buying some extra ornaments. You get it set up, and I'll grab my bags from the back room."

I give Ma a high-five, then head into the living room.

CHAPTER 6

Z AIRE

~

I stare at the rippling waters of Lake Lasso in the distance and try to force the retched memories of the day from my mind. There's nothing worse than an online-only business having its website crash on Cyber Monday.

Or self-destruct.

Even though I don't understand how that's possible.

My cell phone hasn't rung all night. The dozen times I've called Wiley were greeted with a full mailbox notification. I thought about texting, but that would leave evidence of one of my biggest professional mistakes. Ever.

I never should have trusted such a critical aspect of my business to Wiley. There's an emergency tech squad charging me absurd prices to resurrect the website and recover the lost sales.

What's worse is that of all the disasters my business could have faced, this is the one area where I have no expertise. I can't code, program, or work around the clock with the team to help diagnose and fix the problems. Sticking around to hover over them would do nothing to make this disaster go away faster.

There's nothing I can do.

It would've driven me insane if it wasn't for my bestie swooping in with a girls' night in. Pouring out my frustration to Harlow-Rose and hearing her perspectives as a fellow business owner helped to calm me down … a fraction.

Harlow-Rose pours her award-winning Cabernet Sauvignon into my wine glass. She gives me a sympathetic smile before placing the empty bottle on the low, custom-made teak wood table, which *should* be for sale on my Kincaid Furnishings website for six hundred dollars.

"That's a lot to deal with." She eases down onto the Adirondack chair, retailing for twelve hundred dollars on the website that is still down and losing sales by the hour. "You hear websites being so popular that they crash and never think it'll happen to your business."

"I thought we had sufficient bandwidth for a spike in traffic, so I don't understand how it could've happened." I take a long, luxurious sip of the fantastic wine. My statement isn't entirely true. Hiring an amateur with a reputation for being "good at computers" to design the website was one of the dumbest business decisions I could've made. But I'm not ready to admit that to anyone. Not even Harlow-Rose. Instead, I say, "Honey, you did the thing with this wine. It is divine."

"I can open another bottle if that would help," Harlow-Rose offers as she tosses a cheese cube into her mouth. A charcuterie board fit for royalty rests next to the empty bottle of wine. The finest cuts of meat, cheeses, fruit, and olives are arranged onto a massive mahogany board.

"No, this is good. Being here with you and having your support is all I need." I gaze up at the night sky. Stars sparkle against the inky blackness, soothing the tension clawing at my muscles.

Placing the wine glass back onto the table, I grab a handful of grapes and turn toward Harlow-Rose. "Enough with my work woes. Let's talk about you and Napa Guy. Things still perfectly blissful?"

Harlow-Rose erupts into laughter. "When are you going to stop calling him Napa Guy? He has a name."

"Yeah, yeah, I know. Stop avoiding the question. Things are good?"

"Amazing. Better than I could've ever imagined," Harlow-Rose says, but the smile on her face, the sparkle in her eyes, and the excitement in her voice say more than those simple words.

My bestie is head over heels in love.

For the first time in a long time, and I mean a very long time, I wonder what it would be like to feel that way about someone. To have someone other than Harlow-Rose, Quan, Simona, or Sydney to call when I have a disastrous day like today. How nice it might be to walk into the arms of a strong, supportive, and caring man and allow myself to feel weak, knowing that there's someone else there to be strong so I don't have to.

I let out a long sigh as Harlow-Rose fills me in on the details of her romantic Thanksgiving weekend with Napa Guy in Tuscany. The story sounds like something out of a Nicholas Sparks book.

And I can't imagine having anything like that in my life.

When would I have time to date while juggling three businesses? Especially when one is on the verge of collapse after only being open for a weekend.

"I know what you're thinking." Harlow-Rose gives me a shrewd stare.

Cringing, I suspect she does. But I try to play it off since I'm in no mood to talk about my nonexistent dating life on the same day that my business is in a crisis.

"That Baker Bros BBQ would go great with this wine and charcuterie board?" I joke.

Harlow-Rose makes a face, then turns serious. "When was your last date?"

I fight against the wave of anger coursing through my body. Not tonight. I cannot do this tonight.

"I'm not trying to be that annoying best friend who falls in love and then wants to make sure all of her friends find love, too, but I can't help it. It's not just me. Sydney and India are married. Persia's getting married in a few weeks. I'll probably be next."

I stiffen in my chair. Did she need to remind me that India was married? Like I could ever forget how that happened.

"So what if you get married, and all of my sisters are married? Does that mean I must drop everything I'm doing and find a man to love me? I get that from so many people. I never thought I'd hear it from you."

"I'm sorry." She raises her hands in the air. "I didn't mean to—"

"Upset me? Too late. I've been upset all day. Why not pile it on all night?" I grab the glass of wine and finish it, then stand up. "I'm going home. I'm tired and cranky, and I don't want to say something I might regret later."

"Zaire ..."

"I know. You love me, and you care. You want the best for me. I feel the same way about you, honey. But tonight is not the night for me to delve into my pathetic love life. I don't have the energy for it."

A sharp ringing pierces the air. My head whips toward the sound as Harlow-Rose's cell phone lights up.

"It's Persia," Harlow-Rose says, confusion in her voice. "Any idea why she'd be calling me?"

"None." I wonder what's going on with my youngest sister. She's in Paris. With the time difference, it's early morning in Europe. "I hope nothing's wrong."

The ringing continues.

"If something is wrong, why would she call me and not you? This is ... odd."

"Only one way to find out." I sit back down on the Adirondack chair. "Answer it and put it on speaker."

Harlow-Rose sits up and answers the phone. "Hey, Persia. What's up?"

"Is Zaire with you? I've been trying to call her, and she's not answering. I'm getting worried," Persia says, her tone anxious and tense.

"Hey honey, I'm here." I plunge my hand into my purse for my cell phone. Finding it, I jerk the device out. I tap the black screen, then punch the buttons. Nothing happens. "My battery died, and I didn't realize it."

I wonder if Wiley has been trying to call me back, and I've missed his calls? I could kick myself for not double-checking my battery strength before coming to Harlow-Rose's home. Checking my phone for missed calls will have to wait until I figure out what's going on with Persia.

"You let your cell phone battery die?" Persia almost shrieks on the other line. "Who are you, and what have you done to my sister?"

"Take it easy on her," Harlow-Rose interjects. "She had a rough day, and I didn't make it any better."

"Oh, I'm sorry," Persia says. "You want to talk about it?"

"Let's talk about why you were trying to reach me instead," I say, grateful for the distraction. Of all my sisters, I'm only close to Sydney. India and I stopped talking years ago, and Persia, the baby of the family, is too self-absorbed and spoiled to keep up with any of us. But as her wedding date draws closer, I've noticed an increase in contact from her … for better or worse. I wonder which it is tonight?

"I don't want to get married."

"What!?!" Harlow-Rose and I yell at the same time. We stare at each other wide-eyed, waiting for Persia to explain.

"Can y'all let me finish?" Persia asks. "I'm still getting married. Yves asked me, and I accepted. I'm not changing my mind about that."

I raise an eyebrow. Harlow-Rose frowns, and I know she's picking up on the same thing I am. Persia was the recipient of my mother's strategic matchmaking with the grandson of a prominent French businessman. They embarked on a whirlwind romance on one of Persia's trips to Paris, where our father is the US Ambassador to France. Four months later, Persia and Yves announced their engagement to both happy sets of parents.

"So, what's wrong, then?" I decide not to mention that she doesn't sound like an excited bride-to-be.

"I don't want to get married in Paris. We had meetings with the wedding coordinator yesterday, and it doesn't feel ... right," Persia says.

"What are you talking about? You said a wedding at the Eiffel Tower was your dream. You insisted on it." I try to remind my little sister of how hard our father worked to get the Christmas Day wedding booking on such short notice. Now, she's saying it doesn't feel right?

"It is my dream, but I also want to get married where I feel at home. I'm surrounded by all of Yves's friends, and they are nice enough, but it seems like we're going through the motions and pretending to be close when we're not. If I could get married where I'm comfortable, surrounded by my family and friends, my wedding could be perfect," Persia says.

"All your friends and family will be in Paris the week of Christmas for the wedding. You won't be alone. There's no reason to give up on your Eiffel Tower dream wedding. It'll all be fine," I say, trying to talk Persia off the ledge.

"No, it won't. I don't want to get married here. If I do, it will be horrible, and that's not how I want to start my life as a married woman. Yves thinks I'm being irrational. Mommy and Daddy think I'm being a brat. Sydney told me I was spoiled to my face, and India was trying to convince me to elope. I thought you might be the one person who could see my side of things. You're always blazing your own trail and following what you know is best for you without caring what other people think," Persia says, with a hint of admiration in her tone. "But you won't help me."

Is that how she thinks of me?

I grip my neck and try to massage the knots away. "Persia, I didn't say I wouldn't help you. Honey, you are a month away from your wedding day. Finding another venue is going to be impossible—"

"No, it won't," Harlow-Rose interjects. "She can get married at my winery."

I frown and glare at my bestie. Shaking my head, I mouth the word "No" and move my finger exaggeratedly across the width of my neck.

"Are you serious?" Persia asks. "You would let me take over your winery for my wedding."

"Persia, your guests have already spent a lot of money to book flights and hotels in Paris. It would be pretty bad to cancel on such short notice," I say, panic slicing through me.

This wedding cannot happen in the Hill Country.

My entire family descending like vultures on Kimbell is the worst thing that could happen to me. The first thing they'll demand is to meet the new man in my life. The man that doesn't exist.

I grip my forehead as the beginning of a migraine takes root.

"Don't be ridiculous," Harlow-Rose says, not picking up on my distress. "Flights can be rescheduled, and hotel rooms have long cancellation periods. Zaire has dozens of contacts with hotels and B&Bs in the Hill Country to find rooms for your guests. I have a few holiday parties booked that week, but I'm sure we can work around them for the rehearsals. Nothing is booked on Christmas Day. So you can get married on the day you want."

"You are the best! Thank you, thank you, thank you!" Persia screams into the phone. "I gotta go. I have a ton of calls to make. I'm so happy to be getting married at home. You don't know how much this means to me, Harlow-Rose."

"It's no problem at all," Harlow-Rose says, then ends the call. She stares up at me and freezes. "What? What did I do wrong? I thought that was the best solution. I understand her wanting to come back to Kimbell to get married."

"Your winery is in Fredericksburg," I say, unable to hide my anger.

"Same thing. Why are you upset?"

"Don't you remember the little white lie I told my family to get out of the annual Thanksgiving dinner? The one where I've been dating a guy secretly, and he surprised me with a trip to St. Barts last week," I say, staring at her like she has three heads. "I could've made up a reason for him not to come to Paris for the wedding. What in the world am I supposed to do now that the wedding will be here? How can I hide that my mystery boyfriend is … imaginary?"

"Zaire! Is that what you're freaking out about?" Harlow-Rose asks, shaking her head at me. "Why don't you try this? Tell your family that you're single and try to find a man to date … for real!"

CHAPTER 7

Z AIRE

~

"I'M SORRY ABOUT ALL THIS," TROY SAYS, LEANING AGAINST my desk. His hand lingers near mine as if he wants to caress it. Wants to provide some kind of intimate comfort to soothe me as the launch of my furniture company grinds to a tragic halt. Every hour the website is down, I lose traction with potential customers. The brand takes a deeper hit, and the cost of luring them back skyrockets.

"Is this all you're sorry about?" I ask, pushing away from the desk and standing. I walk over to the glass windows that make up my office's back wall and stare at a family of ducks swimming across Lake Lasso. The sun casts a shimmering orange glow over the rippling waters.

Troy's hand rests on my shoulder, turning me to face him. "I don't regret anything I did last week. But now is not the time to get into anything ... personal. We have a business crisis on our hands."

Fuming, I push away from Troy and cross the room. Breathing the same air as him is threatening to choke the life out of me. "What are our options?"

"A forensic tech team has started the search for the orders that came in over the weekend. They are optimistic that all of them can be located, but the search will take several days, and we'd still need to verify what they recovered with the purchasers. Something about being unable to tell the difference between items abandoned in the cart and those purchased."

"You should be able to cross-reference with accounting to confirm the sales. I don't want to bother the customers with this. It's not their fault, and they shouldn't get pulled into helping us clean up our mess," I say, turning around to face him.

Troy stiffens at my rebuke, likely because he should've thought of this before I said anything.

"You're right."

"And the website?"

"Whatever company built it for you incorporated complex coding beyond anything they've ever seen for an e-commerce shopping page. A lot of predictive analytics and machine learning of customer behavior is embedded that the new guys think will take months to replicate. Plus, they aren't sure they can recreate the self-destruct feature that seems to be embedded in the site," Troy says.

"Self-destruct feature? What are you talking about?"

"Some code they found that impressed them. It protects customer sensitive information like credit card numbers and addresses if there are signs of a cyber attack," Troy says.

"Do they think the site was hacked?"

"Not sure. I don't think there are any definitive signs to say."

I bite my bottom lip, thinking about the long nights I spent at my house pacing back and forth as Wiley Alexander and I discussed my wish list for the Kincaid Furnishings website. Things I wasn't sure were possible, but he'd listened and encouraged me. The handsome playboy had given me his undivided attention, brainstorming ideas until the sun rose. No matter how many times I tried to tell him we could call it a night, he insisted there was nowhere else he needed to be. We were in sync, our creativity feeding off each other until we'd settled on the final specifications. Then Wiley had set off to make my dreams come true. That's why Black Friday and weekend sales had already surpassed our goals.

I wish I knew what went wrong.

What did he miss that caused the website to crash on the busiest online shopping day of the year? Was it as simple as too many visitors? Had the predictive analytics caused the site to shut down? Was there a cyber attack by hackers trying to steal my customer data? What was going on?

And why hasn't he returned any of my calls?

It's been months since we've talked, so he has to be curious to know why I've called so many times over the past twenty-four hours. His stupid cell phone is going straight to voice mail, which is full. Combine that with my pride of not wanting anyone else to find out I let an amateur build my e-commerce website, and I'm stuck. I can't call around and ask for him. People will wonder why. They'll assume I've turned into one of his many Kimbell groupies when I don't explain. Not a good look for me ... at all.

"It's your call," Troy says, snapping me out of my wayward thoughts.

"What?"

"Building a simpler website from scratch, which they can have up in about three days, or reaching out to the company that created the site to get them to investigate how to get it back working," Troy says, slower this time.

I pause, not sure what to do.

I should focus on getting the website back functioning by any means necessary. Even if that means simplifying the site.

But I don't want a simple site.

I want the website Wiley created for me. The website he promised me and convinced me he could make. He was probably too busy sweeping some woman off her feet over the past two days and didn't care that my business was going down the drain. Didn't care the money I was losing by the minute was his fault!

It's time for me to face the truth and move on.

I let out a loud sigh, then say, "Tell them to build a new website."

There's a knock on my door, and Simona pops her head in. "Your mother is on line four. She says something is wrong with your cell, and she can't get through." Her eyes are wide and full of concern. "She sounds upset."

And I know why.

CHAPTER 8

W ILEY

I'M LATE FOR MY SHIFT AT THE FIRE STATION AT NINE IN the morning as I turn my F-150 into the back parking lot. There's no excuse I can give Ronan that won't have him ripping me a new one in a few minutes. Working a one day on, two days off schedule leaves no wiggle room for tardiness. Especially since I have no pets, elderly parents, or kiddos to use as an excuse.

Parking next to Nate's Porsche, I open my door and leap down to the ground, slamming the door shut. I sprint toward the front entrance and yank the door open, stepping into the cool air conditioning. The sound of Christmas music fills the air. Since our last shift, the city crews have added festive decorations to the interior.

Erin Newman, our dispatcher, looks up and blushes as I head toward her. The digital clock behind her head reads 9:13.

"How bad is it?" I peek through the glass window to check if she got my stash this morning.

She lowers her voice. "Something happened yesterday that has them all concerned. I don't know what it is, though. Ronan is too distracted to notice that you are late. If he asks, I'll cover for you." Erin reaches over, grabs a white bag with the Elevation Cupcake Shop logo on the front, and hands it to me.

Since my relationship with Brianna ended a couple of years ago, it's been too awkward between us for me to go into the shop and get one of my favorite to-go breakfasts. That's where Erin's generosity comes in handy.

The smell of the gooey cinnamon roll wafts from the surface, making my stomach rumble. I grab the bag, then push my torso through the window to give her a loud smacking kiss on the cheek. Erin giggles and flushes a deeper red as she swats me away.

"You're the best. Thanks." I wink, then swipe my badge on the side door and head upstairs to the break room. As I approach the doors, I hear a hushed discussion between Ronan, Nate, Luke, and Darren. They are huddled around the table, looking more serious than I've seen them in a long time.

I head straight for the counter, where a coffee machine gurgles, and fill a cup to the brim. I barely slept last night, wondering whether I would get any new matches from the influx of subscribers to the dating app since Darren's social media post went viral. I checked my profile at midnight and still didn't have any matches. To stop myself from going bonkers, I decided to only check in every twelve hours. That means I need to keep myself busy for three more hours before I can check in again.

"It's such an enormous blow," Darren says. "I'm sure Zaire is—"

I fumble my coffee cup. The blazing hot liquid splashes against my leg. Yelping in pain, I leap back as all eyes turn to me.

"What happened to Zaire?" I hop on one leg to the table.

"Good morning to you, too. Don't think I didn't notice your truck speeding into the parking lot at 9:07." Ronan gives me a perturbed glare.

"I'm ready to take my punishment," I mutter, then turn to Darren. "Did something bad happen to Zaire?"

My best friend frowns at me, confusion in his eyes.

Nate says, "Calm down, man. Your unofficial mentor is fine. Her latest business venture took a pretty nasty hit yesterday."

"Unofficial mentor?" Luke asks.

"Wiley's been fanboying after Zaire for years. He follows all her blog posts on the Kimbell Business Bureau website that helps local small businesses and religiously listens to her monthly Q&As," Nate says.

Darren looks surprised. "Didn't know that. And you made me think all those good business ideas were your own. I should've known better."

"Yes," I agree. "You should have."

"I'm sure it helps that she's very easy on the eyes." Luke takes a long sip from his coffee mug. "Every few months, she comes by the farm to ask me to sell some of my grandfather's land close to Lake Lasso. My answer never changes, but those pretty brown eyes and batting lashes have made me think twice a few times."

"Trust me, Zaire is too intelligent, innovative, and persistent to need her looks to seal a deal," I say, sitting in the chair beside Darren. "An influential and important entrepreneur like her shouldn't be objectified over her looks."

"You saying you never noticed?" Ronan asks, giving me a pointed stare.

Memories of Zaire slam through my head from the amazing month I spent sneaking over to her house to work on the e-commerce website for Kincaid Furnishings. The doe-like brown eyes, mile-long lashes, and pouty lips on a stunning deep brown, heart-shaped face. Short hair has never looked sexier on any woman. They say beauty is in the eye of the beholder, and I was beholding a lot as we worked side by side for weeks. I'm surprised I stayed focused long enough to create the website.

I scoff. "I'm not blind."

"Does she know you're online stalking her?" Darren asks.

Nate growls. "Don't bring that athlete mentality into the business world. It's not uncommon for up-and-coming entrepreneurs like Wiley to follow more successful business people from afar. Happens all the time in industry. You don't have to know a person directly to gain lots of insight from them."

"Thank you, Nate." I stick my tongue out at Darren. Grabbing the cinnamon roll from the bag, I take a bite, then say through chews, "Now somebody tell me what happened with Zaire."

"Her website crashed," Nate says.

The cinnamon roll tumbles from my hand and lands with a splat on the floor.

"What's up with you this morning?" Ronan asks. "You know you're going to clean up this mess you keep making." He points to the spilled coffee across the room, then to the cinnamon roll smashed onto the floor.

I give a dismissive wave of my hand. "When did it crash?"

"Worst possible time. Yesterday. Cyber Monday. The biggest online shopping day of the year. That was after she'd wracked up record sales on Black Friday and the weekend. I heard those were all lost, too," Nate explains. "She has an army of tech teams working round the clock to figure out how to get things back up and running. Not a good start for a brand new business."

Stuffing my hand in my pocket, I grab my cell phone and scroll through the missed calls from the phone number I didn't recognize. The person didn't leave a message, but that was because I hadn't cleaned out my voicemail in months. I'd thought it might have been psycho Amanda "Don't Call Me Mandy" Tucker, which is why I ignored the calls like the plague.

Could Zaire have been the one trying to reach me?

I never saved her number in my contacts since I knew she didn't want word to get out that she trusted me to create her e-commerce website.

It's been months since we've spoken or texted.

Since I created the website, it would make sense that she'd reach out to me now. I know I can figure out how to fix it. But I can't do anything until my shift is over.

Tomorrow morning at nine.

"What's her number?" I ask Nate.

"I know you think you're a mini tech genius and you can help fix some simpler websites," Nate says. "But Zaire needs actual experts on this one."

I bite my tongue, not wanting to give away that I was the actual expert that created her cutting-edge website.

The website that has crashed and maybe wasn't as great as I thought?

She must hate me right now.

I pinch the bridge of my nose.

"If you want to help somebody, start with yourself and clean up all this food you've wasted on the floor and the rest of the kitchen." Ronan tosses his empty plate into the trash can several feet away. "After that, you're on bathroom duty, Playboy. That's for being late."

I groan, in no mood to do housekeeping to kick off my shift.

Ronan doles out the rest of the assignments to Luke, Nate, and Darren—equipment check, vehicle check, and inspecting the personal protective equipment. Our fearless leader will be holed up in the computer room, completing the required mountain of paperwork for the incidents we went out on during our last shift. This is the real life of firefighters that never makes it into the glamorous television shows.

"Let's go, fellas. Wiley has some scrubbing to do." Nate chuckles under his breath, then staggers out of the break area. Luke and Ronan follow him, and I'm left alone in the break room with Darren.

"Any luck with the app?" Darren drums his fingers against the table. The repetitive sound fills the silence between us.

"No matches when I checked last night. I'll check again around noon."

How did my life become a dumpster fire in the span of twenty-four hours?

Darren nods. "Three weeks is enough time for us to be ready for Heather. If the social media post doesn't help, we have time to come up with a Plan B. We'll figure this out. Alright?"

"Yeah," I mumble under my breath.

Darren ruffles my hair like I'm a kid, then leaves the room.

I don't want to figure this out.

What I want is a time machine app that can take me back to the meeting with Heather. I want to vaporize the idea that seemed so perfect but, in hindsight, was the stupidest thing I could've ever done.

What woman in her right mind will go along with a crazy plan like this? And if I could find that insane woman, three weeks wouldn't be long enough to convince her to be my fake fiancée.

Darren is wrong.

We won't be able to come up with a way to fix this mess.

I know what the right thing to do is. I just need to force myself to do it.

CHAPTER 9

Zaire

Blocking my mother's number temporarily wasn't my best idea, but I was trying to avoid the exact conversation I'm trapped in now.

"How could you do it? Tell me, Zaire. I count on you to be the voice of reason with your crazy sisters. But you supported this wild idea of moving the wedding?" Mommy's voice is strained and frazzled. I can't imagine what the fallout has been as Persia explained to everyone how she made the unilateral decision to move the wedding venue from the Eiffel Tower in Paris to a winery in Fredericksburg, Texas.

"There was no talking her out of it, Mommy," I say, folding my arms across my chest. "And Harlow-Rose was on the line, and she offered her winery—"

"Do not blame this on Harlow-Rose. If you had stood your ground and told Persia no, we wouldn't be in this predicament. We were so close to getting your sister to drop this foolish idea of moving the wedding, then she has one conversation with you, and the wedding is going to be at Harlow-Rose's winery," Mom screeches. "I have spent the entire day with Yves's parents trying to do damage control. They are horribly upset, as expected. We had a thousand guests coming to this wedding. Now we have to whittle it down to one hundred. One hundred! I swear my hair has turned white overnight. That's the only good thing about coming back to Texas. I can get my hair done by a woman who knows how to handle these kinky coils."

"Do you want me to to book you an appointment with Quan?" I ask.

"Would you, dear?" Mommy says, then sighs. "There will be nine hundred influential and powerful guests upset about being removed from the guest list. I'm fit to be tied."

I swallow hard and slump over my desk, massaging my temples with my fingertips. "As stressful as this will be, we can't forget that this is Persia's special day. She wants the wedding to be here. I thought you'd be glad I was a supportive big sister."

"Your sister is spoiled, and we all know it! I'm afraid Yves's family will think she's more trouble than she's worth. What if they convince Yves to call it off? Can you imagine the shame? Persia will never be able to come back to Paris."

I stifle a chuckle. As if that's some horrible consequence.

"Now, who's being melodramatic?"

"Fine. Perhaps you're right."

"If Yves is the kind of man that would allow his parents to convince him to walk away from the woman he loves, then he's not the man we want for Persia," I say, trying to appeal to Mommy's more rational side.

"Yves's father owns the largest freight shipping company in France. The man's connections have worked wonders for your father in setting up favorable economic deals between the US and France. He's been amenable because of his son's relationship with Persia."

"With you by Daddy's side, he'll find new connections if that one evaporates. It's what you do best."

Mommy is a sucker for unadulterated praise. I can almost hear the tension easing from her body.

"Yes, it is. Yves would be a fool to walk away from Persia, no matter what a frustrating little brat she can be. But if he does, we will survive whatever the Voltaires dish out. They are no match for us."

"Of course, they aren't."

"Since that's settled, I'm assuming you'll be able to convince your new beau to come to the wedding? We're all looking forward to meeting him," Mommy says, then lowers her voice a bit. "Plus, I'm sure you'll need the support with India and Kei coming. Seeing them again for the first time in five years won't be easy, honey."

"Tell me about it," I say, stifling a scream.

"This will be hard for you, but I need you to put aside all your anger and let us welcome India back into the family. As much as I was disgusted by her actions, I never imagined that would mean I'd lose my daughter for five years."

"You want me to forgive her?"

"Or pretend to, honey, to keep the peace. India is so headstrong, and if she senses for one second that we're taking your side over hers, she'll vanish again. I don't think your father could handle that," Mommy explains. "Plus, now that you have a new love in your life, that should be so much easier to do. Right?"

Now would be the perfect time to kill the idea of the mystery man. Make some excuse like he got eaten by a shark when we went snorkeling, or a bat bit him, and he's one of the undead. Or maybe a simple, he bailed on the trip, and I went alone. Something. Anything. But I don't. I'm frozen.

"Zaire? You are going to introduce him to the family, aren't you?"

"I don't know, Mommy," I say, my voice low and strained.

"What do you mean, you don't know?" Her breaths quicken over the line. "Who is this man? You haven't told us his name or anything detailed about him. Please tell me he isn't some ex-con or, God forbid, a rapper."

More like a firefighter, entrepreneur, and brilliant computer coder.

When I'd come up with the dumb idea to lie to my family, the first person who came to mind as the stand-in for my imaginary boyfriend was Wiley Alexander.

No, not because he's the Playboy of Kimbell and has women swooning over him throughout Lasso County. He's stunning. I'll give him that. But that's not why I thought of him.

It all tied back to that one month we spent secretly working on the Kincaid Furnishings website. If we could hide that from everyone in town, I could've also hidden a romantic relationship.

Thus, the mystery man was born.

Loosely based on Wiley.

But I can't tell Mommy this.

She'd be on the next plane to Texas, ready to commit me to a mental institution for going through such an intricate ruse. Harlow-Rose was right. This was a bad idea, and now I'm stuck. Persia's wedding is in four weeks. There's no way that I can find a man to fall madly in love with me that quickly—

My cell phone dings.

I glance down at the notification floating on the screen.

A social media post by Darren Manning promoting the Ladies Love Country Boys dating app. A dating app that uses artificial intelligence to match you with the love of your life. Success rates are through the roof. The number of likes and hearts on the video is in the thousands already.

I say, "You know what happened the last time I brought a man home to meet the family. Can you blame me for hesitating?"

"Honey, of course not," Mommy concedes. "But you're not a passive person. You take life by the horns even when you get knocked down. You make gourmet lemonade out of old, moldy lemons. You always have. That's why you're my favorite child."

"You're not supposed to have a favorite," I remind her.

"Too bad. I do. It's not like you to avoid confrontation. Something else must be going on. You can tell me. What is it? What is it about this guy that is worrying you?"

I glance back at the social media post from Darren. Maybe that's my answer. An idea sprouts in my mind.

"Nothing worries me about him," I say before I can stop the words from slipping out.

"I would think not. A man who would whisk you off on a holiday vacation to an exotic island is taking this relationship seriously. Serious enough that it's time for him to meet your family. You will talk to him?"

"Yes, Mommy," I say, then click on the link in Darren's post. The App Store loads to the dating app, and I click download.

"Great. I'll work out the arrangements for our travel to Texas and let you know when we'll be in town."

"Sounds good," I say as I open the app.

"Love you, honey."

"You, too." I hang up the office phone and take a deep breath.

I'm not delusional.

Finding true love before the wedding is not happening. But Harlow-Rose is right. I need to get back out there. And if this app is as good as the reviews claim, maybe my soul mate could be my date to the wedding. Maybe?

"What are you doing, Zaire?" I mutter under my breath. "This is crazy."

But maybe crazy is what I need.

CHAPTER 10

ILEY

GETTING UP FROM THE TABLE, I CROSS THE ROOM, GRAB THE cleaning supplies from the utility closet, and make my way to the restroom. I'd already tackled the break room and kitchen. Took almost two hours, but it's sparkling clean. I glance at my reflection in the glass window as I turn the corner toward the bathroom. Shaking my head, I almost laugh out loud. This is the stuff of women's fantasies. A hot guy who is attentive *and* keeps the bathroom clean so they don't have to … yeah, that would put me at the top of their list.

I pause, wondering if I should take a selfie and post it on my social media. With everything going on with my app, it's been a while since I've been on a date, despite what the whole town thinks about me. People assume that since I'm a big flirt, there's a bunch of dating backing that up. But I've been focused on trying to make the dating app profitable. I love firefighting, but it doesn't pay enough to afford me the things I want in life. I'm tired of riding on the rich boys' coattails. The scrub friend of Darren and Nate.

I want money and success of my own.

Pushing the restroom door open, I stop in my tracks as a rotten stench slams into my nose.

"Really, guys!" I scream, stepping out of the restroom to breathe fresh air. "Which of you unloaded in the place right before I had to clean it?"

I hear snickering from down the hall, but none of them own up to it.

I wouldn't be surprised if all four made a deposit from the smell of things. Propping the door open, I grab the can of Lysol and spray my way inside. Forcing my dry heaves down, I slip on yellow rubber gloves and attack the first toilet like Mr. Clean.

It's scary how quickly the rank odor dissipates, and I don't notice it anymore as I run through my options again. My moment of weakness, where I considered telling Heather the truth, had been replaced fast with a dose of reality. She's a social media maven. I can't give her ammunition that would torch my business.

I'm back to the drawing board of figuring out who would be easiest to convince to go along with a fake relationship.

Maybe hiring an actress to play the role of my doting fiancée could work after all. I could make up a story about the match coming from one of the earlier iterations of the app, which would stop Heather's tech team from being able to check the validity of my claims. It's conceivable that some of the earlier results wouldn't have been saved. Then I could take Darren's original suggestion, make the woman sign a non-disclosure agreement, and spend the next three weeks pretending to be in love.

I fling the sponge into the trash can as I finish up the toilets and grab a fresh one to clean the urinals.

The only problem with that is I am the Playboy of Kimbell.

The favorite pastime of the women in this town is to keep up with who I've dated, who I'm currently dating, and who I may be secretly dating. If I introduce a complete stranger as my fiancée, the women will leave no stone unturned until they know everything about her. They'll uncover my secret and expose my lie.

An NDA is no match for this small town of nosey women.

I lean back and admire the shining gleam of the porcelain urinals, then turn my attention to the two shower stalls. Spraying them down with scrubbing bubbles, I watch as the foam slides toward the floor, doing most of the work for me.

The most important thing is to make the fake relationship look as authentic as possible. Sticking close to the truth, so everyone will be convinced that the engagement is real.

I drop the sponge into the bucket of sudsy water and make quick work of the showers. Slipping the gloves from my hands, I toss the water from the bucket and pack up the cleaning supplies.

Pulling my phone from my pocket, I glance at the time.

It's past noon.

I can check the app again to see if I have any matches. I open the developer version of my app and scroll through the most recent metrics.

My mouth drops open as I take in the impact of Darren's video on sign-ups to the site and new subscriptions. My best friend has given me my highest single-day sign-ups since I launched the app, getting in one day what usually takes a month.

Yep, I'll have to buy him a donut in the morning for his trouble.

I chuckle under my breath, then tap the button to open up matches for my hidden profile.

I inhale, waiting for the data to load.

A green bubble pops up with the number 1 inside.

Stumbling backward, I bite down on my fist and resist the urge to hoot and holler in the middle of the bathroom.

I have a match!

Tapping the bubble, stats of the match populate the screen:

98% match

Black female
Entrepreneur
Location … Kimbell, Texas
"Huh?" I stare at the location.
This can't be right.
I swipe the screen to see a picture of the woman.
"Holey Moley …"

CHAPTER 11

ILEY

Darren slaps his hand down over my coffee mug.

"What are you doing?" I ask, looking from him, then to Ivy, the waitress at Gwen's Country Cafe, then back at Darren.

"You're cut off. The last thing I need is you pumped full of more caffeine when you're already bouncing off the walls." Darren shakes his head at Ivy. "Give him some orange juice instead."

I stare down at the remnants of my breakfast—Gwen's Special, which includes four pancakes, three eggs cooked to order, home fries, and a heaping bowl of bacon. All that's left on my plate are a few bacon crumbs and the crispy edges of the fried egg I refuse to eat. My stomach growls as if I haven't eaten a breakfast big enough for two. I contemplate ordering a side of pancakes. Stress eating is not something I'm ashamed of.

As if sensing my needs, Darren pushes his side plate toward me. I grab the homemade biscuit and container of honey butter and slather it on top.

Ivy laughs under her breath, pours juice into my glass, then refills Darren's mug with coffee. "Anything else I can get for you two?"

"No, we're good," Darren says.

As Ivy walks away, I turn back to Darren. "Nothing about this situation is good. Of all the people I could've been matched with on this earth, I get the one woman who would never give me a shot." I look around the near-empty restaurant, making sure no one can hear me. "How on earth am I going to convince her to agree to be fake engaged to me?"

Darren turns his head to scope out the place, then leans forward. "The real question is, why did she fill out a profile on your app?"

I grab my phone and glance at the screen again.

Zaire Kincaid's gorgeous face stares back at me. Her smile is genuine and inviting. Her hair is different. Still short, but she has glossy curls now. I wonder what it would be like to run my hands through them.

These results are baffling.

Lucky for me, we had a quiet shift with no calls, which gave me too much time to fret over what to do next.

I never would've guessed that the woman I had a secret quid pro quo arrangement would be my love match. We sneaked around for weeks as I designed her website. In exchange, she helped revamp the business plan for my dating app and gave me pointers on how to turn a profit.

It was by far the most enjoyable month of this year. Spending late nights into the early morning in her home office working side-by-side and talking for hours about business strategy. Being in the presence of a confident, intelligent, and stunning woman was the best kind of torture. I fought every urge to ask her out on a date, knowing she'd decline in the most polite way.

I was shocked no one ever found out about our covert meetings.

I'm sure the last thing Zaire wanted was to become town gossip as the latest woman on my arm.

Now I need her to be precisely that.

Or at least pretend to be.

"Maybe she's looking for love like everybody else." I pick up my glass. I take a sip of the freshly squeezed juice, calming the rumbling of my stomach.

Darren's eyes narrow. "Last I heard, Zaire isn't single. She's been dating some guy for months and keeping the relationship a secret."

"Since when?" I slam my glass of orange juice on the table. She was single when I was building her website, but that was several months ago. A lot could have changed in that time, and obviously, it had. If Zaire was dating someone, getting her to pretend to be my fake wife-to-be was a dead end.

I suck in a sharp breath, then freeze.

A rush of an emotion I haven't felt in years flares within me.

The telltale signs of unabashed jealousy.

Why am I jealous that some other guy is with Zaire? It's not like I want to date her, regardless of what my app says. This arrangement would strictly be for Heather Grimley's vlog. A complete game changer for my business. Nothing more.

I clench my jaw and stare at Darren, waggling my hand at him to hurry and explain this bomb he dropped.

"Nate said that Harlow-Rose told him that Zaire went to St. Barts for Thanksgiving with some new guy she's dating." Darren stuffs a heaping spoonful of steel-cut oats into his mouth. "So, it doesn't make sense that five days later, she's filling out an online dating profile, does it?"

"She had to have broken things off with the dude. Maybe he was trying to get too serious too soon." I'm hoping for the best. I need Zaire to be single. She's my only match in the thousands of profiles that flooded the site in the past twenty-four hours. I don't have time to wait and hope there could be another. "Or she found out he was a con artist after her money. Either way, she dropped him like a hot potato,"

I say, convinced I still have a chance to talk Zaire into going along with a fake relationship, although I don't have a clue how to do that.

"What if she got dumped, and she's looking for a rebound fling?"

"What idiot would be stupid enough to dump Zaire Kincaid?"

"There's one guy who walked away from her, and it was a scandal."

Now I'm intrigued.

"Anyone I know?" I ask, but I doubt it.

"Nope. Some friend of Harlow-Rose's from Stanford. Guy named Kei Yamamoto. It was a long-distance thing, but everyone knew how close they were getting and expected them to get married."

"Why don't I know any of this?" I chomp on the last bite of the biscuit. The buttery flavor paired with the sweet honey soothes my frayed nerves.

"Excelsior Prep alum don't air dirty laundry to the townies," Darren points his spoon at me.

"Oh, this is some prep school versus public school crap? I thought we had left high school over a decade ago. And if I remember correctly, you spent your last two years in public school."

"Only to get the attention of the scouts so I could get into Alabama. Old habits die hard," Darren shrugs. "But I'll make an exception for you. Zaire took Kei to her sister Sydney's wedding because she wanted to introduce him to her family. But after introductions, Kei had love at first sight with her other sister, India. India fell for Kei, too. I heard she caught them … " Darren wiggles his eyebrows.

"No!" I grimace. "That's shady."

"It gets worse. The next weekend, India and Kei eloped in Vegas. That was about five years ago. I don't think Zaire and India have talked since."

"Can't say I blame her." My heart breaks for what Zaire must have gone through back then. I lean back in my chair, tipping onto the back two legs.

"Well, the first thing we need to find out is if Zaire is or isn't in a relationship," Darren says.

"I could ask Nate to ask Harlow-Rose. You think she'd tell him?" I wonder aloud. Everything about Zaire's secret relationship works to my advantage, especially if it's over now and the town hasn't caught on yet. I could step in and fill that void.

That's pretending to be a couple through the end of February. Three months isn't a long time. With our busy schedules, it would hardly be an imposition for her. She would barely need to be around me, which could be my biggest selling point to get her to go along with the ruse.

"Maybe. But Nate will want to know why we're asking. Do you want to tell him what's going on?"

"No way," I say. "The fewer people who know, the better."

"How about her assistant, Simona? Didn't the two of you date a while back?"

"Those weren't actual dates." I give him a dirty look. "But yeah, I could get the details out of her."

"Now that we have that base covered, we need a plan of how you'll convince Zaire to be your fake fiancée if she is single." Darren pushes his empty bowl to the center. "She can't be bribed with money. She won't lie to her friends and family so you can be on the most popular love guru's vlog. Plus, she's the last person in this town that you can charm. Honestly, she won't have pity for your predicament."

"Now, you're forgetting one thing," I say, unwilling to let Darren rain on my parade. "She joined my app for a reason. Deep down, she believes it's her best shot of finding someone she connects with, and guess what? I'm that guy. The AI don't lie, my friend." I point at my chest. "Ninety-eight percent love match right here. I'm the future love of her life. Of course, I can get her to help me."

"Do you hear yourself? Do you believe what you're saying?" Darren lays a stare on me that sends ice through my veins.

"What are you talking about?"

"Wiley! You didn't rig the AI. You didn't create a fake profile or manipulate the results." Darren hammers in each point. "You are a bona fide, real ninety-eight percent love match for Zaire Kincaid. She could become the love of *your* life. What do you think about that?"

I stare at Darren and wait for some thoughts to slam into my head, but I got nothing. My mind is blank. I got ... nothing.

"I think I don't have time to think about that," I say after a long, excruciating pause.

"You should make time. Do you want to take a chance of ruining something good between the two of you to promote your dating app?"

I fling my hands in the air. "Yeah. Yes. Absolutely."

"Fine," Darren says, staring out the window at a family giggling and chatting as they head toward Bell Park.

"AI or no AI, I'm not fooling myself to think that she'd ever take the results seriously. She won't give me a shot. So, why would I waste my time? When instead, I could try to appeal to ... I don't know yet. But I gotta convince her to go along with this so I don't lose this feature that will put my app in the black. My business needs this."

Darren sighs. "Go to Kincaid Real Estate and talk to Simona. Before you do anything, we need to know if Zaire is still dating the mystery guy."

My cell phone rings.

Darren and I stare at the illuminated screen and see Kincaid Real Estate.

"It's a sign!" I point at the phone. "It's got to be Zaire."

"She probably wants you to delete the profile she made yesterday. I bet she did it as a prank or in a drunken rage," Darren hisses under his breath.

"The match came through around noon. She doesn't strike me as the day-drinking kind," I hiss back as the phone continues to ring. "This is my one chance to pitch the idea to her."

"And what is your pitch? What are you going to say? She's a shrewd businesswoman. You get one shot at this, and you can't mess it up," Darren warns.

The phone continues to ring.

He's right, and I have no clue what to say.

Winging it with Heather is what got me into this mess.

I can't blow my one shot with Zaire.

"You better think fast," Darren says.

Ivy interrupts, hollering across the restaurant, "Wiley Alexander! Answer that phone or put it on silent. It's annoying the other customers."

I glance around. There are two other tables filled with people. One couple in the opposite corner is in an intense conversation, and a family nearby us helps their elementary school-aged children pick out crayons from a box.

"Nobody cares about my phone ringing," I yell back at Ivy, shaking my head as the phone stops ringing. "Crap!"

CHAPTER 12

Z AIRE

~

A WEEK LIKE THIS DESERVES A DRINK.

And not the run-of-the-mill kind.

I'm about to dust off one of my vintage bottles.

Slamming the door to my convertible BMW, I power walk through the antique Spanish door of the garage. My purse falls to the tufted bench of the mudroom as I move with purpose through the kitchen and around the corner to my wine cellar.

The door is ajar as I yank it backward. It bangs against the door stopper before swinging back to slam behind me. I march down the three steps to the main area. Two plush cashmere chairs are arranged around a carved marble table in the center of the room. A glass decanter, crystal glasses, and a wine opener adorn the surface.

Let's see.

Monday, my website crashed.

Tuesday, the tech team started to rebuild the site while the forensic accountants scrambled to find records of my weekend sales.

Wednesday, both teams struggled to accomplish their tasks, predicting delays in achieving both.

And today?

Today I got a call from the furniture production facility about a flood in the warehouse that ruined a million dollars worth of fabrics and materials.

Yes, I'd say this is a Malbec kind of misery.

Moving closer to the curved wall of mahogany wine shelves, I gaze at the labels of the bottles lined in rows under the soft, golden light. I grab a Malbec from Argentina and swipe at the dust coating the label. Several years ago, I bought it on a research trip with Harlow-Rose to the Mendoza region. Popping the cork, I ease onto the chair and pour one of the crystal glasses almost to the brim with the dark purple liquid. The heady scent of blueberry and black pepper teases my nose as I swirl it around in the glass. Goosebumps pepper my skin from the chilled air.

It isn't enough that my new furniture business is suffering from setback after setback.

I still need to figure out what to do about the new man in my life, who doesn't exist, before my family gets into town this weekend. I can't believe I was desperate enough to join a dating app to find a man before the wedding. I'm glad I came to my senses and deleted my profile before the AI matched me with someone.

After all that, I am absolutely entitled to wallow in self-pity for a night.

Okay, maybe a night is too long.

An hour or two should be enough.

I got work to do.

Taking a long sip, I allow the wine to cloak me in warmness as the faint hum of the cooling system lulls me. I forget all my problems as I close my eyes.

I envision being back on the beach in St. Barts. The warm sun basks my skin as I sit on the sand. Balmy ocean waves crash against my body as I—

A loud creak pierces my memories.

The hairs on the back of my neck stand on end.

The sound gets louder as if someone is opening the door to my wine cellar.

My eyes fling open, and I grab the bottle of wine as panic slices through me.

Oh, God.

Someone is in here.

I'm about to be robbed. Raped? Killed?

No way, not tonight.

Whoever tried to prey on me picked the wrong night to mess with Zaire Kincaid.

CHAPTER 13

Z AIRE

~

I PIVOT ON THE CHAIR, THEN HURL THE BOTTLE OF WINE AT the door as it swings open.

A bloodcurdling scream pierces the air. The sound feels distant and disconnected from me, but I know I'm the one screaming as a dark figure steps into the room. It's a man, large and imposing, filling the entire door frame space. He raises his arms to protect himself from the shattering glass as dark wine soaks him. I reach for my glass of wine and throw it at him for good measure, then stumble backward from the chair, looking around for something else to defend myself with.

"Zaire! Wait!" the man says. Glass crunches under his feet as he comes closer into the room.

"Don't come near me!" I yell, then reach for another bottle and raise it above my head.

He doesn't stop, closing the distance between us. My heart pounds in my chest, and my arms feel heavy and weighed down. The closer he gets, the more I worry I won't be able to throw the bottle in my hand. Fear grips me like a vise as he comes nearer.

I say with a trembling voice, "I swear, I will knock you out …"

A shaft of golden light from the wall sconces crosses his face.

His extremely handsome face.

I freeze, then lower the bottle to my side as I stare at him.

Heat blazes over my skin as I take in all of him.

The piercing, brilliant blue eyes stare back at me with amusement as he wipes wine from his chiseled jaw. His lips curve into a seductive, playful grin as he licks droplets of wine from his mouth. The move sends butterflies fluttering through my stomach.

His white Polo shirt, stained purple from the wine, clings to his muscular chest. Strong, flexing biceps move efficiently as he squeezes his shirt to remove the excess liquid.

Has Wiley Alexander always been this drop-dead gorgeous?

Yes, of course, he has.

How else would he have become the Playboy of Kimbell?

I shake the thoughts away.

"Wiley! I almost killed you!" I scream, then lower the bottle of Harlow-Rose Cabernet Sauvignon to the table, grateful I didn't have to sacrifice my bestie's best wine to save my life. "What are you doing in my house?"

"You left the garage door up. Your back door was wide open," Wiley says, a deliciously sexy grin growing wide on his face that causes my stomach to do another flip-flop.

Had I left my house open? Did I remember to lock the doors when I got home? Or had I been too consumed with wallowing in my misfortune that I forgot?

I shake my head.

"I was coming in here to save you from some bad guy," Wiley says, stepping over the broken shards of the wine bottle to close the gap between us. "But obviously, you're fine."

69

"Well, I don't know about that," I clap back. "You scared the crap out of me."

"Didn't stop you from going on the offensive to take me out. Guess you don't need a hero after all." Wiley eases down into the chair, staining the fabric with wine.

I wince, but instead of complaining, I sit in the chair across from him. My mind races with calls I'll need to make to get the wine cellar cleaned up, and I add upholstery cleaning to my mental to-do list—and the bill will be sent directly to Wiley Alexander.

"So, this is some kind of safety check? I thought only cops did that," I say, still confused about why Wiley is here.

He shakes his head, an embarrassed sheepish look playing in his eyes. "I came over to talk about the website for Kincaid Furnishings."

I press my hands against the cool marble and give him my best penetrating stare. "I am so pissed at you. Your website crashed on Cyber Monday! Cyber Monday, Wiley! It's the biggest shopping day of the year. The Kimbell Furnishings site was replaced with one of those annoying 404 error pages," I say, then raise a finger before he can interrupt. "I'm not finished. I also lost all the sales from Black Friday and the weekend. Poof! Gone into the black hole that is the internet. Hundreds of thousands of dollars of custom furniture orders have vanished. And I call you to fix the mess, and you ignore me for days!"

Wiley leans across the table and places his hands over mine. The smoothness of his touch belies the roughness I expected from him being a firefighter. He caresses my hands in his and gives them a squeeze, then says, "Your website is back up, and the sales have all been recovered from the weekend. All six hundred forty-one thousand dollars of them."

"You're kidding? You fixed it … all?" I grip his hands.

"Of course I did." Wiley winks at me. "But the problem wasn't my website. Hackers got in through one of your servers and corrupted a critical part of the code that took the site down. I had built a self-destruct trigger to protect your data if that ever happened, but I forgot to tell your tech team how to access it. Everything was still in the back end once I cleared the virus."

"The experts I hired told me the sales were lost for good. I wouldn't get them back. They said it would take over a week to build a new e-commerce site for Kincaid Furnishings."

A confident smirk crosses his face. "That's what Simona told me when she called yesterday. She suspected those companies were preying on your panic and milking how long it would take to drive up their fees. So, I suggested she fire them and let me take over. Everything is back working. I gave my info to your head of technology, so if there are any other glitches, he can reach me."

"Simona called you yesterday," I say, easing my hands from his. It's impossible to hide my shock and relief.

"Yes. It was easy enough for me to work on it remotely without worrying you. When you got called out to the furniture warehouse today, Simona let me know. I went to the Kincaid Real Estate offices and worked with your tech guys to triple-check that everything was in order. I asked that they let me be the one to tell you the good news." Wiley leans back in the chair, balancing it on the back two legs. He crosses his arms over his chest as his eyes drink in the sight of me. I feel myself blushing and cross my arms to mirror his position.

Hackers. A virus. Experts that aren't experts.

Wiley didn't ruin my business. He saved it.

"I owe you big time," I say, deciding not to charge him for staining my cashmere chair with wine. Excitement floods my veins at the unexpected turn of events. I'm willing to pay a premium rate for the magic Wiley produced. I'll give him twice what the tech firm was going to charge me. "You saved my business. I was going to have a P.R. nightmare if you hadn't fixed it. Name your price."

A sly smile spreads across Wiley's face. "I don't want your money. You know how we do things."

"Quid pro quo," I nod, resting my elbows on the table. "You help my business, so I help yours. What do you need this time?"

Wiley returns the chair to the floor and slips his hand into his pocket. A second later, he's clutching a small dark blue velvet box, which he places in the middle of the table.

"What's that?" I ask, reaching for the box.

Wiley blocks me from grabbing it.

"First, tell me about this guy you're dating," Wiley says, a hint of a challenge in his aqua blue eyes. "Is it serious?"

I freeze.

How could news of my fake boyfriend have gotten all the way to Wiley? I swear, living in a small town can be so annoying.

My mouth goes dry. This is not good. Wiley knows.

Why in the world did I join that stupid app? Wiley designed it. It's his company. He probably has some kind of alert when anyone in Kimbell joins, spying on our profiles to see if we're getting hits or not.

No, come on, seriously?

Wiley Alexander is too busy to stalk dating profiles. He spent the last twenty-four hours fixing my website, not checking up on the new subscribers to the Ladies Love Country Boys app.

Paranoia is not a good look, Zaire. Stop it.

Wiley continues, "From what I hear, the guy took you to St. Barts for Thanksgiving last week, right?"

I cringe. He knows. I don't know why he would pay attention to the profiles on his app, but he absolutely knows that I completed one. Now I have to explain why I joined a dating app if I'm already in a relationship. How in the world am I going to explain this? Think, come on.

"Or maybe the guy isn't so amazing," Wiley says, his tone full of ... empathy and ... concern. "Maybe things didn't go well last week, and he dumped you. Or you dumped him. Or y'all decided amicably to part ways—"

"Why don't you just say it? You know I joined your dating app a couple of days ago, don't you?" I say, still not sure how I'm going to explain why. "Well, it doesn't matter because I deleted my profile immediately after creating it."

"It does matter. It matters more than you know," Wiley says.

There's a raw vulnerability in his words that I've never noticed before. His aqua blue eyes brighten as he stares at me, but I can't read his expression. The cocky playboy vibe is long gone, and I feel like I'm looking into the face of a man who ... needs me. But why?

"What's in the box, Wiley?" I ask, desperate to understand what's going on.

"The key to everything I ever wanted in life," Wiley says, turning the box over and over in his hands.

"You're not making any sense."

"Are you in a relationship, Zaire? Can you tell me that?"

"No, okay!" I fling my hands in the air. "I'm not in a relationship."

My curiosity about Wiley's unusual behavior overrides my desire to protect the lie I've told my family. The lie that has somehow spread across Kimbell like wildfire.

Wiley relaxes. He bites his bottom lip as a sexy twinkle sparkles in his eyes. He pushes the box toward me.

For the first time, I register that it's a jewelry box.

A ring box.

"Open it," Wiley urges.

My hand trembles as I flip the box open.

A gasp escapes my lips.

"Zaire Kincaid," Wiley says. "Will you marry me?"

CHAPTER 14

W<small>ILEY</small>

Z<small>AIRE'S LAUGHTER RINGS THROUGH THE AIR AS SHE</small> clutches her stomach.

It's the most delightful and infectious sound I've ever heard, causing me to smile when I should be ... hurt? Offended? Pissed?

More like relieved that her reaction is what I expected.

When I returned the call from Kincaid Real Estate, my initial disappointment that it was Simona reaching out and not Zaire quickly vanished. I knew saving Zaire's website was my ticket in. The open door of opportunity that, if timed right, could help me convince Zaire to take on the role of my doting and loving fiancée.

The only wildcard was the mystery man she was dating. The one who'd swept her off her feet and surprised her with a romantic holiday in St. Barts. The guy I wasn't sure she was still dating. Sure, she'd created a profile on the Ladies Love Country Boys app, but my records showed she deleted the profile thirty minutes later. As I worked like a madman to figure out what had taken the Kincaid Furnishings website down on Cyber Monday, a thought tormented me. What if they'd had a lovers' quarrel but had made up now?

If Zaire was in a relationship, my entire strategy had to be scrapped. I hate to celebrate the end of a relationship, but whatever broke up Zaire and St. Barts Guy is my salvation. I hope he doesn't come back before I convince her to do me this not-so-little favor.

"Who put you up to this?" Zaire asks as her fits of laughter die down. "Harlow-Rose is too sweet to pull a prank on anyone, and Simona would be too afraid I'd fire her when I found out what she'd done." She stares at the ceiling. "Do you know my hairdresser?"

I chuckle. "Everybody knows LaQuandelier."

"Aha! She told you to do this, didn't she? She's been badgering me about my love life."

"Wait. Let me get this straight. You didn't tell Harlow-Rose, Simona, or Quan about St. Barts Guy?" I ask, unable to hide my suspicion. My thoughts wander into crazy places like the guy is in the C.I.A. or worse, he's a clown in a traveling circus, and Zaire doesn't want anyone to know she's fallen head over heels in love with him. I feel a sharp pang in my chest at the thought.

Zaire coughs, then sputters before responding, "Of course, they know about him. But I never told them his name, and they haven't met him."

"Not even Harlow-Rose?"

"Oh, well, umm, of course, my bestie has met him. But no one else. Doesn't matter anymore since he's out of the picture."

I lean back in the chair again. This works out better than I hoped. If Harlow-Rose is the only one who knows St. Barts Guy's identity and what he looks like, it'll be much easier for me to swoop in as Zaire's secret man. Darren is in on my plans and bringing Harlow-Rose into the fold wouldn't be the end of the world. In fact, it could help convince the rest of the town that the fake engagement is real.

"You want to talk about it?" Curiosity gets the better of me. Who is this guy who let a smart, brilliant woman like Zaire Kincaid slip through his fingers? If I had been in his spot, I wouldn't have made the same mistake. But Zaire would never take me seriously as a love interest. Good thing I don't need her to. I need to convince her it's in the best interest of both our businesses for her to be my fake fiancée.

A sexy frown emerges between her eyebrows. She picks up the box that contains my grandma's ring and turns it toward me. The sparkling two-carat nearly flawless round diamond sparkles under the soft lights of the wall sconces. It sits within a halo setting, encircled by smaller diamonds, and accented within a channel-style band filled with more diamonds. Grandma loved to tell the story of how her feisty and somewhat of a con artist husband won the ring in an illegal Texas Hold'em poker game in Galveston from a wealthy widower, then drove for hours back to Kimbell to propose to her at sunrise. She always dreamed of seeing this ring on the finger of a woman I loved as much as grandpa loved her.

A part of me feels guilty for using this special ring as part of my scheme, but if Zaire was really my fiancée, everyone in town would expect this to be the ring on her finger. The whole town knows grandma left it to me to give to my future wife. It sells the story better than anything else can.

"What I want to talk about is why you're proposing to me out of the blue with this gorgeous engagement ring?" Zaire places the ring back on the table and pushes it toward me. "Start talking. What's going on here?"

"Funny how someone can be right in front of you, and you don't realize it." I search her face for an opening. A glimmer of interest that I can grab onto. Instead, I get back a blank look of utter confusion. "Come on, Zaire. We've hung out a few times in the past, and we've always gotten along."

"We have *worked* together on a few projects. We share the same passion for our businesses and have complimentary work ethics."

I suck in a breath, then push a little more. "And along the way, we became friends."

"More like acquaintances," Zaire corrects.

"And you find me irresistible." I give her a wink.

"Like every other woman in Kimbell," Zaire counters, unfazed by my attempt to flirt. "I doubt there's a woman on this planet who can resist your charms, Wiley Alexander. But if I remember correctly, you were doubling down on making your dating app business a success. Cutting out all distractions, including women, so you could turn a profit. Now, six months later, you expect me to believe you're interested in getting married? And not to any person in Kimbell. To me?" She scoffs. "Stop insulting my intelligence and tell me why you decided I should be your wife."

Zaire laces her fingers and rests her chin on top, giving me a curious glare. She is gorgeous. I can't deny that. But I can't get distracted by her. It's time for me to go all in on my pitch.

I lean forward, closing the distance between us, and look her in the eyes. "An opportunity has come up that I think would benefit both the Ladies Love Country Boys dating app and Kincaid Real Estate."

As if on queue, she raises an eyebrow and leans in closer. If there's one thing I can count on, it's Zaire's ambition and drive for success. It's the reason why I sought her out months ago to become my mentor for my business. I could only get so far following her talk and articles for the Kimbell Business Bureau. I needed direct advice from the entrepreneur queen. Sure, I had to sweeten the deal by offering my services to create an e-commerce website grounded in predictive analytics for her new business venture, but the weeks I spent making it were worth every second.

"Keep talking," Zaire says.

I launch into the story of the opportunity to be on love guru Heather Grimley's vlog, my conference call with her, and the competition in place to decide which AI-based dating app will become the feature for her vlog.

"So, you see that this could be huge for me."

"It's the kind of publicity you can't pay for. It would give your app national recognition and no doubt boost your bottom line. Are you making a profit yet?"

"No, but I'm close. I scaled back on the operating costs and changed my advertising strategy to rely more on content marketing than paid ads. I'm no longer throwing money down the drain, and forecasts show I can be in the black in about another year."

"This article would accelerate that." She taps her fingers on the table.

"Exactly!" I clap my hands. "I knew you'd understand—"

"I understand why this is good publicity for a dating app. I do not understand how a love guru, even with millions of social media followers, could help Kincaid Real Estate. It sheds no light on why you showed up here with an engagement ring and proposed. Care to explain that?"

I take a deep breath. "I needed to stand out from the other apps. So, I may have told her I found the love of my life through the app and that I'm engaged right now."

"You did ... what?" Her hands fall to her sides as she looks at me like I've lost my mind.

"When Heather heard that, she gave the feature to me on the spot. In hindsight, not my finest moment, but now I'm stuck. If I come clean, I won't just lose out on the feature that could bring more business to my app—"

"You could become the story, which would bankrupt you for sure." Zaire leans back in her chair.

"Now you see why I need you to marry me?"

"No, I do not."

"Come on, Zaire," I plead with her. "We wouldn't go through with the marriage. I need you to pretend to be my fiancée until a few weeks after the vlog is posted. It's a Valentine's day thing, so that's only about three months."

"Three months? Wiley! Dozens of women would trip all over themselves to be your fake fiancée. Let's start with your high school sweetheart, Izzie. Or how about Erin at the fire station, Brianna at Elevation cupcake shop, or half a dozen nurses at St. Elizabeth's? Shall I go on? How on earth did you pick me out of all the women in town?"

"Wow. Didn't realize you were keeping score," I give her another wink.

Zaire rolls her eyes, not impressed by my attempt to joke, although I am feeling some kind of way about the fact she knows the women I've dated in the past. She's been paying closer attention than I thought. Not that any of that matters. I need Zaire to enter this fake engagement to help boost my business. Nothing else.

"Kind of hard not to when you're the playboy of Kimbell. News of your exploits travel fast," Zaire snaps back. "Why not ask one of them?"

I drag a hand down my face. Honesty would be the best policy in this case, but it's not a card I'm willing to share. Especially since Zaire has no clue that the dating app matched us. To convince her to go along with my plan, I have to appeal to her brain and not her heart.

"Because I need someone with a similar incentive to see this thing through and be able to keep their ... feelings in check," I admit. Asking one of my exes to be my fake fiancée would be an epic disaster. It's bad enough that none of them can take the hint that our relationships are over. I still get calls from them, even though I've moved on.

"You want this to be like a business deal?"

"Yes. We worked on the Kincaid Furnishings website for a month, and not once did you fall for any of my attempts to flirt with you." I remember with a tinge of disappointment that Zaire seemed immune to my charms. In reality, if she'd hinted that she was interested, there's no way I would have passed on the chance to ask her out, even if I was supposed to be on break from dating to focus on my business. "You're a machine, incapable of letting matters of the heart distract you."

"I wouldn't go that ... far," Zaire says, scowling.

"The vlog is going to focus on the creator of the dating app as much as the app itself. Heather will want to hear all about our story, including the fact that we are two successful entrepreneurs."

"Two?" Zaire laughs under her breath. "I'm the only successful entrepreneur in this room. You're still trying to get there."

I raise my hands and give her a smile. "You got me there. But think about it. As Heather is interviewing you, she'll have no choice but to cover your career. You'll talk about your businesses and how it's the reason we spent time together after growing up in the same town and never knowing each other. Kincaid Real Estate, Kincaid Construction, and Kincaid Furnishings will all be highlighted as much as my dating app. We can have the filming done in a Kincaid lake house filled with Kincaid furniture for perfect product placement. It's a win-win for both of us with no hearts getting involved."

"And all fifty million of her followers across the U.S. and the world will think that we're in love."

I can tell she's still struggling with the idea. I have to nudge her toward what I know will benefit both of us. "Yes, while we count the money rolling in from the increase in our businesses. In March, we can fake a break-up, end things, and move on with our lives."

"You think it's that simple?" Zaire shakes her head. "It's not. My sister, Persia, is moving her wedding to the Hill Country. She and Yves are now going to get married at Harlow-Rose's winery on Christmas Day. My entire family is going to descend on this place like vultures."

I walk over to her and kneel by the side of her chair. Reaching for the box with the engagement ring, I push it back toward her hand. "So, won't you be glad you have me by your side when India and Kei show up?"

The air between us shifts. A tangible force radiating intense and undeniable energy as Zaire turns toward me. Her features soften, and I see the flicker of hurt and embarrassment in her dark brown eyes. I reach a hand toward her and caress the side of her face, wanting her to know that I understand and I can be the support she needs. Not only to get more recognition for her business but to be her shoulder to lean on when her family comes to town.

"You heard about that, huh?" Zaire asks, her voice low and soft.

"Small town, you know," I say, although I got a crash course in Zaire's man-stealing sister from Darren a couple days ago.

She glances down at the ring sparkling in the box and takes a deep breath. When she looks back at me, I sense the change in her. The lightbulb has gone on in her mind. She's found value in my proposal. Different from how I tried to pitch things, but beggars can't be choosers.

I pull the ring from the box, then grab her left hand. A flutter of nerves race through my body. The moment has gone from being rehearsed to feeling ... real. I'm down on one knee in front of the woman my dating app shows is a ninety-eight percent love match for ... *me*.

I can't stop to consider what any of that means.

Instead, I slip the ring on her finger as I hold my breath, waiting for her to protest.

She doesn't.

"So, will you be my fake fiancée?"

CHAPTER 15

Z AIRE

~

"CAVEMAN STYLE OR WEDDING NIGHT STYLE?"

An army of butterflies takes flight in my stomach. I look up into Wiley's sparkling aqua eyes as he reaches a hand down toward me.

"What are you talking about?" I ask.

"I need to carry you out of here," Wiley says with a wink, then leans over to wrap an arm behind me.

"Whoa! Wait a minute," I say, pressing my hands into his chest.

A rock-hard, muscular chest. Well defined and toned beyond belief.

I bite my bottom lip, then say, "Sweeping me off my feet won't change my mind. My answer is still no."

Wiley shakes his head at me as if I'm some foolish girl, then glances back toward the door.

My eyes follow his movement, and I see why he wants to carry me out. The floor is trashed with spilled wine and shards of broken glass from the wine bottle I threw at him. A quick glance down at my bare feet and his in sneakers confirm that his approach is better.

But I still resist.

Do I want Wiley to carry me out of here?

No. Don't answer that, Zaire.

"I'm not giving up yet. It's better if we discuss this over dinner before you give me your final answer." Wiley leans against the table, then asks, "You must be a piggyback kind of girl?"

A laugh bursts from my mouth despite all my efforts to hold it in. "None of the above. I can avoid the broken glass. The chunks are so big, I'd be blind to step on one."

To prove my point, I take a bold step onto a dry block of travertine. No sooner as my foot contacts the cool floor, I feel a sharp, searing pain. I recoil and stumble backward, cursing under my breath.

"Caveman style it is," Wiley says, shaking his head at me.

Before I can squeal in protest, he lifts me into the air and throws me over his shoulder. Patting my butt with two quick hits, he says, "This is one perk of being my fake fiancée. Getting free rides."

"Wiley!" I squirm in his firm grasp. My arms dangle down his back, close to his rear. I force myself to resist returning the favor with a few smacks. "Put me down. This is ridiculous!"

"I will. Soon enough."

Boy did soon enough come too soon.

Moments later, he lowers me onto a chair in the dining nook next to the kitchen. His hand grips my calf and raises my foot into the air.

"How bad is it?" I ask, trying to ignore the sting. "Is it bleeding?"

"Wow, if you don't have the prettiest feet I've ever seen." Wiley turns my foot to one side, then the other. "And soft, too."

"Can you stay focused?" I demand, wondering if I can stay focused. The man is an incorrigible and incurable flirt, but I never thought I could get caught up in his shenanigans.

And I must admit I am caught up.

I'm thinking about agreeing to Wiley's fake engagement despite my protests.

I don't have any other options.

Wiley inadvertently solved all my problems with his fake proposal.

It's the perfect solution to my imaginary boyfriend fiasco.

He could be the stand-in for the mystery man I told my family I spent the Thanksgiving holidays with in St. Barts. He'd be by my side as I faced seeing India for the first time since she betrayed me five years ago. I would get a reprieve from disaster.

I grimace as Wiley adopts a serious expression, then squeezes my foot.

"I'm a professional. You're in expert hands," He says. With his fingernail, he swipes against the bottom of my foot, then declares, "Got it."

Leaning forward, I stare at the glass shard about the size of a mustard seed and flush hot with embarrassment.

"No blood. You don't need a band-aid." Wiley lowers my foot to the floor.

"I swear it felt like a boulder had sliced through my foot. Is that all it was?"

"You were lucky. Maybe you'll listen to me the next time I try to warn you."

I grab my foot and raise it close to my face, thankful for my nightly cocoa butter and sock wrap routine. If I stare intently, I can make out a tiny puncture on my skin dotted red. Shaking my head, I let my foot drop to the floor.

Wiley grabs a chair and puts it in front of me, then sits. Only inches separate us. He looks relaxed … and drop-dead gorgeous.

My gaze lingers on his face. The square jaw and full lips. The aqua blue eyes are the color of the Caribbean Sea. A smile spreads across his face. He's enjoying this. He's the kind of guy that has had women gawking over him since he could waddle out of his crib. Nothing about my stares is making him the least bit uncomfortable. Not only is he okay with it.

He expects it.

And yet, his expression is far from cocky or arrogant.

He's downright ... endearing?

I push the thoughts from my mind.

"What's your biggest concern about being my fake fiancée?"

"Where do I start? How would it work? People will want details about this relationship. What would we tell them?"

Wiley scratches his blonde locks and frowns. "Honestly, I didn't think past pitching the idea to you. No way I thought you'd go for any of this."

And if Persia's wedding was still in Paris, I wouldn't have. But my family will be here soon, and I can't endure the incessant questions about this new man in my life that doesn't exist. All the preparations for Persia's wedding won't stop them from berating me about getting the secret man to come to the wedding. Coming clean is not an option. Telling them we broke up while in paradise will usher in a wave of nauseating pity.

This is my only option.

Wiley continues, "You're better at project management than I am. You can come up with a solid plan. It's why you've been as successful as you've been."

Right. He goes in for the kill with praise. I am my mother's daughter.

I rub a hand along my neck as the thoughts fall into place in my mind. The best way to handle this is like any other business project. We need a business plan that outlines the background of the idea, objectives, and end goal.

I say, "We'd need to stick as close to the truth as possible. We don't have to come up with some crazy way that we met or try to memorize a lot of useless details about each other."

"Nope. We know each other very well."

"I wouldn't say very well. I mean, we knew of each other growing up but didn't hang with the same people."

"But it's a small town, so it doesn't matter if we hung out or not. You know a crap ton about me, and I do about you."

"True. So, after all these years, how could we have gotten to where we shifted from acquaintances to ..."

"Lovers?" Wiley wiggles his eyebrows at me.

"Oh, you would go there." I fling my hands in the air.

"Only if you let me."

My mouth drops open as I stare at Wiley. "What kind of fake engagement are you expecting? Casual hook-up while we lie to people? Acquaintances with benefits?" I ask, my voice reaching a soprano.

Wiley raises his hands in surrender. "Zaire, I know you wouldn't, and I respect you too much to seriously suggest it. I was teasing you. If we do this, there would be no hooking up."

"What about kissing?" I ask, trying to understand the boundaries of the arrangement.

Wiley hesitates, tilting his head toward the ceiling.

"Wiley! You think we should kiss all over town to prove to people that the fake engagement is real?" I ask although the idea of it doesn't repulse me as much as my response would suggest.

"Of course not, but I'm an affectionate guy," Wiley leans back in the chair, balancing it on the back two legs. "How about this. No mouth-to-mouth kissing, but if I need to kiss your hand or your cheek or something to sell it to whoever we're around, then that's allowed." He raises an eyebrow at me.

"Fine. I suppose some public displays of affection would be expected," I say, satisfied with the compromise.

"Does this mean you're going to do it?" Wiley asks, rummaging through the Christmas-decorated sugar cookies in the bowl on the table. He settles on a gingerbread man and slides it out of the plastic wrapper. Popping the head off, he tosses it in his mouth, then looks back at me. "You'll be my fake fiancée?"

"You haven't answered my question. How will we explain to people how we started dating in the first place?"

His eyes dance with excitement. I know he knows I'm only moments away from caving. Still, I'm not sure I should compound one big lie with another massive lie. This could get out of hand quick and leave me looking like a fool if it all comes out.

"When I showed up at your office to fix the website, your team was shocked that I was the one who created it in the first place," Wiley says. "None of them knew I'd spent a month holed up here designing it with you. That means we've already had a secret relationship."

"Secret *working* relationship."

Wiley winks at me. "Close enough. So that's when we fell in love. We realized we were soul mates as I spent every waking hour I wasn't on shift here with you working on the website."

"But you have a reputation for being a flirt, a ladies' man, and a playboy who goes through women like tissues. So, I wanted to make sure it was real before we went public."

Wiley grimaces. "I'm not that bad."

I raise an eyebrow. "You haven't paraded any girlfriends around town in months since you've focused on growing your dating app business. That helps with the story."

"You're in that social media group, too?"

I refuse to confirm or deny. Instead, I say, "That means we've been together for about six months?"

"Right. We kept it a secret, except Darren knows about us," Wiley says.

"He does?"

"He was there when I blurted out to Heather that I was engaged. He knows I need a fake fiancée. No one would believe I'd keep something like this from him," Wiley says, then stuffs the rest of the gingerbread man into his mouth. "Which brings us to Harlow-Rose. How do we get her to believe this?"

"I tell her the truth. She'll keep our secret." I say, knowing it won't be that easy. My bestie is going to flip out when she hears about this charade.

"Good, because trying to explain to her how you rebounded from your breakup with St. Barts guy and now claim that I'm the guy you've dated for the past few months would be a tough sell."

"Impossible. So, how did you propose?"

"Stick to the truth," Wiley says, grinning. He reaches for my left hand, which still has his grandmother's ring on it.

"What does that mean?"

"You were pissed because the website I built for you crashed. I spent the past thirty-six hours getting it back up and running because of my undying love for you. When it was fixed, I came over to surprise you but scared you. You threw a wine bottle at me." Wiley leans back and points at his stained shirt. "I gave you the good news. You were ecstatic, but that was nothing compared to the look on your face when I placed the ring on the table."

"You're better at this than you thought," I say.

"Of course, you laughed and thought I was joking. I assured you I wasn't. Got down on one knee and proposed, and you said yeah!" Wiley raises a hand toward me.

I give him a reluctant high-five. Then freeze. "There's one problem with all this."

"Just one?"

I roll my eyes. "Everyone knows about my trip to St. Barts for Thanksgiving with my boyfriend," I say, flexing my fingers with air quotes. "It's going to look like I lied about that."

"You're safe."

"How?"

"I spent Thanksgiving alone in a vacation rental on Padre Island. Didn't feel like being around my sister and her husband and all her kids and my mom. They would've been on me like crazy about settling down and finding a good woman and having kids."

"You too?"

"Women aren't the only ones who have to suffer. Especially when your mother is Sally Alexander," Wiley says, chuckling. "I needed time to focus on upgrades to the dating app. If I can get this off the ground, it could be my ticket to financial security. After that, I'll find a wifey. Not before."

"Money isn't everything."

"Says the multi-millionaire."

"Touché." I shrug. "And how would we break up when you no longer need me to be your fake fiancée? Who would be the bad guy?"

"Me, of course. I have lots of practice at it." Wiley rolls his eyes.

"What reason would we give?"

"You want kids, right?"

"Of course."

"I've learned that's a pretty big deal breaker for women. I've used that card a few times to get out of clingy relationships. It will work for this one, too. I'm sure a few of those exes will come out of the woodwork to commiserate with you on doing the right thing by dumping me."

Wiley looks impressed with himself.

"So, you don't see yourself as a father?"

He laughs. "Of course I do. I'm going to be an awesome dad, and I'm looking forward to it."

"You lied to get out of relationships."

"It's a rare excuse I use when the woman I'm with isn't letting go," Wiley says, then squirms under my glare. "Don't hate me."

"I have no words for this." I cover my face with my hands.

Wiley pulls my hands away. "I got you. We can do this."

"Wiley, you'll have to be very convincing that you're head over heels attracted to me for people to believe we're in love."

"Won't need to fake that ... at ... all," Wiley says. He strokes a finger along my thigh.

I slap his hand and push it away.

"Ow! That hurt."

"Keep your hands to yourself."

"For now," Wiley says, then reaches for the bottom of his shirt and pulls it over his head.

My mouth drops open as I gawk at his bare chest.

"What are you doing?" The words are breathy, coming from my mouth.

"I need to get this sticky wine off me, and you need more time to get comfortable with the idea of being my fake fiancée. Can you toss this in the wash?"

Wiley throws the shirt at me. I try to duck, but it lands on my head. As I fight to get the fabric off my face, I can't help but notice the faint smell of wine mixed with Wiley's cologne. It's intoxicating in more ways than one.

I snatch the shirt away and hold it away from my body. "Sure."

"Shorts too, but I'll toss those outside the bathroom door. Can't show you all my goodies yet," He says, then heads toward my master bedroom.

"The guest bathroom is that way," I yell after him, pointing in the opposite direction.

"I know, but I want the overhead Vichy shower with aromatherapy. Think I'll go for lavender …"

CHAPTER 16

Z AIRE

~

Holding my hand up to the light, I stare at the gorgeous ring once again.

The hum of the washing machine can't drown out the sounds of Wiley singing the old 1950s hit Splish Splash, loud and off-key, floating from my bathroom.

Wiley was right.

I need time to weigh the pros and cons of going along with his scheme.

I glance down at the flawless round diamond sparkling under the recess lights of my living room and let out a low whistle. It's stunning. Not something that should be used as a prop for a fake engagement. Wiley should save this for the woman who will capture his heart. How will his future wife feel about me wearing her ring for months as a ruse in the fake engagement? Wiley is too focused on growing his business and not thinking clearly. Shouldn't I look out for his future love and refuse to wear the ring?

Or maybe I should let go of my petty beef with India and stop lying to my family about being in a relationship. After five years, I should've moved on by now. Every relationship since then has sputtered and collapsed while India was off living her best life with the man I thought would be my husband. As the years ticked by, it's like I lost my love mojo until I stopped trying.

That didn't stop my family from pressuring me to find a new man.

I know they felt awful for me and what I endured when India stole my boyfriend. The extra pressure from them to hurry and move on didn't help. Especially since I'd hit a relationship dry spell.

Who cares if I haven't been able to snag a husband in that time? Doesn't mean I need to lie about being in a loving relationship when I'm not. Right? But that's what I felt forced to do. I made this bed, and now, I need to decide if I'm going to lie in it … or not.

I need a voice of reason.

Grabbing my cell phone, I call Harlow-Rose. It goes to voice mail. I end the call, then try the direct number to the winery. Knowing my bestie, she's working late in the vineyards.

She picks up on the first ring.

"Hey you, I've been meaning to call but got caught up in examining the chemical analysis of my merlot. It's off a bit, and I gotta figure out what to do about that," Harlow-Rose rambles.

"Why were you going to call me?"

"Your website for Kincaid Furnishings is back working. Word spread like wildfire across town that Wiley swooped in and saved the day," Harlow-Rose says, a subtle curiosity in her tone. "And he was holed up in your house for about a month creating it earlier this year."

I pull my shirt from tucked into my pencil skirt and hike up the form-fitting knee-length fabric as I slump down, cross-legged, onto the couch. "That's a lot of detailed information."

"That's not all."

"What else could there be?"

"People are wondering if Wiley might have a crush on you."

I sit up straight. "You're joking."

"Nope. There's a target on your back with the ladies in town. Some ladies are worried that you'll become his next amour."

My mouth gapes open, but no words come out.

She continues, "But others are convinced you'd never give him the time of day because you're smitten with the guy who took you to St. Barts. You know, the guy you and I both know doesn't exist."

"It's only been a couple of hours since he fixed the site. How on earth has all this gone on?"

"You know how bad it is in Kimbell with gossip," Harlow-Rose says, giggling under her breath. She lowers her voice, then says, "I want to know why you never told me about this secret website project with Wiley. Did something happen between the two of you?"

"Nothing happened with Wiley ... back then." I pause. The shower is still running, and Wiley has switched to singing Waterfalls by TLC in falsetto. I drag my hand down my face and shake my head.

"Back then?" Harlow-Rose asks. "Wait a second."

I hear her footsteps racing along the stone floor of the winery, then up the back stairs that lead to her apartment on the second floor.

"Okay," she says, panting. "Spill it. What's going on with you and Wiley?"

Wiley will be out of the shower soon, so I waste no time. The words tumble from my mouth a mile a minute.

Harlow-Rose is unnervingly quiet.

"Did you get all that?" I ask.

"Sorry. Stunned. Perplexed. Dazed. Confused."

"And reduced to speaking in disparate single words. That's great. My Stanford degreed best friend has lost all intelligence after hearing what I'm contemplating. I need you to talk me out of this."

"You think you can pretend to be his fake fiancée for three months?"

"I didn't think that part all the way through. I was only focused on the benefits of being his fake fiancée for Persia's wedding when I'll come face to face with India for the first time since she stole my boyfriend from me."

"This is Wiley Alexander. The charming playboy of Kimbell."

"Yeah. And?"

"Aren't you the slightest bit concerned that you're going to fall for him ... for real?"

I snort and fall over on the couch. "You mean the guy singing TLC songs at the top of his lungs in my shower right now? Not a chance."

"No ..."

"Oh wait, now he's transitioned to gangster rap. Sounds like old school Snoop Dogg."

Harlow-Rose laughs. "Okay, maybe that's not a risk. How are you going to feel when the fake relationship ends? Won't it be just as bad telling your family that you couldn't make things work with Wiley, especially after your face is blasted across the country on love guru Heather Grimley's vlog?"

"He has a foolproof exit strategy," I say, then tell her the reason we'll give for the breakup after the vlog is live.

"Not bad," Harlow-Rose says. "He's funny and charming and serious eye candy. Definitely will impress your family, being a firefighter. Your folks hold civil servants in high esteem. You could do worse."

"Wait? You're okay with this? You're not going to give me a hundred reasons why this is a bad idea?" The shower stops. I strain but can't hear Wiley singing anymore.

"Oh, it's a bad idea. Worse than lying to your family about going off to St. Barts for Thanksgiving with a mystery man," Harlow-Rose says, then adds. "For the record. I do not think you should do this. It makes an already complicated situation crazier. You don't need that right now. But my heart hurts thinking about what you'll go through seeing India in a few weeks. So, do what you think you need to do to survive that. If that means being Wiley's fake fiancée, then I got your back. Okay?"

The doorbell rings. My head jerks toward the door where a massive silver and gold decorated wreath hangs in the center.

"Okay, I got to go," I say, scrambling up from the couch. "Someone is at my door."

I wouldn't be surprised if Wiley ordered take-out to be delivered to the house. From what I remember, he has a voracious appetite. Not that you could tell from his stunning physique.

Pressing my face against the door, I stare through the peephole and see the last three people I want at my door right now: my mother and my sisters, Persia and Sydney.

My heart drops to my stomach as I watch them talk on the front porch.

They weren't supposed to be in town until the weekend.

Why are they early?

I do not want to open the door.

The doorbell rings again.

This time, they call out my name in a chorus. "Surprise! Zaire, open up!" Then break out into a fit of giggles. Sydney steps forward and pounds on the door.

Dread seeps deep into my bones, and I know there's no way out.

No way for me to avoid letting them inside.

I unlock the door and open it. My heart pounds in my chest as their beaming faces greet me. The twinge of guilt I feel for wanting to avoid them fades as Sydney and Persia rush forward and swallow me in a big hug. Jumping up and down with excitement, they scream "Surprise" over and over as they twirl me around.

A huge smile erupts on my face as I squeeze them back.

"Why didn't you tell me y'all were coming in early? I would've picked you up from the airport," I say, taking a step back from my sisters.

"Well, it wouldn't have been a surprise if we told you," Sydney says. "And we didn't want you to give us some lame excuse for why we couldn't come over midweek."

Persia adds, "I told her you're a workaholic who hates surprises and won't have time for us. Sydney wouldn't listen, so here we are."

"Whatever." I squeeze her round cheek with my fingers like I used to when we were younger. "I will make time to hang out with my sisters—"

"Oh my God, Zaire!" Mommy says, sending a jolt of alarm through me.

"What is it? What's wrong?" I ask.

Sydney and Persia turn around to stare at our mother, who squeezes past them and jerks my hand forward.

My left hand.

The one with Wiley's grandmother's ring on my ring finger.

"Sweetheart, you're engaged!" Mommy says, grinning from ear to ear as she wraps me in a big hug and peppers my cheek with kisses. "Your secret beau proposed! I'm so happy for you!"

I freeze, squeezing my eyes shut.

Sydney and Persia squeal and pounce on us, smothering me in another hug. I can barely breathe as I extract myself from their grasp a moment later.

"Can we meet him now?" Sydney asks, giving me a shrewd look.

"Wait. Your mystery man from St. Barts? He proposed?" Persia asks.

"Oh my," Mommy says. A soft sigh escapes her lips as she fans herself.

Her eyes are locked on something behind me.

Or … someone.

"Oh, you did good, sister," Sydney says, raising an eyebrow.

"Really good," Persia whispers as she looks past me.

I turn around to see Wiley.

He's standing in the middle of my foyer, draped in nothing but a towel. His body is to die for—ripped six-pack abs, massive muscular arms, broad chest, and powerful wide shoulders. Beads of water coat his smooth skin, sliding down his legs and dropping into small puddles on my teak hardwood floors. His full lips part into a wicked smile as his gaze shifts from Mommy to Sydney, then Persia, until resting on me.

I can't think straight, losing myself in the aqua blue pools.

I force myself to look away but find my gaze sliding down his body toward the plush Egyptian cotton towel sitting low on his waist.

My skin flushes with a blaze of heat. Blood rushes through my ears as my heart beat thumps in my chest.

"You're engaged to Wiley Alexander?" Mommy asks.

I glance at her, and I'm struck dumbfounded by the unabashed hope in her eyes. She's happy that I'm engaged to Wiley?

"Really, Mommy? Why else would he be standing half-naked in the middle of her living room if he wasn't the one who put that rock on her finger," Sydney says.

Persia is quiet as her gaze bounces between Wiley and me. A goofy grin plastered all over her face.

I swallow hard, still not able to force myself to speak.

Wiley approaches me, wrapping an arm around my waist. I melt into his strength as he presses a kiss to my temple.

"Not the way we wanted y'all to find out," Wiley says, then blesses my family with another devastating smile. "Yes, Zaire and I are most definitely engaged."

CHAPTER 17

ILEY

~

"MA?" I PLACE A HAND ON HER BACK. I CAN FEEL HER trembling as she takes a deep, shaky breath. "Are you ok with ... this?"

For the first time since I came up with the idea of the fake engagement, I feel a tinge of guilt in my gut. It was all fun and games and lighthearted when I was only focused on Zaire, me, and Heather's vlog. I never considered the impact sharing this news would have on our families.

After Zaire's family assumed we were engaged, with a lot of help from me, I got Zaire alone in her bedroom to make sure she was okay with participating in the scheme. She was shell-shocked but otherwise committed to continuing the ruse. When we returned from her bedroom, Zaire's mother, Felicia, was on her way to planning a celebratory dinner where our families could meet. We settled on a catered dinner on Sunday evening after Zaire's father, Otis, Persia's fiancé, Yves, and Sydney's husband, Matthieu, were expected to arrive in town. I was directed to invite Ma, my sister Hayley, her husband Robert, and their four kids. We'd all descend on Zaire's house in our first official family get-together.

And that meant I had to be at Ma's house before my shift on Friday morning to break the news to her before she heard about it around town. News like this spreads faster than lightning in Kimbell. She took it as well as expected. I was late for my shift as I waited for an hour for her to say something, anything, about my big announcement. That's how overcome with emotion she was, which I later found out was a good thing and not that I'd given her a stroke.

With Darren's help, I weathered the storm and barrage of questions from Ronan, Luke, and Nate during my shift. The congratulatory calls and texts have been nonstop for the past three days. Sure, there were some drunk dials of women cursing me out and crying uncontrollably. Can't say I didn't expect one, or two, or a dozen of those. Overall, once everyone got past the shock of Zaire being in love with me, they were thrilled and supportive of our fake union.

Ma turns toward me with tears glistening in her eyes. The moon shines bright overhead, reflecting off the rippling waters of Zaire's infinity pool that blends with Lake Lasso only a few dozen feet away. The sounds of the guests laughing and talking from inside the house are a faint hum as all my focus is on Ma.

"I'm happy for you, baby," Ma says, reaching a hand to caress my cheek. "Never in a million years did I think you'd end up with a woman like Zaire. You're a good-looking boy, but it takes much more than looks to snag a woman of that caliber."

I wince. "So, you think she's—"

"Out of your league? How about out of your universe, baby," Ma says, caressing my face. "That's why I'm so excited for you. You're going to be a Kincaid!"

"Zaire is going to be an Alexander," I say, not wanting to belabor the point since, in reality, it's moot. Zaire and I will never make it down the aisle.

Ma frowns. "You should think about becoming a Kincaid. Or an Alexander-Kincaid. Has a nice ring to it."

"You're serious?"

"As a heart attack. If you think for one second that woman is going to ditch her name for yours, you're crazy. You're crazier if you don't take advantage of all the opportunities you'll have as a Kincaid. I don't have a problem with you ditching my last name."

"Okay. I'll talk to Zaire about it," I say, hiding a chuckle.

"And the ring looks gorgeous on her finger. Your grandmother would be as proud of you as I am. You picked an amazing woman, and I'm glad she picked you back."

"Got it. She's out of my league, and I'm lucky to have her."

"And don't you forget it. Do not mess this up, Wiley Templeton Alexander," Ma says, then smacks me on the back of the head.

"Ow! Ma!"

"Come on, let's get inside. The dinner should almost be ready." Ma leads the way back into the house.

I make my way to where Otis, Yves, and Matthieu admire a collection of first-edition classics on Zaire's bookcase. Lucky for me, I'd passed Otis's withering one-on-one inquisition with a bit of help from pointers Zaire had given me when we talked last night. Her dad is practically my best friend now. Yves has trapped the men in a boring conversation about the early years of French printing presses in the publishing industry. I pretend to listen, but my gaze drifts to Zaire.

And she catches me looking. Busted.

Zaire raises an eyebrow at me as Hayley, Persia, and Sydney talk animatedly around her. My brother-in-law is busy trying to stop his four kids from destroying the expensive Christmas decorations around Zaire's home.

My fake fiancée is stunning in a simple pale yellow sheath dress with a low neckline that fails miserably at hiding her curvy body. I allow myself this luxury of drinking in the sight of her. She exudes confidence, but it's balanced by her infectious, cheerful smile and soft, welcoming brown eyes. She's both powerful and approachable at the same time. No wonder she's brilliant in business. She has the smarts to make people respect her and the allure to dazzle them. Her soft dark curls accentuate her lovely face.

There's no reason to worry about faking an attraction to this woman. The hard part will be not letting my attraction to her derail the goals of this fake engagement.

"Oh my God, Wiley! Can you stop making goo-goo eyes at my sister? I swear you are completely in love with her," Persia says, walking over toward me with her hands on her hips. Sydney nods in agreement while Zaire stares at me with eyes wide as saucers. "I swear, Yves never looks at me like you look at Zaire."

"No point in hiding how I feel. She's mine now," I say, using this as an excuse to head over toward the ladies.

"Not quite," Sydney chimes in. "She won't officially be yours until the two of you say I do."

I shrug. "Technicality. Isn't that right?" I slip past the Kincaid sisters and reach for Zaire's hands. They're soft. I stare at the contrast of our skin next to each other as I stroke her fingers in mine.

"That's right," Zaire says.

Her smile obliterates my ability to think clearly. I reduce the space between us to nothing and stroke a hand down her face. I should stop while I'm ahead, but I wrap an arm around her waist and pull her to me. She leans into my chest, and I smell the intoxicating scent of her perfume. As if I have no control over myself, my lips find her temple and kiss her.

Zaire tenses. I promised not to kiss her lips, but a few strategically placed kisses every now and again will make the whole thing look real. As long as I don't take things too far. Which, of course, I won't because none of this is real.

"Dinner is ready," Felicia announces and ushers us into the dining room.

CHAPTER 18

ILEY

I WALK BEHIND ZAIRE AND WATCH AS FELICIA DIRECTS Zaire and me to chairs at the head of the large rectangular table. I grab my collar and try to push away the feeling that we're about to sit in the hot seats.

Pulling the chair out for Zaire, which causes a wave of approving nods, I wait until she sits before I sit. The sight of my family commingled with Zaire's takes my breath away. Everyone is getting along so well. I almost forget it's all a giant fraud we are perpetrating on the people we love most. The hired wait staff circles the table, filling our wine glasses with Harlow-Rose's award-winning Cabernet Sauvignon. As soon as my glass is filled, I grab it and take a few long gulps.

The catered dinner prepared by Thorn's owner and head chef showcases the best the restaurant offers—Vichyssoise, followed by a rack of lamb in mustard sauce with stuffed artichokes and couscous with crème brûlée for dessert.

Ma giggles and nervously stares at the arrangement of silverware around the plate. She's as clueless as I am about which fork to use. Hayley and Robert are too busy wrangling my nieces and nephews to behave than to care about what utensil to eat with which course. I make a mental note to pick one first, so any correction can come my way and spare Ma the embarrassment.

"Shall we toast?" Felicia announces, beaming at me and Zaire.

"Why not," Zaire says, lifting her glass.

"Can I?" I ask, which does the trick. Otis gives me a nod of approval, and Felicia swoons. A quick glance at Hayley and Ma fills my gut with butterflies. I haven't seen them this proud of me since I graduated from the Firefighter Academy.

Zaire whips her head toward me.

I give her a reassuring smile.

"From the moment I got close to Zaire, I was drawn to her intelligence, passion, and commitment to everything she does in life. She is a role model for entrepreneurs, pushing the envelope and never settling for second best. That drive and determination hooked me ... and the fact that she can pour an entire bag of plain M&M's into her mouth and eat them without gagging when she's stressed doesn't hurt either."

I sneak a glance at Zaire.

"Wiley! You promised you wouldn't tell anybody about that," Zaire hisses, slapping my biceps. Hard.

My heart leaps in my throat, and I give her a wink. Laughter fills the dining room.

"As we spent more time together," I continue, "I saw beyond those outer layers to the parts overflowing with generosity, caring, and loyalty. It didn't take long for me to realize what a special woman she is and how lucky I am to be with her. Love is inevitable between us. I'm thankful she said yes."

Zaire doesn't hide her smile. Her eyes light up, sending a flood of warmth through my body.

"Oh, you are too perfect, Wiley!" Persia says, grabbing her napkin and dabbing at her eyes. "That was so beautiful."

We all clink glasses.

Zaire stares at me, but I don't turn to her.

I can't.

I know she wants to know where that toast came from, and I don't know the answer.

None of what I said feels like a lie.

In fact, what I said reflects what I felt when I ran into her at Elevation Cupcake shop several months ago. The fateful moment when we talked about websites and algorithms and predictive analytics led me to offer to create an e-commerce website for her when I'd never done it before and wasn't sure I could pull it off.

Zaire motivated me to try.

To push the edges of what I'd done in the past and stretch to create something beyond anything I'd tried before. To show myself I could be better than I thought I could be.

The wait staff refills our glasses with wine, and we settle into a mundane conversation. The Kincaids are kind enough to not make a big deal about the Alexanders using all the wrong forks and spoons as we lose ourselves in the delicious food.

The lamb is disappearing at a break-neck pace from my plate.

Zaire notices and pushes her plate toward me. I grab a slice of lamb by the bone and take a bite, chewing the tender meat.

"My sister may be generous with her lamb, but she won't be generous with her money," Sydney says, raising an eyebrow. "Have you contacted your lawyer about the prenup?"

"He asked me a few days ago, Sydney," Zaire says, shaking her head. "I didn't race to the phone to call Lance after saying yes."

"I don't think Zaire needs to worry about her business or go into the marriage assuming that it's going to end," Felicia says, looking at Ma, then Hayley, to gauge their reaction.

Hayley's jaw clenches as she lays her fork down on the table.

"That's not your call," Sydney challenges. "My sister has worked hard for everything that she's accomplished. She must protect her legacy."

"My brother is not in the market for a sugar mama," Hayley says. "If he wanted one of those, he would've gotten married when he was eighteen. There's been plenty of women in and out of his life with tons of money to make him a kept man. But he's not shallow."

I cringe at her not-so-glowing defense of my character.

"Business is not worth creating tension between her and her fiancé," Yves chimes in. "Persia and I decided a prenup wasn't necessary for us, and no one seems to have a problem with me putting my money at risk."

Sydney rolls her eyes. "Your inheritance is a fraction of my sister's net worth, Yves. Your father wants you to make your own way like my sister has already done." She turns toward Zaire. "Matthieu is licensed in Texas and can handle the paperwork for you."

Matthieu becomes extremely interested in eating his artichokes.

"I don't want any of Zaire's money," I say, stopping the debate. "Whatever she needs me to sign, I will."

"You will?" Zaire asks, biting her lower lip.

"Yeah, you need to be protected. If you dump me, can't promise that in my haze of being brokenhearted that I won't try to fleece you."

Everyone in the room erupts in laughter, breaking the tension.

Zaire says, "Good to know."

I toss my napkin on the table. "Well, I hate to do this, but I have to work in the morning."

The chorus of regrets fills the air. Zaire is noticeably quiet. At least to me.

"It's been a pleasure meeting all of you," I say, then stand up. "Hayley, would you mind dropping Ma back home?"

"Of course," Hayley responds.

I walk around the table and give hugs and handshakes.

Zaire stands. "I'll grab you a crème brûlée to-go and meet you outside."

Minutes later, I lean against my F-150 as Zaire hands me a bag containing dessert.

"That was quite the speech you gave earlier," she says, tilting her head at me.

"You liked that?"

"You played the part of doting fiancé well. Sydney and Persia love you to pieces, and I dare say Mommy and Daddy want to adopt you."

"I meant every word I said. None of that was fake. Okay?"

"Sure, Wiley," Zaire says, fighting off a smile.

She swats a hand at me, which I grab. My fingers brush over hers as I tug her closer to me. She doesn't resist as I pull her into my arms.

"Don't let them stay too late."

"I won't." Her words are muffled against my neck. Her breath caresses my skin.

"I'm serious. It's almost midnight. Kick them out."

"I promise. They'll be gone before you get home."

I close my eyes and shift against the truck into a more comfortable position. My arms still wrapped around Zaire, pressing her body into mine. I don't want to leave her alone to fend for herself, but she's more than capable. I know that, and she knows that. Being fake engaged will be tougher than I think we both realized.

"Wiley?"

"Yeah."

"Why are you still holding me?"

"Umm ... well, because it feels good."

"Not a bad answer."

"Good, cause it's the only one I got."

Seconds later, she extracts herself from my embrace.

"Good night, fiancé," she says, walking backward away from me. Her hips sway seductively as she waves good bye. The sparkle in her eyes is so cute that I have to force myself to stop wayward thoughts from entering my head.

Of all the things I could see before heading home to fall asleep, Zaire smiling at me as she walks away is the best yet.

CHAPTER 19

Z AIRE

~

"YES, I UNDERSTAND THAT. I ASSURE YOU THAT THIS IS NOT an unnecessary buildup of inventory. We have legitimate orders coming in faster than we can keep up with. Staying on top of the custom orders is imperative." I shift the headset on my head, then cross my arms over my chest. "Plus, this will allow you to compensate for your shortfalls earlier this year. Your employees can enjoy an extra bonus right before the holidays if you can meet my targets."

Troy slumps in the chair on the other side of my desk, eyes downcast as he listens to every word. I resist the urge to stomp over and slap him across the head. Jimbo Barnes, the owner of our furniture manufacturing facility, sounds wary, but after almost two hours of negotiating, I think I've gotten him on board.

"Yes," Simona whispers, pumping a fist in the air when we get verbal agreement.

"Thank you. I'll have my attorney draft the terms and send them to you later today. The orders will be on your desk first thing Monday morning, and I expect the team to start working on them by Wednesday," I say, leaving nothing to miscommunication.

Snatching the headset from my head, I fling it across the room, sending it skittering to a stop near the edge of the wall. This was not how I envisioned spending the entire morning and most of the afternoon. I needed to catch up on my work after all the distractions of my engagement with Wiley. Not swoop in and resolve issues for an executive that I pay too well.

"Simona, be a dear and get the terms over to Lance. Tell him I'll pay whatever it takes. The amended contract must be signed today."

Simona nods and heads for the door. Troy rises to follow her.

"Not so fast," I say, walking toward him. "You and I need to discuss what happened."

"Can we do it tomorrow? I'm spent," Troy says, not meeting my gaze.

"Can't imagine why you're so fatigued? You barely worked on anything in the past few hours."

His head jerks toward me. Green eyes flash with anger.

"Have a seat," I command. Walking back to my desk, I ease into my chair and try to keep my emotions in check. "We discussed yesterday that we needed to be prepared for a flood of orders now that the Kincaid Furnishings website was back up and working. I asked you to negotiate additional capacity with the manufacturer to avoid delays. What happened?"

Troy shrugs and glances away. "I wasn't as optimistic as you that the sales would be that robust. I thought we had plenty of time."

"You ignored my expertise."

"You have no experience in the furniture business. I do. That's why you hired me."

"And remind me, again? Whose instincts turned out to be correct?"

Troy is quiet, waves of anger wafting from him. We've never had this kind of contentious conversation. Ever.

"You used my name to try to bully Mr. Barnes into the deal. That's not how we do business down here. You never know when his sister's boyfriend's aunt's cousin could be the one to get you out of a jam later," I say, crossing my arms over my chest. "Don't roll your eyes on this or be arrogant enough to think you know better. Trust me. Situations like that are common place in Kimbell."

Troy's jaw clenches tighter as he looks past me to the lake outside my windows. I can't help but feel that something else is going on. Something not related to work. Definitely … personal.

I'd hoped he would have the good sense to keep his feelings and disappointments under wraps, but it looks like I was wrong.

"I guess I was distracted and off my game," Troy admits. "Won't happen again."

"It can't, Troy. The website Wiley created optimizes upselling. Predictive analytics steer buyers to things similar to their interests but also presents them with something out of the box to challenge their curiosity. The combination results in more sales than the typical furniture start-up. I need you to recognize that my company isn't like the old-school furniture retailers you worked for in the past. You need to be innovative if you want to survive working for me. It's the reason I connected with Wiley—"

"Look, I get it. You're so in love with your white boy toy. The arm candy for the rich, black woman that gives you instant status and respectability. Guess you made it now," Troy says, venom dripping in his tone. "Black men aren't good enough for you anymore. You need a white tech nerd with a hero complex to make your life complete."

I push up from my chair with such force that it topples over. My body is ice-cold with fury. "You have no right to speak to me that way or to belittle my relationship with Wiley. This is not about race."

"Isn't it? I've been tripping all over myself since I moved to this podunk town to show you how much I want to be with you. Everything I did a couple of weeks ago was to prove I'm the best man for you."

I cringe, refusing to let the memories of Thanksgiving week play through my mind. I say, "Don't stand there like you're some injured party. I told you from the moment we discussed your employment with Kincaid Furnishings that I was not interested in a relationship. You said you were okay with that."

"If I had known I'd never be enough because a light-skinned brother is still not white, maybe I would have thought twice about taking the job," Troy says, pointing a finger in my face.

"Maybe you should think twice about staying at this job."

Troy's scowl grows deeper.

I can't contain my anger anymore. "And my personal life is none of your business." I stab a finger back toward his face. "Who I choose to marry is none of your business! And who I choose to love—"

"Is all of my business." I hear the playful hint of Wiley's words before I see him emerge in the doorway. He's dressed in a pair of loose cargo pants and a blue tee shirt with a Kincaid Furnishings logo on the front, exposing his powerful arms with the sleeves rolled up to show off his biceps. Wiley's hair is tousled with rumpled blonde waves clinging to his forehead like he's just rolled out of bed. The sexiest five o'clock shadow has overtaken his face. "After all, I am your fiancé."

My heart stills then races as he walks toward us. I haven't seen him since he held me in his arms late Sunday night.

Troy looks like he wants to rip Wiley's head off. Wiley approaches Troy with a goofy grin and pats him hard on the back. "You didn't think you had a shot with Zaire, did you? Do you know how hard it was for me to snag her? You're better off trying to get blood out of a turnip." He chuckles under his breath, shaking his head with mock pity.

Troy jerks away from Wiley, then takes a step back and almost stumbles over the chair. Wiley doesn't bother hiding his laughter.

"I'm glad you find this amusing," Troy says, the anger in his voice turning hostile. He motions to me with a disgusted wave. "I'll have my stuff out of the office and my resignation letter on your desk before I leave today."

"That's for the best. I'll tell accounting to process your severance package—"

"No need. I'm sure there are plenty of companies who would appreciate my services," Troy says, barreling toward the door. He pauses before leaving. "And when this white boy breaks your heart, don't come crying to me." With a haughty tilt of his head, Troy leaves, slamming the door behind him.

My knees wobble, and I sway.

In the blink of an eye, Wiley is by my side. He wraps an arm around my hips, pulling me close. His aqua gaze peers down at me. "You okay?"

A charge of electricity emanates from his touch, and my face flames with heat. I take a deep breath, trying to force these pesky, unwanted feelings for my fake fiancé away. Everyone knows Wiley is a good guy, through and through. His moniker as the Playboy of Kimbell was never said with disdain but more playfulness. I shouldn't be surprised or wooed by this kindness he's showing. He would do it for any woman in this exact situation.

But I can't pretend I'm not happy he's here.

I look back at him and smile. I'm not sure I trust myself to respond to him without melting into a puddle of goo at his feet. I need to get a grip on these strange emotions. The way Wiley handled Troy with his typical jokey nonchalance was brilliant. It helped diffuse a conversation that was headed for an explosive end. One that could have had ramifications not just for me but for my sister, Sydney, since Troy is her brother-in-law.

And I would never forgive myself for that.

"Is what he said true?"

"What?" I falter.

"I mean, I heard his thoughts on you being a successful black woman and not wanting a black man. Is that how all black men feel? Are you going to endure more conversations like that because of me?"

Relief floods through me. "No, not at all. It's a very vocal, tiny percentage of the population of black men who share that distorted view. It's not worth giving a second thought."

"You sure? Because the way he talked to you was out of line. I was going to step in earlier, but you showed me that you don't need a man to swoop in and save the day."

I laugh. "But it is nice to have a guy here to hold me after I've fought the battle and won. I appreciate your support."

"Anytime," Wiley says. "Another question for you."

"Okay ..."

"What's wrong with Troy? Why weren't you interested in him?"

"Nothing is wrong with him, per se. He was great at his job when he stayed focused and applied himself. I had a lot of respect for him professionally," I say, noticing that Wiley hasn't stopped holding on to me. In fact, he's tightened his grip as we stand mere inches from each other. "Sydney got it in her head we could be sisters married to brothers. I went to Atlanta a few times to go out with Troy, and the vibe was wrong. He's so serious and talks about work all the time. Every other word out of his mouth was about his material possessions like he was trying too hard to impress me. What I wanted was someone who wasn't afraid to let their hair down and have fun. Work hard, play hard, you know. Troy couldn't do that. I couldn't force chemistry between us where none existed."

"I see. So he didn't make you feel all giggly inside." Wiley whips his free hand toward my abdomen and tickles me. "Giggly like this."

I screech and try to fight him off, but it's no use. I'm cramping with uncontrollable laughter as a flood of endorphins washes away all the negativity of the encounter with Troy. I maneuver around enough to catch my balance and grip the sides of Wiley's face. His face is smooth underneath the light stubble.

His eyes lock on mine, and it's like time stops. We stand there for several seconds, lost in each other. The giggly feeling continues to bubble inside me despite his fingers ceasing their tickling assault on my stomach. I want to kiss him. I want him to kiss me.

But that's against the rules we set for this fake engagement.

No real kisses allowed.

Wiley frowns, then breaks into a playful grin as he releases me from his grasp.

"And I guess not giggly like St. Barts guy made you feel. How's he handling the news?"

I freeze, not sure how to respond. I shrug.

"Have you heard from him?"

"No," I blurt out. "And I don't expect to."

"I wouldn't be so sure about that. If a guy who had a crush on you is struggling to deal with our engagement, I can't imagine what the guy who had you feels like right now. Especially since we got engaged a few days after y'all broke up."

"He doesn't know any people in Kimbell except me, so it'll be a while before the news gets to him. If it ever does."

"No chance he shows up out of the blue and calls B.S. on our story that you and I spent Thanksgiving together?"

"Nope."

Wiley's eyes narrow, and he swallows hard. "As much as I want this feature on Heather's vlog, it's not worth you sacrificing what you want for me to get it."

"What are you talking about?"

"If St. Barts guy comes back and you want to make things work with him, then we can call this whole thing off—"

"Will you forget about him?" I walk past Wiley and pick my chair up from the floor. Setting it upright, I take a seat and wake up the computer monitor. "There is no chance he'll come back into my life."

Because he is a figment of my imagination … based on you. But Wiley can never know this.

"Guess that settles that," Wiley says, leaning on my desk. "Shut down the computer. It's time for us to go."

"Go? I can't go. I spent the entire morning and afternoon handling a negotiation that Troy should've done. Now I need to find a new COO for Kincaid Furnishings."

"That can wait until tomorrow," Wiley says, reaching down underneath my desk.

A second later, the computer powers down with a distinct whine as Wiley yanks the plug from the socket.

"You need to let off some steam and have fun. I'm going to take you on our first date tonight. We gotta have a good story to tell Heather when she comes to town."

"Can't we make something up? I'm great at memorizing speeches. If you write what happened, I promise I'll rehearse every detail and deliver it perfectly."

"Nope. That's not what we agreed to. You said that it's better if we've done all the things we talk about with Heather." Wiley taunts me with my strategy. "Your rules and great ones."

"It would be more authentic that way," I admit.

"And I get to take you on the best first date of your life," Wiley declares.

"The best? You know I have high standards."

"The highest, and yes, I know," Wiley says, reaching a hand toward me. "Trust me, it's going to blow every other date you've ever had out of the water."

After enduring the disastrous argument with Troy, getting away from the office would be refreshing. Slipping my hand in his, I say, "Okay, let's go."

CHAPTER 20

Z AIRE

~

WILEY HOLDS THE DOOR OPEN FOR ME LIKE A PERFECT
gentleman.

I rush down my driveway, tugging my leather jacket closed as an
icy breeze rustles through the pine trees surrounding my house.
Despite only being a few minutes after six p.m., the sky is an inky
dark blue.

Glancing down at my Ferragamo ankle boots, I feel a smidgen of
regret for not choosing my Louis Vuitton sneakers. This might be a
fake first date, but it doesn't mean I didn't take the time to select my
outfit with care. I paired dark skinny jeans with a cashmere lavender
sweater. Very form-fitting to show off my curves in the best possible
way.

I hesitate as I approach his Ford F-150 with a six-inch lift kit
resting on giant tires. The step board is above my knee. I stare at the

massive height and wonder if I need to take a running jump into the truck.

"Need some help?" Wiley asks as if reading my mind.

"That would be nice," I say, extending my hand, which Wiley ignores.

He leans over and lifts me onto the step board. The heady scent of his cologne wraps around me, alluring and sensual. Every touch enthralls my senses. His warm, firm grip of my hips as I steady and balance myself on the edge of the warm leather seats. The subtle hint of peppermint wafting from his mouth as his breath caresses my skin. I shiver and wonder if it's because of the forty-degree Texas winter or from Wiley's body so close to mine ... again. After I'm seated comfortably, I reach for the seatbelt as Wiley closes the passenger door.

Inhaling a deep breath, I'm thankful for the reprieve from the perfection that is Wiley Alexander. He rounds the front of the truck, gets inside, and cranks the engine. His lips are twisted into a goofy smirk that is as sexy as it is adorable. I try to look away, but those gorgeous, kissable lips are making it almost impossible to do.

"Do I get the details of this best first date ever now?" I ask, pulling myself out of my daze. I hope I don't sound as anxious as I feel.

His aqua blue eyes shine in the darkness as he rests a hand on my leg. The warmth radiating from his touch shoots through me. "Not yet. It's a surprise. You'll see when we get there."

"But this has to be a date we could've done months ago when we were supposedly dating in secret, so it can't be close by where anybody from Kimbell could see us."

"That's right. Everything I planned is several towns away and fits into the folklore we created. Trust me, no one would've seen us back then, and nobody will see us tonight."

We ride in silence as he speeds down the quiet, tree-lined private road that leads from my lake house. He merges onto the highway traffic of 290 West toward Austin, then says, "We'll be there in thirty minutes. Hope that's not too long."

I sink into the comfort of his truck and cross my legs. A move that captures Wiley's attention. I'm about to tell him to put his eyes back on the road, so we don't crash when he abruptly looks away. Why am I so pleased that Wiley can't seem to take his eyes off me tonight? It shouldn't matter since everything we're doing is to have authentic dating stories to share with the love guru. We're not supposed to enjoy this. Right?

Tapping a finger on my chin, I say, "There's no way we can get to Austin in thirty minutes. So I'm guessing we're headed to Chappell Hill or Brenham. People from Kimbell rarely go there at night since the sausage company and Blue Bell are closed in the evenings. That makes it the perfect place to sneak off without being detected."

He laughs. A rich, deep velvety sound that echoes within the truck. It makes me smile though I'm fighting not to … hard.

"You are working overtime to figure this out, aren't you? Don't like not being in control, do you?"

"Hate it. How'd you notice?"

"Well, no more work for the rest of the night. You're completely mine, with no distractions."

Completely his?

I don't correct him. I don't want to correct him.

Wiley extends an open palm toward me.

"What? What do you want?" I ask, staring at his hand.

"Cell phone."

"You're confiscating my cell phone? I'm never without it. Ever."

"I remember. That's why I'm locking it away since our first date has begun."

"What if there's an emergency at work and my team needs me?"

"They'll be fine for the night. Nothing you can't handle later."

Despite my better judgment, I ease my phone out of my jacket pocket and place it in his hand. I agreed to this arrangement. When I commit to something, I'm in one hundred percent. This fake engagement will be the most productive and effective fake engagement for both of our needs. I'll make him look great with Heather, and he'll be my gorgeous buffer at Persia's wedding when I have to face India for the first time in five years.

"Was that so hard?" Wiley teases as he turns off Highway 290 onto a back country road. The area is bathed in darkness, with only the lights from his truck illuminating the asphalt. I figure he's taking a detour to stop me from guessing our final destination, which is fine with me. Even at night, the rolling hills and miles of ranch lands are a beautiful sight. Cows are bunched in clusters to conserve heat in the cold.

In the distance, I see three wind mills turning, triggering a memory from my childhood.

"I've been on this road before," I say, easing out of my leather jacket. The heat is on in the truck, but I'm positive that's not why I'm so flushed. "Up ahead, maybe three miles or so, there's another dirt road that leads to an old drive-in movie theater. It was ancient when we were little girls, but I guess there was enough nostalgia from folks in all the towns around here to keep it up and running. My parents used to take us to see a movie there every month. Did I tell you about that when we were working on the website?"

Wiley's eyes narrow as he takes a quick glance at me. "Does sound vaguely familiar. You, Sydney, India, and Persia stuffed in the back of the family minivan?"

"I thought we'd talked about it. Don't remember how it came up in conversation, though." Those movie nights were one of the few sister memories that I cherish. It's been a long time since the four of us have been that close. I doubt we'll ever be again.

"Tell me about your sisters. From what I've seen of Sydney, she's intense and scary. Couldn't get a read on Persia."

"Despite being the number two daughter, Sydney is the protector of all of us. No one will ever take advantage of the Kincaid girls under her watch. But she's balanced. She has a loud bark but is very slow to bite."

"And you're closest to her. It's pretty obvious."

"And I'm not very close to Persia, who is a spoiled brat. She was on her best behavior the other night. I think she's nervous about becoming a wife."

"Last but not least … India."

"Do we have to talk about India?" I roll my eyes and cross my arms over my chest.

"Not if you don't want to," Wiley says.

"India and I don't see eye to eye on most things in life. She's a strict vegan and committed to various environmental causes. She works for a think tank in D.C., lobbying Congress on environmental issues."

"Caring for the environment is noble."

"Noble is not a word I'd use to describe my sister. I caught her having sex with my boyfriend at Sydney's wedding reception, remember?" I shake my head, disappointed that the simmering anger is still there. "India is radical. She believes in going to extreme measures and has organized various events that put people's lives in danger to prove a point. But more importantly, she believes I'm evil because of the development I'm spearheading at Lake Lasso."

"The improvements of the lake front that have boosted the economy of Lasso County and brought jobs for all skill levels while still protecting the wildlife and nature in the area," Wiley says, frowning. "Has she bothered to understand how your actions have benefitted our community?"

"I doubt it," I say, touched by the vehemence in his defense of my work. My legacy. It's what I want to leave behind to the town I grew up in and love so much.

Wiley reaches over and caresses my thigh. "Hey, what she thinks doesn't matter. Everyone in Kimbell is proud of you and everything you've done to put our little town on the map. Those opinions are the ones that count."

"Didn't realize you cared," I say, trying to lighten the mood. "Maybe I should hire you to sing my praises."

"I'd do it for free. You're amazing."

"Alright, save all of this for when we have an audience. It's just you and me right now."

Wiley laughs, but it sounds different. Hollow.

I wonder what he's thinking.

I wonder if he's struggling as much with getting used to this fake engagement situation as I am. The lines of pretending to be in love and actually falling in love can blur if we're not careful. I can't afford for either of us to become confused about what we're doing. This is a business arrangement. Nothing more.

A bright light shines in the distance. I lean toward the front window.

"Wiley, do you see that? It's the old drive-in theater. I thought it closed down a decade ago, but it looks like they are about to show a movie."

"They're showing one of the most romantic movies of all time tonight," Wiley says as he slows the truck and turns on the dirt road that leads to the drive-in.

My hands fly to my face, covering my mouth. Tears prick at my eyes, but I blink them away.

"Just for us." Wiley flashes that gorgeous smile, and I melt on the spot.

CHAPTER 21

ILEY

~

"THE PRINCESS BRIDE? YOU THINK THIS IS ONE OF THE most romantic movies of all time? It's a goofy comedy," Zaire balks, laughing at me, as she eases into her leather jacket, covering up her amazing body.

Unfortunately.

A woman rarely distracts me for long, but Zaire is doing exactly that. The lavender cashmere sweater paired with skinny black jeans clings to her curves. I can't stop looking at her.

Putting the truck in reverse, I park in the dirt, marking the front of the area for viewing, then say, "It's a *romantic* comedy. Cult favorite of the eighties and considered one of the best movies of all time. How can you not love this movie?"

"I can't love something I've never seen."

"Stop ... you've never seen this movie?"

"Nope."

"Well, Ms. Kincaid, you are in for a massive surprise. By the time this night is over, you're going to see the error of your ways," I say, leading her around my truck to the back cab. Opening the latch, I lower it to reveal an air mattress covering the truck bed with a bunch of blankets on top. Near the back of the truck, down pillows are spread across, and a picnic basket filled with all of Zaire's favorites—courtesy of a quick call to Sydney this morning—is tucked in the corner.

I place a foot on the back ledge, reach a hand toward her, and adopt an English accent. "After you, milady."

"That's the worst English accent I've ever heard," Zaire says, without a hint of humor.

"Fine," I say, allowing my Texas twang to come back in full force.

"Much better. I want my fiancé to sound like me. Not some weird European." She places her hand in mine and climbs into the back of the truck. My eyes linger on her, crawling across the air mattress, fighting back every wanton impulse coursing through me.

All of this is a lie. We're pretending. This is nothing more than an orchestrated, staged experience to give us shared memories to discuss with Heather when she comes to town to film her vlog on dating apps of the future.

That's the only reason I need to crank up the romance on this date.

But I can't let it go too far.

For my sake.

Zaire grabs the picnic basket and pulls it onto her lap. "What's in here?"

"All of your favorites from when you used to come here as a little girl," I say, climbing in behind her.

"I doubt that," she says, then gasps. "Oh, you got all of my favorites!" Her face lights up as she finds the unhealthy snacks from the nineties. "Lunchables, Junior Mints, Jujyfruits, Buncha Crunch!" She squeals, then digs around the basket some more. "Capri-sun! So perfect, and oh my goodness ... did you talk to Sydney?"

"You found the peppermints and sour pickles, didn't you?"

"My guilty pleasure. I sneak and eat these at home once a month, no lie." Zaire giggles.

"I thought only pregnant women ate stuff like that."

"Yeah, and me and Sydney."

"Now I know."

"What's next?"

"I start the movie with this app," I say, wagging my cell phone at her.

"Wiley ..." she hesitates, biting her bottom lip. "How in the world did you pull this off? This place looks like it hasn't been operational in years. This is all so ..."

"Like the best first date ever?"

She swats a hand at my biceps, but her fingers linger. I flex, not minding if she wants to grope my arm. Typical behavior for a first date. She licks her lips, sending a jolt through my body. Before I can enjoy the feeling, her hand has moved, and she's rummaging through the snacks in the basket. Settling on a handful of Pixy Stix and a bottle of water, she eases back onto the pillows, wiggling to get comfortable.

I swear, I can almost see ten-year-old Zaire doing the same thing, and it's the most endearing, adorable sight ever. I grab the layers of flannel blankets and cover our bodies. A whole other person could fit between us, making it too cold as the temperatures drop south of forty.

Closing the distance, I fluff a few pillows and move next to Zaire, allowing our body heat to keep us warmer. She doesn't flinch or move away. But she doesn't lean into me, either. That disappoints me.

"Ready?" I ask.

She nods.

With a tap of my cell phone, The Princess Bride is projected onto the sixty-foot screen. As the opening scenes begin, Zaire goes through a transformation. She's trying not to like the movie, but I can tell she's getting into it, which is the point. The debate over whether this is one of the top romantic movies of all time could be excellent fodder for our interview with Heather.

"Okay, pause it right there," Zaire says, grinning. "I know that kid. Wasn't he on some t.v. show?"

"Yeah, that's Fred Savage."

"Right! Wonder Years! I remember commercials for that show when it was in syndication," Zaire says, nodding her head.

Confusion rifles through me. "You never watched that show, either? I thought everybody did."

"Nope, never saw it. But I heard it was good," Zaire says, shifting underneath the blanket. Her body inches ever so closer to me. I fight the urge to wrap an arm around her waist.

"Were you anti-television and movies growing up?"

A laugh bubbles from her lips. "No, I watched shows with black people, mostly. You know, like Moesha, Sister Sister, Fresh Prince of Belaire, Martin. Bet you never watched those."

"You'd lose that bet, Gina," I say, squeezing her nose.

"Ha! Well, alright," Zaire says. "Guess there's more to you than I expected. Like you think the way Buttercup treats Westley is romantic. What guy would fall in love with a girl who bosses him around?"

"He's not in love with her because she bosses him around. He lets her boss him around because he is already in love with her. Duh!" I say, shifting into a more comfortable position that erases all distance between me and Zaire. "Kind of like you and me, right?" I lean my head against Zaire's.

"Explain yourself," Zaire says, bolting up. A rush of cold air flushes against my body, but it does nothing to quench the heat blazing within me. Her dark brown eyes sparkle with the excitement of a debate. She's enjoying this. And I'm enjoying her.

Zaire asks, "How could this be anything like us?"

"We have a long history of you ordering me around," I say, thinking back on all the times our paths have crossed over the years. "I've always been on call for any tech issue you were having. Remember when your laptop crashed and you thought you lost your business plan?"

"I told Simona to take care of it. I had no clue she reached out to you."

"Fine, you knew I updated all the software on the Kincaid Real Estate computers after you fired your tech manager."

"Forgot about that."

"And that day your VPN wouldn't connect from your house. Who did you call?"

Zaire shrinks back, a cute furrow on her brow as she sees where I'm headed. I pile on a bit more. "Don't forget I recovered your password that time you forgot it, and I changed the light bulbs outside your garage when they blew out, and you couldn't find Ace Lallo to ask him to do it."

"Okay, perhaps I've had more than a few moments of requesting your help over the years—"

"Ordering me around. Don't think I got paid for any of that."

"I seem to remember you declining payment because all of that was so easy for you to fix," Zaire says, mocking my speech.

I laugh. She does a great job at it, too.

"You sure that's why I didn't charge you?" I tease.

Zaire's eyes grow wide, then narrow. "Trust me, there were no 'as you wish' responses to my requests."

"How can you be sure I wasn't secretly in love with you?"

"Because you were too busy dating half the town to notice I was alive."

I can't lie and say I'm not enjoying this fake relationship with Zaire.

I'd thought long ago she might be fun to date.

Now I get to do that with no strings attached.

No confusion about what's happening between us.

We both know that none of this is real, which is why we can relax and enjoy spending time with each other.

It's a refreshing change of pace for me.

If I had a dollar for every time a woman claimed I was the love of her life before our third date, I could retire. I could never understand how love comes so quickly for some and not at all for others. I learned to stop feeling guilty about the lack of reciprocity a long time ago. When I find a woman that makes me feel that way, she'll know I haven't been tossing out that line to a dozen women before her. She will be the only one.

"Maybe back then, Buttercup, but definitely not now …"

Our eyes lock, and my breath catches in my throat.

A definite and distinct vibe transmits between us.

I raise an eyebrow and tilt my head, wondering if Zaire notices.

She responds with an exaggerated eye roll.

"Buttercup? Is that the term of endearment you're going to use for me?" Zaire scrunches her nose.

"I think it's a perfect fit. What are you going to call me?"

"Let's see," she says, glancing up at the stars peppering the night sky. "Buttercup calls Wesley … Wesley. So I guess I can call you … Wiley!" Zaire cackles with laughter.

"I need something better than my name."

"No, sir! We are going to follow the most romantic movie of all time. You'll be Wiley, and you'll know how dear you are to me every time I say it." Zaire rests a hand on her heart.

I narrow my eyes as I gaze at her. There's a playfulness in her voice, but something in her eyes is giving off a different vibe. One that is pure and genuine, and real.

"Fine. I'll go with that. But you need to give up some goodies in return."

Her eyes grow wide. "What'll it be? Buncha Crunch or Jujyfruits?"

"Jujyfruits."

She tosses the box at me, which I catch with one hand.

I give her a big grin as she snatches the cell phone from my hand and starts the movie again. She flips over to face the massive movie screen. My hands have a mind of their own as they find a place around her waist, pulling her body flush with mine. She doesn't complain or pull away, to my surprise.

She pushes a pillow away and replaces it with my chest. Her head presses against me as she relaxes in my arms. I could get used to this.

No, I can't.

Because this is a fake date.

We are playing out our respective parts of this charade, so it will be believable when we tell our story to her family, my family, and, most importantly, Heather Grimley.

Sounds from the movie blast through the speakers. But I'm not watching it. I don't need to. I've seen this movie more times than I can count because my sister, Hayley, was obsessed with it. She wore the VCR out, playing the movie repeatedly when we were kids.

All my attention is on Zaire. Over the next ninety minutes, I watch her fall in love with the goofy story with tender romance. She pokes me in the gut as clever banter is exchanged on screen and doubles over with laughter at the corniest parts. As the closing credits flash on the screen, Zaire turns to face me. In dramatic fashion, she begins a slow clap that increases in tempo. Her eyes twinkle as she gives me the most gorgeous smile.

And for the first time, I realize I'm in over my head.

CHAPTER 22

ILEY

It's eight in the morning, and I'm still restless. Tossing and turning in my bed. Trying to push thoughts of Zaire from my mind. Last night had been the perfect date. Everything going better than I'd planned ... except for one thing.

I hadn't expected it to feel like a *real* date.

And I hadn't expected to think about Zaire all night after dropping her off at home. It took every ounce of restraint I had not to kiss her as we stood outside her front door.

She gave me a hug.

A *friendly* hug and told me to drive home safe.

As she shut the door in my face, all I could think about was how much I wanted to devour her full, sensual lips. The urge grew so strong that I almost banged on the door. Almost.

Then reality struck, and I remembered we had a strict no-kissing rule. I reminded myself for the thousandth time that all of this is fake. She's playing along to help me out, but she's not feeling anything for me. Didn't that hug say it all? It was the most platonic and distant hug a person could give another, like a wimpy handshake that makes you frown in disgust.

That was her way of checking me.

She was saying without saying that I needed to remember that none of this is real.

So why have I tortured myself by thinking about her all night long? Why can't I get her off of my mind?

Last night, I'd seen the other side of Zaire. The intelligent, shrewd but approachable 'work hard' woman had been replaced by the carefree, fun-loving, 'play hard' woman. She'd taken all of my antics in stride and threw back a few of her own. I'd seen this side of her when we'd worked together on her website months ago, but that was the tip of the iceberg. She left all seriousness at the office and was in the moment with me, all-in on the fake first date and enjoying every minute. There were no "be serious, Wiley" or "stop joking" or "you play too much" moments. She laughed when I was funny and called me corny or lame when I bombed. We bantered back and forth, paused the movie dozens of times to discuss our thoughts on the comedic and romantic elements, and re-enacted some scenes after it ended. The ninety-minute film took us over three hours to watch because we were having a great time together.

And that's why I can't stop thinking about last night.

I grab my phone and stare at the screen, debating whether to contact her. I know she's up. She's probably been at work for the past few hours, running multiple businesses. Successful people like her don't get to where they are by sleeping in. Isn't it enough that she's going along with this charade and carving out time to get to know me? Should I bother her while she's working?

On the other hand, we have a limited number of days to get to know each other. Shouldn't we spend more time together to make sure we're ready to convince folks our engagement is real?

I sit up in bed, clutching the phone as if it's a magic eight ball that can deliver the answer I need.

Yeah, magic eight ball.

That's what I need.

Scrolling through the App Store, I find a magic eight ball app with the most positive reviews and download it. Within seconds, I'm typing my question: Should I text Zaire?

Following the instructions, I shake my phone, then stare at the answer. *Outlook good.*

I pump my fist in the air, then lean back on my pillow and text.

> morning buttercup

ZAIRE KINCAID
> morning, that's growing on me now

> I knew it would

> not typical at all. more special that way ...
> Wiley ... ha!

> we need to renegotiate what you call me

> suggestions?

> Big Daddy!

> LOL!!!! Are you always this silly?

> not always ...

> I like it.

And I like you, Zaire. But I can't type that. For this fake engagement to work, I can't introduce any awkwardness. There's nothing more awkward than unrequited interest. I should know since

I've been on the other end of that too many times. Keep things light and easy. Don't give Zaire a reason to bail on being my fake fiancée before Heather swoops into town to interview us.

I turn on my side and clutch my pillow to my chest as another risky thought enters my mind. Opening the magic eight ball app again, I type: Should I ask Zaire for a picture?

I shake my phone.

Cannot predict now

Well, that's as good as a yes in my book.

I text again.

> send me a pic of you

ZAIRE KINCAID

why

> your fiancé would have tons of pics of you, but I just need 1 or 2 or 9 or as many as you can send

you think someone is going to check your phone for pics of me?

> have you met Nate, Ronan, Luke, and Darren?

good point. Guess I need some of you, too

> of course. With shirt or without?

wow!

> without it is

I take a candid shot of myself in bed, add heart emojis and a for your eyes only label, then send it to Zaire.

Her response is more than I hoped for—a line of flame emojis. It's followed by a couple of photos of her, with clothes, unfortunately, but gorgeous no less.

you're soooo beautiful

ZAIRE KINCAID

you're sooooo silly

and you like that, remember?

how could I forget?

free for lunch? I want to see you

too much work, sorry

dinner ... do NOT say no

no

fine you suck

j/k pick me up at 6 from my office

My response?

CHAPTER 23

Z AIRE

~

Shutting the door behind the last group of my employees, heading home for the evening, I turn the lock and press my back against the door. Slipping my cell phone from my pocket, I turn toward the window and watch as Simona makes small talk with a few of the agents before getting into their cars.

Can they leave already?

After enduring another day of relentless focus on my *fake* engagement, we made little progress dividing up Troy's work. Productivity for the rest of the week will be ruined if they see Wiley pulling into the parking lot to pick me up for our dinner date.

Our dinner date!

A date I couldn't believe he'd suggested.

Not the suggestion, but the way he suggested it.

It wasn't the "we need to do more to convince this town we're engaged, so let's go out so people can see us" type of date proposal.

In fact, nowhere in his request did he mention where we'd go for dinner.

What he had said made all the hair on my body stand on end.

An electric jolt of satisfying proportion.

The only reason he'd given for suggesting that we meet up for dinner was, "I want to see you."

I want to see you.

What does that mean?

Do I want to know what that means?

As the ladies enter their cars, cranking the engines to drive out of the parking lot, I tap on my phone to call my bestie. The line rings twice before she picks up.

"Harlow-Rose! I don't have much time. It's almost six o'clock, and Wiley will be here any minute," I say, peeking through the blinds facing the parking lot in front of Kincaid Real Estate offices. I give her the run-down of the texts exchanged between Wiley and me today, then, with a dramatic sigh, I ask, "So, what do you think it means?"

"I'm less interested in what Wiley meant and more interested in what you want those texts to mean," Harlow-Rose says.

I cringe. Of course, my bestie would turn this around and try to get me to explore what I'm feeling, which I'm in no mood to do. It is not in my best interest to allow any deeper reflection on my date with Wiley last night or the back-and-forth texts all day today. What's the point? Just because our engagement is fake doesn't mean I can't or shouldn't enjoy his company and that he shouldn't enjoy mine. It's been a long time since I've had such carefree fun with a guy.

Rubbing my temple, I say, "Obviously, he didn't want to have any texts floating around that would give away that this engagement is fake. So, just like we need to pretend in front of people, we need to pretend in our texts, too. Right? What if Nate or Ronan were nearby and looking over his shoulder? He had to stay in character."

"Is that what you think?" Harlow-Rose asks in an annoyingly suspicious tone.

"Yes, that's the only thing that makes sense. I don't know why I got confused. Probably because the entire office has badgered me nonstop since finding out about our engagement. They are shocked I kept my relationship with Wiley a secret for so long. Bless their hearts. They couldn't be happier for me, which makes me feel so guilty about lying to them."

"Zaire, do you want Wiley to ask you on a *real* date?" She asks, ignoring my attempts to distract and deflect.

I'm quiet.

"It's okay if you're attracted to him. I mean, beyond the physical. Who isn't attracted to Wiley? He's gorgeous. He's a great guy. Maybe there's a reason that you two got forced together this way. Maybe something could—"

"He's here," I say, grateful for a reason to stop her from saying what I'm not ready to hear. "Gotta go. Bye."

Glancing down at my light blue strapless maxi dress and denim jacket, I'm satisfied that one, I look stunning, and two, I can blend in at an upscale or down-home restaurant. I walk to Simona's desk, grab my Burberry purse, and then head toward the door as Wiley jumps from his truck.

My mouth falls open as I see him in all his gorgeous glory.

How in the world can a man look this good?

It's that rare handsomeness you never get to the point of *not* noticing, no matter how often you see or are around him.

He saunters toward the door with a cute frown, likely because all the lights are off and there's no sign of my car since Simona picked me up this morning. A sneaky move by my assistant to trick me into thinking we'd cover work on our way when she wanted to pump me for information about my engagement to the dreamiest man in Kimbell. Her words, not mine. Although, I'm finding it hard to disagree with her as I continue to watch Wiley come closer.

A gust of wind rustles his blonde hair, tousling it against his forehead. He's dressed in an aqua blue Polo shirt and a pair of blue jeans. I take another quick glance at my clothes and freeze.

We match.

His shirt. My dress. The same color.

Denim in the same dark shade of blue.

We look like we planned this, but nothing could be further from the truth.

I shake my head.

Just a coincidence, Zaire.

This doesn't mean a thing.

I open the door as he's about to knock.

As the door opens wider, he stumbles, unprepared for the door to move, and topples inside, bracing himself by wrapping his arms around me. We stagger backward, fighting to keep our balance, but it's no use.

I shriek as the floor comes closer to my face.

Shutting my eyes, I land with a thud ... on the firm, strong muscled chest of Wiley Alexander.

My eyes fling open.

His eyes are flirty as a sexy grin spreads across his lips.

I'm instantly aware of his hands on my bottom.

"Breaking your fall is the best thing I've done all day."

"You can move your hands from my butt now," I say, although I'm not sure I mean it.

"As you wish," Wiley says, winking.

I laugh and roll my eyes at him. Sliding off of his body onto the floor, I stand up and extend a hand to him.

He doesn't budge. His eyes roam over me from head to toe and back again, causing my entire body to sizzle with excitement. When he grabs my hand, I can't tell if he's trying to pull me back down on top of him or to help himself up. He licks his bottom lip as if he's contemplating that exact thing, then stands instead.

"You okay?" He asks.

"You broke my fall, remember?"

"Ah, yeah, I won't ever forget that."

"Save the flirting for when we have an audience to convince, okay?"

Wiley shrugs then slips an arm around my shoulder. "You look lovely."

"Thank you. You're handsome as usual. Can't believe we're matching, though," I say as he leads me back toward the office door.

"I cheated. You texted me a photo earlier, and I thought couples in love dress alike. So, I wanted us to do that."

"You wore the same color as me on purpose."

"Yeah." Wiley holds the door open for me. "Jeans were easy. Finding a shirt to match this dress," he pinches part of the fabric. "That was tougher until the nice lady at the department store looked at me and said, 'Oh, you want a shirt to match your beautiful eyes.' Then I wondered, does Buttercup know she picked that dress because it matches my beautiful eyes?"

"That is not why I picked this dress to wear. I didn't know we would see each other today."

"Exactly," Wiley said, chuckling under his breath. "You did it subconsciously because we had such a wonderful date last night. I was on your mind."

"You're ridiculous, and I'm not taking part in this conversation," I say, then pause as Wiley opens the passenger door of his truck for me. I raise my arms and brace myself for his touch as he lifts me onto the step board and helps me inside. Like last night, that jolt hits me, and I can't hide my body's instant response to him. It's something I'll have to get used to.

Minutes later, he's inside, grinning at me as he starts the engine. Wiley asks, "How was your day?"

"Good." I cross my legs and lean my head against the seat.

"Zaire?"

"Yes."

"How was your day?" This time he says it, I get it. He doesn't want an automatic, meaningless response. He's genuinely interested. He wants to know how my day was. The good, the bad, or the ugly.

When was the last time a man showed this kind of interest in me?
It wasn't Kei.

Or any of my boyfriends before or after him.

"Crazy busy." I rub my eyes. "It was hard to keep my team focused on divvying up Troy's work load because they were too busy badgering me about being your fiancée. To top it off, Troy leaving is putting me in a bind. I wasn't aware of all the stuff he was taking care of. He was an exceptional performer. It's going to be hard to replace him. Kinda wish I wasn't so hasty in pushing him out the door."

"I'm not. He needed to go. No one should ever disrespect you like he did. I don't care how good his work is," Wiley says. "Plus, I wouldn't be comfortable with you working with a guy who had romantic feelings for you. Can't let a wolf in the hen house with my woman."

Laughter bubbles out of my mouth, and before I know it, I'm cackling and doubling over in my seat. "Do you hear yourself?"

"Come on, I have a reputation to keep up here. Ronan and Nate would become suspicious of our engagement if I put up with Troy working with you. They'd expect me to put my foot down and at least try to limit your interaction with that douche."

"Is that right?"

"Keeping it real."

"You would what? Forbid me from working with the COO of my furniture company?"

"Not sure," Wiley admits, looking forlorn. "So it's good that he took himself out of the equation."

"Right," I say, smiling despite myself. If Wiley and I were really a couple, he wouldn't have needed to worry. I would've set Troy up with an office at the manufacturing plant instead of inside Kincaid Real Estate to limit our daily interactions.

"And how was your day? Did you do anything exciting on your day off?"

"Thought about you ..." Wiley stops. I can see his muscles tense. He keeps his eyes on the road. "I mean about the fake engagement and what our next moves should be to convince the town that we're a real couple, you know."

"Of course," I say, but I'm not so sure I do know.

"Which brings me to where we should go for dinner. Wednesday nights are legendary at Baker Bros BBQ."

"The renowned game night. Anyone who's anyone in Kimbell will be there."

"Which is why it'll give us the biggest bang for our buck with public exposure," Wiley says. "Heather is known for adding local color to her vlogs, and I'm sure she'll interview some people in town about us."

"Being seen in public recently will give them lots of good things to say. Good move, Wiley."

"So, you're game?"

"Absolutely."

CHAPTER 24

ZAIRE

~

"Have you talked to Izzie since our big announcement?" I fall into step next to Wiley as we start the trek toward Baker Bros BBQ. Cars are lined up along the curb of Main Street and most of the side roads. All the surface lots are full. We were lucky that Wiley had his access card for the gated parking lot behind the fire station, or we would've had to walk a mile to get to the restaurant.

"Not exactly," Wiley says, avoiding my gaze.

"What ... exactly? I'm sure she's working tonight, so what will I walk into?"

The last thing I need is for one of Wiley's most vocal exes to ruin our night. The entire town knows Izzie is still in love with Wiley, even though their relationship ended a year after graduating high school.

She's made a point of interfering with every relationship he's had since then.

Not that her antics stopped Wiley from moving on.

"I texted her. Her response was … not safe for work. But she won't make a scene while I'm with you."

"And if you aren't with me?"

"Let's say you should only get takeout for a while. And have Simona place the order for you," Wiley says, then gives me a sheepish grin as he slips his hand in mine.

I flinch, then force myself to relax. Every touch makes me yearn for him in a way I don't want to acknowledge.

"Do we need to … hold hands?"

"Is my hand sweaty?" Wiley drops my hand to rub his vigorously against his jeans.

"No, your hand feels … nice. Strong and smooth."

Wiley frowns. He grips my hand and pulls it to his chest, pressing the back of my palm against his heart. I can feel the soft beating increasing in pace. Is that because he's holding on to me?

"Alright, you caught me," he says. "I got hooked on this fancy French moisturizer that Hayley uses. Every time she buys more, she gets me a small bottle."

"Who knew you had a high-maintenance skincare routine?"

"Shh. Don't tell anybody," Wiley whispers, leaning close to my ear.

I giggle as we make our way to the packed restaurant. As we get closer to the entrance, I stop abruptly, jerking Wiley to a standstill a few steps ahead of me.

Draped across the upper windows of the restaurant and woven between the lighted garland is a wide banner that reads: Congratulations Wiley and Zaire. An intricate balloon arch is tethered to the entrance, with beautiful lace ribbons blowing in the wind.

I point at it, not able to believe what I'm seeing.

"Did you know about this?" Panic grips me.

"Maybe," Wiley responds.

"Wiley! Why didn't you warn me?"

"Because you wouldn't have come if I did?"

I let out a low growl through gritted teeth.

"Here they come!" I hear the unmistakable voice of LaQuandelier. She peeks out the door and waves at us with a big smile.

Darren, Wiley's best friend, is behind Quan with a huge grin on his face.

Wiley turns toward me and grips my other hand. He leans close, and for a split second, I think he's going to kiss me. My heartbeat quickens. We agreed not to kiss, so why do I want nothing more for him to do exactly that?

I get lost in his aqua eyes, not registering the words he's saying. Shaking away the hypnotic fog of this handsome man, I focus.

"I'm sorry. I should've let you in on the surprise when Darren and I cooked it up earlier today. Please, can you go along with it? I promise it won't be horrible."

"I don't have a choice, do I?" I say, pretending to be pissed when I find the idea very sweet. If we were engaged and he'd surprised me with an engagement party, I'd be over the moon with happiness.

Wiley wraps me in a quick hug, then spins me around. His arm drapes around my shoulders as we make our way to the doors. The smell of delicious smoky meat hits me, and my mouth waters. Cheers and clapping hit a fever pitch as we walk inside and are swallowed up by the crowd. We stop to hug and chat with dozens of people before being ushered to a table near the back wall that's been elevated and decorated with balloons and streamers.

I swear the whole town has come out to celebrate our engagement. I glance to my right and see my family sitting with Wiley's mom and sister at a long table. In my periphery, I catch Harlow-Rose tiptoeing up to me.

"Don't be too mad. I was sworn to secrecy," she says, then hugs me.

"You will pay for this." I wave at Santos, her boyfriend. They are seated on the opposite side of our family at a table with the firefighters from Wiley's shift. Releasing my bestie, I head over and give all the guys—Nate, Luke, and Ronan—hugs and thank them for coming.

I feel a tug at my elbow and turn to see Simona. "Were you in on this, too?"

"Not at the beginning, but Quan needed to make sure someone kept you away from downtown as they decorated the place. So I was texting her regular reports," Simona says, giving me a hug. "I'm so happy for you. I don't think I would've put you and Wiley together. Now that I see y'all, it makes sense. You're the perfect complement to each other. Like peanut butter and jelly."

"More like peanut butter and ... chocolate," Wiley says, then leans down to hug Simona.

I leave them to head over to my family's table.

"This is wonderful. It's so amazing to see how much the town is coming together to support you and Wiley," Mommy says as she stands up and hugs me.

"I'm surprised," I admit, sliding down to hug Daddy.

"You shouldn't be. Everybody loves you, Zaire." Persia gives me a hug next.

"And it doesn't hurt that you're engaged to the hottest guy in Kimbell," Sydney says, following up with a tight hug. I cling to her, enjoying this moment. I push away the disappointment that all of this joy is because of a lie that Wiley and I have constructed. A part of me, and not a small one, wishes this was a real celebration for a real engagement with the real love of my life.

"You did good, Zaire," Sydney continues. "Every time I see how Wiley looks at you, it gives me goosebumps. He's so in love."

"You think so?"

"When y'all got here, even as you hugged and greeted other people, his eyes were rarely off you," Sydney says. "The Wiley I remember would have been winking and flirting with every woman here. But not anymore. Looks like those days are in the past because he only has eyes for you."

"Alright, love birds," Quan says, stomping toward us as she wields a microphone. Not that my loud mouth friend needs one. "Take a seat so we can get this engagement party started."

"The best way to start our engagement party is with a Baker Bros tradition. Where are our mugs of Elm Beer?" I ask. I need some liquid courage to make it through this night.

Hoots and hollers ring in the air at the restaurant's tradition that involves getting the first round of beer for free when you yell out a toast and chug the beer until your mug is empty. If you fail on any criteria, two rounds of beer get added to your tab at the end of the night.

The sassy Latina waitress I was hoping to avoid stomps over and scowls at me. Her face is a mask of dark smoky eyes and bright red lips curled into a disgusted sneer. "I can't believe you're suggesting this. What are you trying to do? Kill Wiley?"

"One mug of beer will not kill Wiley," I say, shrugging off her interruption. I knew showing up at the restaurant where Wiley's most well-known ex worked was going to be awkward.

Wiley winces.

"Zaire, he has celiac disease!" Izzie places a hand on her nonexistent hips. "Do you want him to be on the toilet all night and damage his intestines for the sake of your love?"

"What?" I turn toward Wiley.

"I'm gluten sensitive," Wiley explains as the table full of his friends snickers. "I don't have celiac disease. I don't." He looks at me with a reassuring smile. "I won't die from drinking beer."

"But you will have diarrhea all night long. Trust me, I know from before he got diagnosed," Izzie continues.

My hands fly to my mouth as I stare at Wiley. Mortified, my eyes search his. I could have caused him a lot of discomfort because I didn't know. What else do I not know about Wiley that his fiancée would? I swallow hard, uncomfortable with all the attention. I can't have another slip-up like this. I hope Wiley knows how sorry I am for almost forcing him to drink gluten-laden beer.

Wiley turns toward Izzie with his hands raised. "Iz, now is *not* the time to share my medical issues with the whole world."

"I'm shocked she didn't know," Izzie says, looking suspiciously at me. A murmur rustles through the crowd.

Now, this is worse.

In front of everyone, I look clueless about an important part of Wiley's life. What fiancée wouldn't know something like this? And are people questioning whether our relationship is real? I need to do damage control.

I shrug dismissively. "Wiley and I drink wine at my place. I don't drink beer unless it's from my bestie," I say, giving Harlow-Rose a nod for the famous beer from her family's brewery. "Makes sense that it never came up in conversation." I tilt my head and give her a sweet smile.

"Well, as his fiancée, you should try to know what things might land him in the hospital. That is if you truly love him," Izzie claps back.

"Oh, I do. That's why he put a ring on it." I raise my left hand in the air and twirl my hand, Beyonce style.

The ladies in the crowd break into the popular song as Izzie's face falls. I didn't mean to embarrass her, but she started it.

And there was no way I wasn't going to finish it.

CHAPTER 25

ZAIRE

~

QUAN GRABS A MICROPHONE AS A HEAPING PLATE OF barbecue with potato salad, and baked beans are placed on our table. She announces, "Keeping with the theme of Wednesday Nights at Baker Bros, we're going to play an exciting game. One that is focused on Kimbell's newest favorite engaged couple! The game is called Guess Who. At everyone's table, there are cards with questions about this wonderful couple. For each question, you need to guess whether it's the bride or the groom. So, for example, question one is, who is funnier?"

Wiley's name rings out in the restaurant. An overwhelming crowd favorite as the answer to this question.

"Then I'll ask the couple, and they have to tell us the right answer," Quan says, then turns to face us.

Wiley and I look at each other and nod, then say in unison, "Wiley."

Quan gives a thumbs up to the crowd. "You have five minutes to complete your cards and give them to our table of graders." She turns and waves an arm toward the table where our families are sitting. "The people who get the most answers correct will be entered into a drawing to win a free barbecue dinner from Baker Bros."

The entire restaurant is in a frenzy, filling out the cards and racing to turn them in. Sally takes the completed cards and divides them among everyone at the table to check how many correct answers.

"This is going to be interesting," I whisper to Wiley.

"Hope we don't get any hard questions," he responds, then stuffs half a sausage in his mouth.

"Confidence in responding is the key. Maybe argue about a few and keep it fun," I instruct. He gives me a high-five, then offers me a piece of his sausage.

Without thinking, I lean forward and allow him to feed me.

The whistles and cat-calls ring through the air at this move.

I chew as Wiley's eyes drop from my eyes to my lips.

Jolts of energy rack through my body, and I look away from him.

"Save that sexual tension for tonight. We need to keep it P.G. up in here!" Quan says, then cackles with laughter. "Let's get to the questions! Who made the first move?"

I point at Wiley at the same time he points at himself. This fake engagement was his idea, after all.

"Who is the most romantic?"

Wiley jumps up this time, pointing both fingers at himself. I agree wholeheartedly. "He's right, y'all." The ladies in the place swoon.

"Who is the best gift giver?"

The crowd screams my name.

Wiley says, "That's only because she's stupid rich!"

Everybody laughs.

"So what did your rich fiancèe give you for your thirtieth birthday?" Hayley calls out.

"Yeah, I'm sure it was something awesome, especially since his birthday was on a holiday," Timmy Quinn yells from the crowd.

"That should qualify for more than one gift if you ask me!" Ace Lallo belts out.

All eyes turn to me as a blaze of fire rushes up my neck. Wiley's thirtieth birthday was this year? I didn't know that, but his fiancée definitely would. I lick my lips slowly and turn toward Wiley. His aqua eyes show all the terror and panic I feel at this moment.

If his birthday was over Thanksgiving, I'm sure that would've come up when we talked about how to convince people he went to St. Barts with me. The only holidays in the past six months are the Fourth of July and ...

"Well, Wiley is a sucker for treats over tricks," I say, confident that my fiancè must have been born on Halloween.

"What does Halloween have to do with his birthday?" Izzie frowns at me.

I pause, gripping the edge of the table, and mentally kick myself for choosing the wrong holiday. "What I meant was there's nothing like extra fireworks—"

Wiley grabs my hand, squeezing it tightly.

My words falter as the murmurs through the crowd grow louder.

"Columbus Day?" I whisper at Wiley.

He squeezes his eyes shut, then whispers, "Labor Day."

I grab the collar of his shirt and jerk him toward me. "Labor Day is on a different day in September every year," I say through clenched teeth.

"No one said my birthday was always on a holiday," He gives me the sexiest sheepish grin.

"How long were y'all secretly dating?" Izzie glares at me, suspicion clouding her face.

The answer I should give is six months, but if I say that now, it would only make things worse. I stay quiet.

"My guess is Zaire doesn't want to admit that she didn't get her man anything for the most important birthday of his life!" Erin says, her tone laced in anger. The crowd goes into a frenzy at the accusation.

Heart pounding in my chest, I struggle to come up with a way to salvage this disaster.

Izzie piles on, "That's horrible. We haven't dated in years, and I still got him a special gift for his thirtieth."

"A collector's edition auto converting Transformers Optimus Prime robot. Best gift ever," Wiley says, a wistfulness in his tone as he nods his head.

"Which is why he didn't get a gift from me," I say, pushing him away. Laughter rings through the air.

Shaken from his reverie, Wiley picks up on my angle. "Zaire was pretty upset about how excited I was over Izzie's gift. We had our very first argument that night, didn't we, Buttercup?"

"Yes, we did, and I may have overreacted and made a poor choice not to get Wiley a gift," I say, breathing a slow sigh of relief as the crowd buys into our lie.

Wiley breaks into a big grin. "But she more than made up for it later, if you know what I mean!"

"Wiley!" I scream and shove him. His body teeters on the edge of the chair from the force, arms flailing in the air before toppling off the stage onto the floor. Wiley is instantly surrounded by his fellow firefighters, giving him high-fives as they help him from the floor. The cheers are deafening as I squirm in my chair from embarrassment.

"Alright, alright, calm down y'all. We still have a bunch more questions to get through," Quan says.

Wiley hops back onto the stage and gives me a wink as he sits down. When the noise level lowers, Quan asks the next question. "Who is the better cook?"

Ronan stands up. "Is this a trick question?"

Harlow-Rose laughs out loud. "I was thinking the same thing. Neither one of them cook."

"Alright, alright, I'll throw that question out," Quan says, shaking her head. "Who wakes up earlier?"

Wiley points both fingers at me. I stand and curtsy.

"Who is the better dancer?"

Both our names are screamed out by the crowd.

Wiley and I look at each other and laugh. I'm sure he remembers that night months ago when we took a break from working on the e-commerce website and danced for hours. He's a great dancer. But so am I.

Wiley speaks up. "It's a tie."

Quan nods. "I believe that." She leads us through dozens more questions over the next half hour until she announces that we are at the last one. "There is a four-way tie for the lead. Timmy Quinn, Ronan O'Reilly, Simona Ivanov, and Gwen Paul all have thirteen of twenty questions correct. Last question is … who initiated the first kiss?"

I stiffen as kissing noises fill the air.

We'll have to make something up, but telling too long a story could be risky. I glance at him, and he looks as stunned as I do. It will seem weird if we don't come up with something soon. I've already made too many mistakes tonight. One more wrong move, and it could torpedo our fake relationship.

"Who cares about which one of them initiated a kiss when they were sneaking around," Darren yells as he jumps on top of the table. "What's most important is where were they when they had their first *public* kiss! Y'all know they spent the past few months sneaking around hiding everything. Don't you think it's about time they show the world their love by kissing in public?"

Cheers ring out within the restaurant.

"And where do y'all think that should happen?" Darren continues, egging the crowd on.

Without hesitation, the crowd responds. "Baker Bros BBQ!" Then chants of "Kiss! Kiss! Kiss!" fill the air.

Wiley gives Darren a look that would detonate a nuclear bomb, but it dissipates as quickly as it flares up.

"You hear that crowd," Quan says. "Let's see them lips locking!"

I stare at the smiling, jubilant faces and know there's no way out of this.

Our "no kissing" agreement has gone up in smoke.

Wiley turns to me, leaning closer, his words low where no one can hear but me. "We don't have to do this? We said we wouldn't—"

"We have to. We don't have a choice," I say through a big smile that hides the pounding of my heart.

"There's always a choice, Buttercup," Wiley says, pressing the issue.

"I'm okay with this," I say, the words rushing from my mouth breathy and soft. I cringe inwardly at the thoughts racing through my mind. The yearning to see what it's like to have Wiley Alexander kiss me.

I want to know more than I care to admit. How many times over the past several days have I wanted this experience? Too many to count. What would one little kiss hurt?

Wiley's aqua blue eyes are intense, shifting a shade darker.

His smile is different like he's genuinely happy with my answer.

Goosebumps pepper my skin as he moves closer to me. His hands grip the edge of my chair, and he slides me closer until only inches separate us. The abrupt move triggers another round of cheers and shouts from the crowd.

"Kiss! Kiss! Kiss!"

As he moves closer, time slows down. The noise fades away. All my focus is on Wiley. It's as if we are the only two people in the room, and nothing matters but him and me.

I close my eyes as his lips press against mine. The smell of him wafts around me, and every nerve ending in my body comes alive from the feel of his soft, sensual lips. His touch is tender and gentle, deliberate and sweet … until my hands wrap around his neck.

One simple move shifts the dynamic of our kiss.

His lips grow more insistent, seeking to devour and delight me, as his mouth moves against mine. My lips part, and Wiley takes the invitation, deepening the kiss. His hands cup my face, thumbs stroking my cheeks as he continues kissing me like it's his favorite pastime, and he's done it hundreds of times. The kiss shifts again and turns possessive as if he wants to show everyone I am his and his alone.

My head is spinning as Wiley claims every part of my heart with the best kiss I've ever had. I never thought Wiley would make me feel this way.

Like nothing about this kiss, or us as a couple, is fake at all.

CHAPTER 26

ZAIRE

~

"YOU OKAY? YOU SEEM DISTRACTED," SYDNEY SAYS, EASING down onto the satin-covered chair next to mine.

I stare at the text message again, wondering what's taking Wiley so long to respond. I take a deep breath. The man is on shift at the fire station. He's probably attending to some real emergency right now. He doesn't have time to deal with me freaking out.

No doubt about it, things have gone off the rails.

A runaway train barreling off the tracks, but headed where?

I don't know.

That kiss last night changed things between us.

Before that kiss, we were friends. We texted. We talked. We goofed around. Everything was light and fun and easy between us. We were working out how to handle being fake in love around our family and friends.

Walking into the surprise engagement party at Baker Bros BBQ had raised all the stakes. Even though we handled the Q&A game without too many slip-ups, the last question rattled me.

One glance at Wiley, and I knew he was rattled, too.

Sure, we were prepared to tell the story of our first date in convincing detail because we'd done it.

What we hadn't done, hadn't thought about doing, was having a first kiss.

When Darren's declaration turned the crowd into raving lunatics demanding a public kiss, we had no choice but to go along with it or risk blowing our cover.

That would mean no chance of a feature on Heather Grimley's vlog for Wiley's dating app and no fiancé buffer to be by my side when I come face to face with India for the first time in five years. The stakes were too high to throw in the towel now.

We did what we had to do.

I just never expected that kiss to be … the best I ever had.

I stuff my phone back into my purse. "I'm fine. Work stuff, but nothing I can't handle."

"Good because you know Princess Persia will have a fit if we don't give her our undivided attention." Sydney grabs a flute filled with mimosa and hands it to me. Taking another from the tray, we clink and drain our respective glasses.

"Where is Mommy? Why isn't she suffering here with us?" I walk toward the minibar to refill our flutes.

"She is with Harlow-Rose, trying to figure out how to expand the guest list from one hundred to three hundred. Yves's mother has convinced most of their guests to make the trek to Texas for the wedding."

"Her winery isn't big enough to seat three hundred people," I say, reaching for the pitcher of mimosas.

Yolanda French, the owner of The French Connection Bridal Boutique, slaps at my hand, then shoves a wedding gown at me. Yolanda and I became fast friends a few years ago when she asked me to step in as her real estate agent and broker a stalemate in negotiations on purchasing this property from the former owner. She had her heart set on this building and this location, which the old owner knew and used that to drive up the value and price. In a couple of weeks, not only had I gotten him to drop the price to within Yolanda's price range, but he also performed several renovations to the building before the closing.

"Hold that against your body," Yolanda commands, then rummages through a side bin filled with bolts of the most gorgeous lace fabrics I've ever seen.

I fumble with the dress, almost dropping it to the floor, before recovering and holding it up against my body.

"Now, with your curves, a mermaid dress is the only kind you should wear on your big day," Yolanda says, giving me a big grin. "This silk is sophisticated, but it doesn't capture your exuberance, which is why I will recreate the gown and use satin with this lace overlay. What do you think?"

I stare down at the delicate lace dotted with sparkling crystals and let out a slow sigh. Running my fingers over the fabric, I say, "This is stunning."

"I got the bolt in from Italy, and I'm saving it for you. Not going to show it to anyone because it has Zaire Kincaid Alexander written all over it." Yolanda gives my arm a quick squeeze, her eyes brimming with happiness.

Zaire Kincaid ... Alexander?

"Yolanda, what are you talking about? I haven't ordered a wedding dress," I say. Nor will I need to order one because Wiley and I are not getting married.

She beams. "After that engagement party, I was inspired. I want your wedding dress to be the dress of the century. More gorgeous than any dress anyone has ever seen, so you can walk down that aisle and snatch Wiley's breath right out of his lungs." She gives two snaps of her finger to punctuate her plans.

I bite my bottom lip as a wave of guilt crashes over me.

Another reminder of how the entire town is enthralled and excited about a wedding that will never be. Wiley and I will break everyone's hearts when we pull the trigger on our relationship escape plan. I never thought in a million years that faking an engagement would be this hard or that so many people were invested in our happiness.

"I don't know, Yolanda—"

"Oh, Zaire. That dress is stunning. Go put it on," Sydney pushes me toward the dressing room.

"I can't. We're waiting on Persia to model her dress. We can do stuff for my ..." I grip the back of my neck, rubbing it fiercely, then continue, "wedding later."

Much later. Later like, never.

"Did you see that Disney princess wedding gown?" Sydney asks. "It's going to take her a good twenty minutes to get into that thing. Go on, try this on."

Against my better judgment, I emerge from the dressing room five minutes later wearing the luxurious couture wedding gown.

"Well?" I say, stepping into the crystal-covered shoes Yolanda places in front of me. I look up and stare in awe at Sydney. She's dabbing at her eyes with one hand and waving a hand at her face with the other. "Are you crying?"

My hard-as-nails sister reduced to a puddle of goo at the sight of me in a wedding dress? What alternative universe have I traveled to?

Yolanda nods her head. "It's perfect for you. Take a look."

Inhaling a deep breath, I turn around to face the mirrors and gasp.

The plunging V-neck tastefully showcases my chest as the silk clings to all my curves. My waist looks smaller, while my hips would make Wiley's tongue dangle out of his mouth.

Or ... whoever my real future husband will be.

Yolanda was right. It's like this dress was made for me and only for me.

"Told you," Yolanda wraps an arm around my waist and leans her head on my shoulder.

"We've been friends for a long time, Zaire. I knew this would be perfect for you," Yolanda continues. "You deserve a longer train, so I'll extend that three feet. Nothing too extravagant. Just enough for that wow factor."

"And the lace?" Sydney asks. "You'll do an overlay with that Italian lace."

Yolanda nods.

"That dress looks amazing," Persia's voice floats across the air, flat and monotone.

We all turn to look at my youngest sister. She stares back at us with a look that could only be described as pure misery.

The princess fairy ball gown swamps her petite figure. The high-neck bodice is covered in floral appliqués. Sheer long sleeves sprinkled with more floral appliqués cover her arms. The tight bodice stops a couple of inches above her waist and explodes into a massive dome of layers upon layers of tulle that stretches out into a wide circle around her body. It's not a terrible dress, but it's not a show-stopper.

"Much better than this hideous thing I have to wear." Persia pouts as she struggles under the weight of the massive gown, moving toward us.

"Your dress is not hideous," Sydney says, rushing over to console her.

Yolanda and I exchange a look. It's going to be a long day. I rush back into the dressing room and change back into my clothes. When I emerge, Persia is crying on Sydney's shoulders as Sydney stares at me with unbridled frustration.

"But Persia, I saw the drawings and the photo inspirations you provided to your designer. This dress is what you said you wanted," Sydney tries to remind her.

"I want to look gorgeous, not like some kid playing dress-up in a big balloon wedding gown. I want a dress like Zaire had on. I'm not wearing this one."

Dragging a hand down my face, I hold in a scream. Persia no longer wants to wear the dress that our parents paid almost six figures for. I have to convince her to keep this dress.

"Honey, you are gorgeous, and this dress has potential, especially after Yolanda works her magic," I say. It needs a few tweaks to make it something a twenty-three-year-old would want to wear.

Sydney squeezes Persia around the waist, then frowns at me. "Part of the problem is that you've lost more weight. You can't expect to look good in your wedding dress when you're nothing but skin and bones."

"I can't help it. I don't eat when I'm stressed," Persia whines.

"What do you have to be stressed about? Mommy, Yves, Yves's family, everybody is jumping through hoops to give you everything you want for your wedding. This dress is what you wanted," I say.

"I don't want it anymore. Yolanda, that mermaid dress Zaire was wearing. Do you have it in my size?" Persia asks.

"No, you're an ectomorph. You need way more curves to pull off a dress like that," Yolanda says, not mincing words. I can tell from the look in her eyes that Persia would have to pry that dress out of her dead, cold hands before she'd let her have it. I stifle a smile at my friend's commitment to me, even though I know I'll never need that dress.

"An ectomorph?" Persia repeats, looking bewildered.

"You don't have hips or a butt, honey," Sydney explains. "That's why this princess-style gown is perfect for you. It just needs to be taken in."

"And maybe make it sleeveless and … strapless. Do you think you could do that?" I turn toward Yolanda.

"In less than two weeks?" Yolanda scoffs.

I whisper, "Name your price. It's yours. Just make her fall back in love with that dress."

"Only because it's you. My holidays will be ruined because of this, so expect a big bill," Yolanda says, ventriloquist style through her smile.

"Zaire, don't lie to me," Persia says, swiping at her tear-stained face. "You think she can fix my dress?"

Yolanda jerks her head toward Persia, insulted.

"Trust me, there's nothing Yolanda can't do."

Minutes later, Yolanda has Persia perched on a tall pedestal as she pins, tucks, measures, and tweaks until the dress takes on a new look. One that is fast approaching the level of stunning.

Sydney walks toward me with a fresh mimosa, then leans against the side table. We clink glasses for the second time.

"Sisters to the rescue," I say.

"Does she always have to create distress so she can be a damsel? I mean, seriously? It's almost like she doesn't want to get married," Sydney huffs. "Do you know what she had the nerve to say after your surprise engagement party?"

I take a sip of mimosa, not sure I want to know.

"It's not fair that you found a guy as wonderful and handsome as Wiley to ask you to marry him." Sydney spits the words with disgust. "As if you don't deserve to have love like the rest of us."

"Why wouldn't she want me to be happy?" I ask, disappointment snaking through me.

"She's jealous. Wiley will be by far Mommy's best-looking son-in-law. Yves, hands down, will be the ugliest."

"Sydney!"

"He's worse than average. The only reason Yves has gotten dates is because the Voltaires are an influential family in France. The needs of their business empire complement Daddy's needs as the US Ambassador to France," Sydney says, then takes a big gulp of her mimosa. "I swear, the only reason she gave Yves a second look is because of his status in Paris society. Now she's here, seeing how Wiley can't take his eyes off you, and she's jealous. Yves doesn't look at her like that."

"That's not true. They are in love," I say, trying unsuccessfully to convince Sydney that she's wrong. "Not everybody has that mind-boggling, can't-live-without-you kind of love."

"Right, which makes it hard for her since that's what I have with Matthieu, India has with Kei, and now you have with Wiley."

My face falls.

"I'm sorry. I didn't mean to mention the persona non grata sister. But you get my point, right?"

There's no way I can get her point because Wiley and I are fake in love.

Fake-in-love people who crossed a line with a kiss that was out of this world. A kiss that has made things weird between us because I don't know what it means. Was it two people who are attracted to each other indulging in the moment? Or could it be a sign of something more?

I can't deny that Wiley and I seem to fit. He understands and accepts me like I do him. I love how unapologetically crazy and silly he can be at one moment, detailed tech-nerdy another, and mouth-dropping sensual the next. All those parts of him make him undeniably appealing.

But I'm one of many who've fallen for his charms.

There's nothing about me that's special to him.

He needs me to do him a favor, and he's doing me one in return.

It's as simple as that, right?

I groan under my breath.

"Okay, I'm being a terrible sister. But you know you're the only sister of mine that counts. I don't know where our parents got those younger two from because they are cray-cray in so many ways," Sydney says.

I look up and see a smile spread across Persia's face as she nods at something Yolanda is telling her. The transformation of the dress is underway. It's already making my little sister happy. Persia gives Yolanda a high-five, shimmies out of the dress, and runs toward Sydney and me.

"Thank y'all so much. The dress is going to be gorgeous, and I couldn't have done it without the two of you," Persia says, wrapping Sydney and me in a big hug. Sydney purses her lips, refusing to return the embrace. I make up for her and return the hug.

"We need a photo to capture this moment," Persia demands, wiggling her hand at Sydney. "Where's your phone?"

"I left it in the car. Where's yours?" Sydney snaps back.

Persia shrugs. "It's around here somewhere."

They both turn to me, expecting my phone to be an extension of my hand, which it is.

I pull it out of my pocket and then try to maneuver us into a position where we can all be captured in the selfie.

"Your arm is too short. Give it to Sydney so she can get a better angle," Persia instructs.

Sydney snatches my phone and takes a series of selfies, making us all look pretty awesome.

"Send those pics to me," Persia says, strutting away.

Sydney taps on my phone then pauses. Her mouth gapes open. "Oh my God! You didn't!" She turns to me with wide eyes full of shock.

Panic grips me.

Did she see my texts to Wiley? Was there something on my phone that shows my engagement is a sham?

I try to swallow past the lump in my throat, but my mouth is dry as sandpaper.

"What?" I eek out.

"You never told us you met Wiley on his dating app!" Sydney hisses. "Now it all makes sense why you gave him a shot. You're a ninety-eight percent love match."

"What!" I scream, snatching the phone from her. I thought I had deleted my profile. Okay, maybe I hid it. I'm not sure. I look at the screen where the Ladies Love Country Boys app is on my phone. The side panel reveals I have one match classified at the highest tier—Exceptional. A picture of Wiley in his firefighter gear is on the screen. One guaranteed to make the ladies fall out in the middle of the street. Below his photo, it reads:

98% love match
White male
Firefighter
Location … Kimbell, Texas

Sydney giggles. "You and Wiley were destined to fall in love."

CHAPTER 27

W ILEY

THAT KISS.

Hot, mind-blowing, intense, tender, and completely unforgettable.

That kiss is wrecking my day.

My mind cycles back to it every few minutes, reliving when I held Zaire's face in my hands. Her full, luscious lips were mine to explore, delight, and ravish.

Because we agreed kissing and intimacy were off limits as part of this fake engagement, I hadn't let myself think about what it would be like. If I did, I knew I'd go for it. The last thing I wanted was to make things awkward between Zaire and me.

Awkward like they are now.

I glance at my phone for the hundredth time.

The text Zaire sent me at six this morning.

We need to talk.

I don't want to talk.

I want ... to kiss Zaire again.

I want to feel her mouth on mine. The blistering and possessive way she deepened the kiss. Her hands kneaded through my hair, pulling me closer, refusing to let me back away. Not that I was going to. With every ounce of desire I felt coming from her, I gave back in double measure ... until Quan disrupted it all.

"Alright, lovebirds. Let's try to keep it P.G. up in here!" Quan said, cackling with laughter.

Zaire stiffened in my arms, pulling away.

I ached to keep her near, but there was no way I could.

She wouldn't look at me, laughing it off as she was surrounded by her sisters and friends. The guys crowded around me, giving me pats and back slaps until there was a mile between her and me.

We never got a chance to talk after that.

I needed to get home and rest before my shift.

Her friends wanted to take her to a bar in The Woodlands to continue the celebration.

While she was out drinking the night away, I was at home in blissful misery thinking about that kiss.

Darren stumbles into our sleeping quarters and bounces on the bed beside mine, interrupting my wayward thoughts.

"You're not still pissed at me, are you?" He asks.

"No," I say too quickly. "I'm fine."

"You're not fine. You haven't cracked a joke since our shift started. That's almost three hours of serious Wiley. It's weird, and it's making Ronan and Nate nervous."

"Luke's not nervous?"

"Nah. He thinks you're missing your woman," Darren says, then raises to look at me. He scrutinizes me with a critical eye, probably trying to read my mind.

I don't respond.

"Is that true? You miss Zaire right now?" Darren prods.

I ignore his question and say, "She sent me a text. I'm not sure how to respond." I toss my cell phone at him.

Darren catches it in one hand, enters my passcode, and taps to open the text app.

A low whistle escapes his mouth.

"And she sent it at the crack of dawn." Darren shakes his head.

"I crossed the line, and it's your fault," I say, then pause. Jumping off the bed, I rush to the door and close it. The last thing I need is Ronan, Luke, or Nate to overhear me. "Zaire and I explicitly agreed there would be no kissing as part of our fake engagement. But you had to force the issue, didn't you?"

"You want this fake engagement to look real, don't you?" Darren asks. "Answer her. It's been almost six hours since she sent that text."

"I don't want her to be mad at me," I admit, slouching against the wall. "I took the kiss way too far."

"Looked mutual to me. To all of us. Trust me, both of you were into that kiss from our vantage point."

I shrug. "Maybe she regrets it now. She could be afraid she's leading me on or something."

"Is she?"

"What?"

"Leading you on. Are you developing real feelings for Zaire?" Darren asks.

I shrug. "Give me my phone."

Darren throws the device like a football. I push off the wall, make a diving catch, and then land on the twin bed against the wall. I type a quick response.

> Sorry for late reply. At work. Free tomorrow or Saturday.

Her response comes within seconds.

ZAIRE KINCAID

> Tomorrow. Let me know when you're free.

Ok

I watch the screen, but she doesn't text anything else. I swallow my disappointment and stuff my phone back in my pocket.

"Are you going to answer my question?" Darren asks.

"Nope," I say, then head toward the door. "Aren't the kids from Kimbell Elementary coming by for a tour today?"

"Yeah, the two kindergarten classes are coming after lunch," Darren says, not budging from his spot. "We'll have forty little tykes taking over the station for two hours."

Usually, I dread the chaos of school field trips to the fire station with out-of-control kids running through the station, being chased by exasperated and tired chaperons. They climb all over the fire trucks and scream and yell as we try to give our safety presentation. Some sneak off and play hide and seek. It takes an hour to pluck them from hiding under the beds or in the kitchen pantry.

But today, I need the distraction.

Whatever it takes to stop me from thinking about Zaire.

"I'm going to grab a sandwich from Gwen's. You want me to bring you something back?" I ask, opening the door.

Darren shakes his head, then grabs a pillow. A nap before the tour isn't a bad idea. If I wasn't starving.

I make my way out of the fire station and walk down the block toward Gwen's Country Cafe.

"Hey, little brother!"

I turn to see my big sister, Hayley, waving at me. Crossing the grass, I jog over to her and lift her from the ground with an enormous bear hug.

"Decided stick around?" I ask, wrapping an arm around her shoulder.

"Ma wants to go to the Cypress outlet mall to get some new clothes to wear to all these events Mrs. Kincaid keeps inviting her to. She says she's tired of showing up in Walmart clothes while they don their fancy Saks Fifth Avenue duds," Hayley says, rolling her eyes.

"The Kincaids are making Ma feel bad about her clothes?"

"Not at all. She says they don't seem to care about stuff like that," Hayley says, looping an arm in mine. "She wants to feel more confident and comfortable around them. I told her having a few new outfits would do the trick. I will drive her down there as soon as her shift is over at the grocery store."

I reach into my wallet. The last thing I want is for Ma to waste money on clothes to feel good around people who will never become part of our family. The least I can do is cover the costs. "Give Ma my credit card and tell her to buy whatever she likes."

"Okay, big spender," Hayley teases.

"What brings you to the town center?"

"Ma had a list of errands she wanted me to take care of to get ready to make gingerbread houses on Saturday. I hope Zaire and her family are excited to come and hang with us. My kids are bouncing off the walls with anticipation. After going to Zaire's house, they want to make a gingerbread lake house. Can you believe that?" Hayley laughs, then turns serious. "What is it?"

"I haven't mentioned Saturday to Zaire. Persia has her super busy with wedding stuff. The whole family has been working with Harlow-Rose at the winery in Fredericksburg to get it ready for the big day. I'm not sure she'll be able to make it," I say, hedging. The truth is, I'm not sure what Zaire thinks of me and if she wants to spend any more time with this charade.

We need to talk can mean a whole number of things.

Most of them not good.

"Wiley, it's the one Alexander family holiday tradition that is uniquely us. At the very least, convince Zaire to come. Everybody is buzzing about you joining her family. I want her to see she's not getting the short end of the stick. Our family has a lot to offer, too."

I drag a hand down my face. "You're right. I'll talk to her about it tomorrow when I get off my shift."

"You better," Hayley says, steering me toward Elevation Cupcake Shop.

"Whoa, you know I can't go in there. I'm headed to Gwen's to grab lunch, then I have to get back to the fire station."

"You owe Brianna an apology in person. Telling her by text that you're engaged to another woman was cruel."

"I texted all my exes. What's the point of having a bunch of uncomfortable conversations?"

"To save your sister from having them for you instead. Brianna is devastated. I talked to her for hours after you texted. Then she called me crying when I was driving in for the surprise engagement party the town was throwing you and Zaire. The fact that everyone is so happy for y'all was making her pain worse."

"Jeez, she was crying?"

"Wiley, that girl is still in love with you, and you know it. Half the women in this town are in mourning over your sudden engagement. You're that irresistible." Hayley tugs at me while I try to divert toward the sidewalk that leads to Gwen's. "If you would talk to her face to face, she could come to terms with things being over between the two of you for good."

"We broke up two years ago, Hayley. She's not my last girlfriend—"

"Please do not mention bat-crap crazy Amanda 'Don't Call Me Mandy' Tucker," Hayley says, eyes growing wide.

"I didn't mention her, but you did."

"Oops!" Hayley frowns and clamps a hand over her mouth. "Did you text her?"

"No! Of course not. I view the restraining order as working both ways. She needs to stay away from me, and I won't contact her either."

"Good," Hayley says, releasing me from her grasp. "Can I say that I'm relieved that you found Zaire? I never thought I'd see you in love, little bro. But I saw that last night. You couldn't have picked a better woman to love or to have love you back."

"What makes you think I'm in love?"

Hayley looks at me like I've sprouted two heads, but I need to know. She's the one person who knows me better than anyone in the world. The only person who can help me sort through these confusing feelings. I'm so close to telling her the truth that Zaire and I are lying to the whole town.

"Well, for one, you proposed to her. You've never come close to doing that before in your entire life."

"But let's say we weren't engaged. Would that change what you thought?"

"Not one bit. If you weren't already engaged to her, I'd be pushing you hard to seal the deal and not let her get away. Lucky for me, you're not as dumb as you look."

"I look dumb?"

"Gorgeous guys are always presumed to lack intelligence. You, little bro, have been stunning from the moment you came out of the womb. I was there. I remember."

"Fine. I've been in love before—"

"If you're calling what you had with Brianna or Izzie being in love, you're so wrong. Wiley, you've dated a ton of women. And I mean a literal ton. In all that time, I'd watch you with these chicks, and you played a role. They were only seeing a part of the brother I knew. It's like you didn't trust them to know the entire you. You wanted to give them the fantasy, but not the other side."

"The other side?"

"The geek. The guy who can lose himself researching a single topic, getting into the minute details that no one else cares about. The guy whose idea of a fun weekend is creating code for a computer program only you will use. Brianna and Izzie never got to be with that part of you," Hayley says.

"They knew I was into computers."

"Wiley, you worked on your dating app and never told either of them about all the research you'd done or that you were building it while dating them. They were as shocked as everyone else when you released it."

"Good point."

"But you shared that part of yourself with Zaire. You should've heard her talking in excruciating detail about how you designed her website with sophisticated predictive analytics. I swear, it's like she was reading from a script you wrote. I knew that you'd found a woman that you were comfortable enough with to show the complete you. And your reward was her complete acceptance of all of you in return— the gorgeous and the geek. It's no wonder you fell in love."

Fell in love? Have I fallen in love with Zaire?

Could that be what's driving all these unruly emotions tearing my life apart?

"But what if I mess things up?" I ask.

Hayley smiles at me. "There are no guarantees in life, Wiley. Many people fall head over heels in love with each other and then end up in divorce years later."

"Or don't make it down the aisle."

"I can't imagine the pressure the two of you are under. Last night proves why it was wise for y'all to keep your relationship a secret for as long as you did. Two of the most popular people in town getting married? It's going to be the event of the century in Kimbell."

I rub my chin, staring off into the distance.

"You can't live your life afraid of making a mistake. If the worst happens and you and Zaire don't make it, you'll be okay ... eventually. Trust me, it's better to have loved and lost than never to have loved at all. Sounds trite, but it's true."

If Hayley is right and I'm falling in love, then wouldn't I be a fool to let myself lose Zaire?

CHAPTER 28

Zaire

~

Is that my doorbell ringing?

I pause in the middle of brushing my teeth, pressing the button to turn off my electric toothbrush, and strain to listen. Sure enough, I hear the distinctive chimes of someone pressing the doorbell repeatedly.

I glance at the artisanal terracotta clock perched on the wall inside my walk-in shower. Fifteen minutes past nine in the morning.

I had the worst night, plagued with insomnia, as I struggled with how to discuss the results of the dating app with Wiley. I passed out around five in the morning. The time I'm usually up and headed out the door for work.

The chimes continue.

God, please tell me it's not Persia.

I cannot deal with another crisis from my baby sister.

I turn the faucet and spit foamy toothpaste from my mouth, then stumble out of my en suite bathroom. Tapping on my phone with one hand, I pull up the security cameras and swipe until the feed from my front door is on the screen.

What in the world?

Minutes later, I swing the door open.

"Wiley?"

Despite the frigid, low fifty-degree temperatures outside, he's dressed like he's headed to a beach in Galveston. He's shirtless, revealing an impeccable muscular chest, and wearing low-hung swim trunks. An oversized beach towel is draped over his shoulder. My eyes travel the entire length of him, then return to his face. That gorgeous face is etched with concern.

"What are you doing here?" I ask, confused by ... everything.

"You said we needed to talk and to let you know when I'm free," Wiley announces. "I'm free."

"I thought you'd text, and maybe we'd talk after I got off work this evening."

Wiley shrugs. "Simona said you hadn't made it into the office yet, so I figured we might as well get it over with this morning. Since this is likely the last time I'll be invited to your house, there's one thing I wanted to do."

"Last time?" I sputter, tilting my head toward him.

"Can I come in?"

I step back and open the door wider. A brisk breeze of cold air follows Wiley inside, and I shiver. He has to be freezing, walking around half-naked like that. But I hold my tongue and decide instead to enjoy the view.

Wiley maneuvers past the ten-foot Christmas tree dominating the center of my living room and heads toward the doors that lead to the pool. I walk quickly to keep up with him. He swings the door open wide, steps out of his flip-flops, and makes his way over to the Infiniti pool that seems to blend into the lake in the distance. An architectural marvel that cost almost as much as the house to have built, but one I wouldn't give up for the world.

Tossing the towel onto one of the lounge chairs, Wiley backs up to the edge of the pool, then pauses.

"You know, I've never seen you without makeup before," Wiley says, tilting his head left and then right. "Don't take this the wrong way, but you're more beautiful like this. Natural. I like it."

"Wiley, what has gotten into you? Wait, what are you doing? Wiley!" I scream as I watch him fall backward. He lands with a loud splash into the water, sinking into the depths, then re-emerging with a huge grin.

"Nate was right," Wiley says, that playful grin that I love spreading across his face. "He said your pool would be heated in the winter."

"Isn't everybody's?" I ask.

Wiley bursts out laughing. "This feels so good." He beckons me. "Come inside."

"You want me to get into the pool?" I ask, looking down at my ratty, old maroon Texas A&M sleep shirt that has seen better days since I bought it as a freshman over a decade ago.

"Come on. One last indulgence with me before ..." He trails off as sadness infects his gaze.

The tug to reassure him takes over me. I'm powerless to resist anything he wants at this moment.

I say, "Why not?"

He looks pleased as I walk straight down the steps into the balmy waters. Wiley swims over to me, stopping mere inches away. We wade next to each other for several seconds, our eyes locked.

I swallow hard, then I say what I've been dying to say since Sydney discovered that Wiley and I are a match from his dating app. A ninety-eight percent love match.

"Tell me about your app."

"My app?"

"Yeah, Ladies Love Country Boys app. You told me about your vision for the dating app. That was how I revised your business plan.

But you never told me how you got started with it. Why you created it."

"That's what you wanted to talk to me about?" Wiley asks, his eyes sparkling. "The origins of my dating app?"

I nod my head. There's so much I want to talk to Wiley about, but I have to know about his app first. Knowing these details will help me determine what I want to speak to him about next.

"Okay," Wiley says, relaxing. The tension and concern dissipate from his face. "You've been in love before, right?"

"Of course. Who hasn't?" I say without thinking. At least at the time, I believed I was in love. Whether I was actually in love is another question.

"With Kei and the St. Barts guy and probably some others," Wiley says, a hint of tension in his tone.

"I suppose so." Kicking my feet through the water, I put some distance between myself and Wiley. "And you were in love with Brianna, Izzie, and probably countless other girls."

"No, I wasn't."

"You didn't love them?"

"I cared a lot about them. They are wonderful women, and I knew they were in love with me. They thought I was the one." He raises his arms and wiggles his fingers in the air quotes motion, sending water flicking on me. "Sorry about that." Wiley swims closer, his hand swiping at the droplets of water cascading down my face. His touch is intimate and gentle.

Wiley chuckles under his breath. "That didn't work. Now your entire face is wet. Want me to grab my towel?"

"Nope," I say, then plunge my entire body under the water. Anything to stop thinking about how good Wiley's touch felt. Rising back to the surface, I swipe my face and lean back against the pool's edge. Wiley follows me, decreasing the distance between us. He's so close. In my space, and I love it. I don't want any distance. "Okay, enough with that. Continue. So, you don't think you've ever been in love?"

"I don't know how to tell if I have or not. Since high school, I've had girls tell me they love me and that I'm their soul mate, but I didn't know how they could be so sure when I wasn't. I know everybody calls me a playboy, but I'm not a bad guy. I don't use women or set out to hurt them. I'm not callous like that."

I rest a hand on his shoulders. "Trust me, I know that. I don't think you're some gigolo. You've dated a lot, but all of your exes still think the world of you because you are a good guy." I move one of my hands to rest next to his heart. "In here."

"It means a lot that you see me that way," Wiley says with a sheepish grin. He clears his throat. "So, I figured if I was ever going to find this elusive love that so many women thought they'd found with me, I needed to know when it was real and when it wasn't."

"I don't think there's a formula for real love, Wiley."

"There is, and I found it." Over the next fifteen minutes, Wiley explains how he used AI and widely available academic, psychological and anecdotal research on true love to build the algorithm for his dating app.

"You saw patterns that could predict if people would fall in love?" I ask, my heart pounding in my chest.

"Well, technically, the AI found them. But I created the AI, so yeah. For example, people are always searching for a mate who likes the same things they like and want to do the same things they enjoy doing, but the AI discovered that the people with the strongest love and longest relationships didn't share a lot of the same interests."

"More like opposites attract?" I ask to confirm.

"Not opposites either. Not on either extreme. More like their interests and views complemented each other. Not the same, which would be boring, and not the exact opposite, which would create too much friction."

"Just enough difference to keep the relationship interesting."

"Exactly. It wasn't long before my app made lasting love matches. I have people who joined the app when it was in beta who email me every year on their matchiversary to let me know they are still together."

"But there are people who join your app and don't end up with a love connection. No app is a hundred percent effective," I counter.

"That's why I gave a rating scale of the match to let people know whether it was worth taking a chance on the person they are matched with or not. As a general rule, anyone below eighty percent match is like flipping a coin. Could work. But might not. Early on, I stopped showing people those matches."

"So, if you have an eighty percent match, there's a good chance the person is your soul mate and the future love of your life?"

"Yes, but only if you give them a chance. Most people aren't successful because they balk at who they are matched with. Something about the person doesn't fit their flawed perspective on who that right person is for them, so they refuse to give the person a try."

"I can totally see that happening."

"Once I realized that, I added categories of matches to encourage people to take a chance. Go outside their comfort zone. What could it hurt?"

"The app has percentage matches and categories now," I say, making sure I understand.

"Right. An exceptional match shouldn't be ignored. That's at the ninety-five percent match level or higher. Anyone with a match that strong owes it to themselves to go for it because the app has a near hundred percent success rate in that range."

"You said above ninety-five percent?"

"That's right."

"And how does the app help your situation?"

"What do you mean?"

"You did all this research and created this great dating app to help others find love, but how does that help you? All these years, you've been worried that you can't tell if you are in love with someone or not. You probably don't trust your feelings or know what it feels like to be in love," I say, rambling. "I get it. You need this app because if you ever felt like you were close, it's a way of validating that it's real this time."

Wiley looks down and squeezes the bridge of his nose. "I guess so."

"Do you believe your app works to match people with their soulmates? I mean, truly, in your heart, do you believe it works?"

Wiley looks back at me with an intensity that delves into my soul.

"Absolutely," He says with such conviction that I know he's not lying.

He gives me the answer I was hoping for. Now, I need the courage to ask what I've been dying to from the moment I saw the results from the dating app. I take a deep breath, then ask, "Has your app found any matches for you?"

"Who told you?" Wiley swims away from me toward the stairs that lead out of the pool. Running up the steps, he shakes water from his body, grabs his beach towel, and dries off. He looks ready to flee when I want more than anything for him to stay.

I swim toward the edge near where he's standing.

"I saw it myself. Sydney was on my phone, and some kind of way opened the app by accident. The results were there."

"I thought you deleted the app," Wiley says, slumping onto the lounge chair.

"I thought I did."

"You weren't supposed to see that."

"Why not?"

"When I told Heather Grimley that I found the love of my life on my dating app, I knew she would send a team to test the authenticity of my app and my statement. I could backdate a match, but I couldn't fake one. Machine learning has advanced to a level I couldn't guess what to put in a profile that would guarantee a match with mine. So, I needed a real match through my app to be my fake fiancée."

"I see."

"I had no clue it was going to be you. In fact, I didn't think you'd go along with this crazy idea."

"But I did."

"Only because you're fresh off a break up with St. Barts guy, who you're in love with, and you'd didn't want to face the last guy you loved who ran off with your sister as a single woman," Wiley says, replaying the deal of our arrangement. "You're on the rebound. I was never going to tell you about the results of the app."

"Makes sense," I say, then ease out of the pool. Wiley is at the edge in seconds, extending a hand to help me out. He wraps the towel around me, then follows me back inside the house.

"What do we do now that I know we're a ninety-eight percent love match?"

"Nothing," Wiley says.

"Nothing?"

"We had a deal that didn't involve knowing the truth about the results from my app. Neither of us is ready to deal with that at the same time as doing the interview with Heather or seeing India and Kei at Persia's wedding," Wiley says, giving me a bitter spoonful of blunt reality.

"You have a point."

"The results of the dating app don't expire," Wiley says, his eyes sparkling.

"Meaning?"

"We have time to think about what all this means after February."

"So, we should wait to see if anything real could develop between us?" I ask, fighting back my disappointment. I have to corral all my deepening emotions for Wiley for three months before we can explore what they could mean? How am I going to do that?

"Only if you're okay with it." Wiley stops and turns to face me.

"Of course. Why wouldn't I be?"

"Great." Wiley gives me a smile, but it's lacking his usual spark. "I know you need to get to work, so I'll get out of here. But I need to put one more outing on our couple's calendar. You free Saturday?"

For you, I'm free anytime. But now is not the time to share that with Wiley. Instead, I say, "Sure. What's the outing?"

"Making gingerbread houses with the Alexanders!"

179

CHAPTER 29

W ILEY

"Uncle Wiley! Uncle Wiley! Come look. It's ready." My
niece, Lydia, tugs on my arm as she points into the dining room. I
swipe another pecan snowball from the dish overflowing with
Christmas treats and follow her. Hayley's sons, Peter and Patrick, hold
up a dingy old throw blanket I used to wallow on as a kid to hide their
masterpiece.

Behind them, Zaire is beaming as she holds the toddler, Becky, in
her arms. I inhale a sharp breath, overwhelmed by how perfect Zaire
looks nestled within my family. When we arrived at Ma's house, it was
like she'd always been a part of our holiday tradition. Rolling up her
sleeves, she listened as my nieces and nephews jockeyed for her
attention, describing how they wanted the gingerbread house to be a
lake house, like Zaire's house.

Of course, Zaire was up to the task, sketching out a construction design on the back of a paper towel, then handing off the patterns to Ma and me to make the precision cuts of the sheets of gingerbread.

Hayley was in charge of decorating duty, arranging the candies in neat piles, and working on the landscaping for the house, which would, for the first time, include a lake made of jellybeans in various shades of blue.

"Ma! Get in here. We're done," Hayley yells into the living room where Ma had collapsed on the couch to take a much needed nap. She'd been baking nonstop since five in the morning to make sure there was enough gingerbread.

Minutes later, Ma leans against me.

The smile on her face is priceless as she gazes at her kids, grandkids, and the woman she is overjoyed will be her new daughter-in-law.

"Wiley, where's your phone? I need pictures of this," Ma says.

"Already got it," I say, raising the phone to take several candid shots of the construction crew.

"And now for the big reveal," Hayley says. "Drumrolls, please!"

The kids and Zaire all join in by making drum noises. Baby Becky adds a chorus of screeches as she struggles to mimic the sound. Peter and Patrick drop the blanket, and the masterpiece is revealed.

Ma gasps.

"Now that's a gingerbread house," I say, stunned by the structure resting on the table. It looks like something that would be in magazines, winning competitions, and featured in special places like the White House.

"You like it?" Zaire asks, her eyes searching mine for approval. I cross the room and slip an arm around her, taking advantage of the situation. I'm her fake fiancé, but only she and I know that. My family would expect me to be affectionate with the woman I asked to marry me. To not be able to keep my hands off her. I resisted the urges consuming me all afternoon because we were busy wrangling the kids and making the gingerbread lake house.

Now that everything is finished, nothing is standing in my way.

"It's amazing, like you," I say, then lean over to give her a soft kiss that I allow to linger, gauging her reaction. I want her to feel like she's mine. Like we belong together. Ninety-eight percent love match together. I'm walking a thin line, but I can't help myself. She kisses me back. Our first kiss was mind-blowing. This one touches me to my soul. It's the feeling I've been chasing all these years, wrapped in our mouths exploring each other. I grip Zaire tighter, then wince as Becky screams and slaps at our faces to make us stop.

"Becky says no kissy face," Lydia says, jumping around with excitement. Peter and Patrick grab Ma's hands and take her on a tour of the gingerbread lake house, sharing all the fun facts and construction details they learned from Zaire in building the delicious structure.

Hayley swoops in and lifts Becky from Zaire's arm.

"I think somebody needs a diaper change," Hayley says, but we both know it's an excuse to give me and Zaire some time alone. I slip my hand in hers and lead her into the kitchen, away from the chaos.

Alone, I stop and look into her gorgeous dark brown eyes.

"This was so much fun. Thanks for inviting me."

"You've spoiled my nieces and nephews. They won't want to go back to the plain old houses we used to create. You raised that bar mighty high."

"Well, they had some great ideas. I'm happy I could show them how to make their dreams come to life."

"Can you make my dreams come to life, too?"

She gives me a look of playful exasperation. "Weren't you the one who said we should wait to …" she checks and makes sure no one is listening, then continues, "see what could happen between us?"

"Now, you want to listen to me?"

"Occasionally, you have some worthwhile ideas."

"I know what I said, but I'll admit, it's hard to think of this as pretending now that we've kissed … twice."

"But both were for show. We had an audience, and we needed to convince people this engagement is real," Zaire says.

I chuckle under my breath. "Is that what you think, Buttercup?"

She nods but doesn't seem so sure.

"Well, this kiss is not for anyone but us."

I lean against her neck and inhale her intoxicating scent of spice and roses. My lips brush against her soft skin. Her hand grips my shirt, pulling me closer as my kisses trail along her jaw to her chin and find her lips. I caress the back of her head, stroking her soft, short curls as I kiss her deeper. The softness of her lips against mine is like heaven.

She loops her arms around my neck as our bodies press against each other. It's like the floodgates have opened. Everything we've been holding back and refusing to say about our feelings for each other is washing over us in this fantastic kiss.

Zaire is tattooing herself onto my heart, and it scares the crap out of me. I pull away, breathing hard, and put some distance between us. She looks as dazed with desire as I feel. Her eyes search mine as her hand brushes wayward strands of my hair off my forehead.

"Wiley—"

"I know." Fear seizes my heart. I can't let her say the words. Not yet. We're not ready. This situation is complicated enough without us bringing genuine, strong feelings into the mix. I don't know what I'm doing. I've never felt this way about anyone. I could easily mess this up. Do something or say something that sends Zaire running and screaming away. I need to keep a clear head and focus on the original agreement—pretend to be engaged until Heather's feature on my dating app goes live on Valentine's Day.

Once that's all behind us, we can figure out what's next. I grip her hands and place soft kisses on her knuckles.

"Come on. After making gingerbread houses, we usually play Candyland with the kiddos," I say.

"Wiley, we need to talk about this."

"Do we? Can't we just … be? For now?"

"Yeah." Zaire gives me a smile that almost stops my heart. "We can."

CHAPTER 30

ILEY

~

THE TRAPEZOIDAL EDIFICE HOUSING KINCAID REAL ESTATE is nestled near the far end of Lake Lasso Center, an upscale development of entertainment venues, retail stores, and restaurants on the banks of its namesake, is like a work of art. It blends seamlessly into the nature surrounding it. Glimmering white Christmas lights adorn the buildings, and oversized red, green, and gold bulbs and massive wreaths wrapped in ribbon are festively arranged in front of each entrance.

Zaire's brainchild come to life in a way that far exceeded everyone's expectations, even her own. A surge of pride flows through me. As if I had anything to do with the legacy Zaire is building for our small town and the surrounding county, which I absolutely don't.

Tightening my grip on the picnic basket, I tuck the oversized blanket under my arm and lean my back against the glass doors of the offices to push my way inside.

"Wiley! What are you doing here?" Simona whispers as she trips over herself to move from behind her desk to block the hallway that leads to Zaire's massive corner office. "I told you Zaire is working late. She does not want to be disturbed. If you go back there, she'll think I didn't do what she asked me to do."

The request from Zaire was for Simona to call me and let me know Zaire was breaking our date ... again. I haven't seen her since the Gingerbread party at Ma's house. Between my shift on Sunday and Zaire canceling our plans on Monday, it's been almost three days. I'm going through withdrawals needing to see her, and she knows it. That's why she asked Simona to do her dirty work. She knew I'd convince her not to cancel our date two nights in a row, which I still fully plan to do. There's no way she'll be able to resist a surprise picnic. I don't care what pressing business she has. I'll keep my visit to an hour, two tops, so she won't fall further behind on whatever work is making her stay late.

I flash Simona a smile and watch her face turn beet red. "Trust me, I'll tell her you followed her instructions and that I'm the bad boy she needs to spank for not following directions."

Simona gasps then erupts in a flurry of giggles. "I swear, you are perfect for her."

That stops me in my tracks. I glance down at the demure woman. "You think so?"

Simona nods. "Quan and I were talking about it earlier. People believe Zaire is super serious because she owns three wildly successful businesses. But she isn't. She's silly and fun. She works hard and has high expectations, but she also likes to joke and keep things light. That's why we all love working for her. You're the first man she's had in her life that made her feel comfortable enough to show that side of herself. We think that's a big part of why the two of you fell in love."

A vision of Zaire walking into her pool fully clothed only because I asked floats in my mind. Every crazy antic I throw at her doesn't rattle her at all. She's drawn to it, and it makes her like me more. I'm not sure we're in love … yet, but there's a knowing inside me we're headed straight in that direction.

I tap my nose and give Simona a wink. "Keen observation. I will neither confirm nor deny your assessment, as it may incriminate my lovely fiancée or me."

"You're so cute!" Simona says, beaming.

"Who else is working late?" I ask, looking around the space. The offices are quiet. The usual hustle and bustle is noticeably absent.

"Zaire and me. The rest of the team went to volunteer at the library's annual holiday book giveaway this afternoon," Simona explains as a yawn escapes her lips.

"You head on home. I'll make sure that Zaire doesn't work too hard tonight."

"Oh, I can't leave her unless she wants me to—" Simona stops, noticing as I wiggle my eyebrows at her. "Oh, okay. Yes, well, let me grab my purse."

"Lock up on your way out," I call after her, then barrel down the hall to Zaire's office. I hear her before I see her.

"You hired him? When?"

There's a tinge of anger in her tone that she's trying hard to hide. Concerned, I pick up my pace until I'm outside her slightly ajar door.

"Well, what can I say? It's your company. You can hire whomever you want. I hope this doesn't impact any arrangements we've already made …"

She's quiet. Her stilettos tap against the wood floor. A few seconds pass, and she comes into my view from the narrow opening. Dressed in a deep red sleeveless dress that hugs her hips and matching four-inch heels, I let out a low whistle and enjoy the view.

"Good. Well, I will ask Simona to arrange for a warehouse visit in a couple of days. Sales continue to spike, and I don't want delays in delivering the custom pieces," Zaire says through gritted teeth. "Wonderful. I'll see you soon, Mr. Barnes."

I push through the door as Zaire hurls the cell phone toward it. I try to duck, but it's too late. The device hits me square in the throat, knocking the wind out of me.

"Wiley!" Zaire screams then rushes toward me.

The picnic basket crashes to the floor as I grip my neck, struggling to breathe past the pain detonating against my neck. Slumping to the floor, I gasp for air. My neck throbs, but I'll live. Not that I need to let Zaire know that right away.

She drops to her knees and presses her hands against my face, forcing me to look at her.

"Honey, are you okay? Oh God, I didn't see you standing there." Her hands stroke the side of my face, then touch my neck gingerly. "Say something, or I'm calling 9-1-1." Panic creases her brow as her eyes search mine.

"Some ... thing," I say, my words raspier than I expected.

"Are you really okay? I can get Simona to bring some ice." She stands, but I grip her arm to keep her close to me.

"I sent Simona home."

"You sent my assistant home. Why?"

"Why do you think?"

Zaire glances down at the scattered contents of the picnic basket sprawled across the wooden floor and the blanket underneath my feet.

"A picnic? Wiley, I have too much work to do. I'm already taking off Friday for final dress fittings with Persia. Then I'll be off again on Monday for cake tasting and the interview with Heather Grimley," Zaire says, but her protestation is weak. She doesn't want me to leave.

"I'm not here to stop you from working late. I'm here to join you," I point to my laptop resting next to the wall. "Plus, I figured you needed to eat to keep your stamina up, so I brought food."

"You're going to work with me. Here?"

"If you let me."

Zaire bites her bottom lip. "Why is it so hard for me to tell you no?"

"Because you like me a little too much," I say, then lean in and brush my lips against hers. Zaire moans against my mouth, sending energy sizzling through my body. "Plus, you owe me for assaulting me with that lethal cell phone. People will think you gave me a hickey."

"Eww, I hope not. That's so juvenile," Zaire says with a haughty air. She touches my neck gently. "Does that hurt?"

"Yep," I lie, feeling like a lovesick teenager.

She leans down and places a soft kiss on the spot. "How about now?"

"So much better," I say, rubbing my hands along her back.

"Good." With a quick kiss on my nose, Zaire helps me up from the floor. We gather the scattered food, courtesy of my favorite restaurant, Gwen's Country Cafe, and arrange it neatly in the center of the blanket.

I dim the lights and pull out a half dozen tea candles. Lighting them, I place them around the office as Zaire opens the food containers.

"I told Gwen to pack up all of our favorites," I tell her, easing down onto the blanket next to her. "I hope she got it right."

"Let's see." Zaire points to the boxes on her left. "These are definitely mine—mushroom quiche, side salad with balsamic vinaigrette. But this must be yours." She lifts a massive triple-decker BLT sandwich from on top of a bed of onion rings.

"Yep, all mine," I say, grabbing the sandwich and taking a big bite.

"I thought you were gluten sensitive," Zaire says, grabbing the plastic utensils and a bottle of sparkling water. She hands one to me, then opens the other.

"Gwen buys gluten-free bread for me. It's safe. I promise."

"Good, because I don't want anything bad to happen to you."

"Like flying cell phones trying to crush my trachea?"

Zaire laughs. "Yes, like that."

"I love your laugh. It's so pure and light and infectious. It makes me smile every time I hear it."

"What else do you ... love ... about me?"

Everything is what I want to say, but I don't. "That you're a boss."

"It's not a turn-off?"

"Not for me. Your confidence and competence are extremely sexy. I remember you presented to the Lasso County Business Association about overcoming imposter syndrome. You were brilliant. I was in awe of you."

"But now you've gotten to see behind the curtains and realize it's all smoke and mirrors." Zaire stares intently at her fork, plunging over and over into her salad without taking a bite.

"I see there's more to the business owner than I thought. There's a lighter side. A funny woman who likes to have moments when she doesn't have to be the boss. She can just ... be."

"Only with you," Zaire says, then stuffs her mouth full of salad.

As much as her declaration has me floating on cloud nine, there's still a part of her she's not letting me in on. The closer we become, the more I want to know.

"Kei didn't make you feel like that?"

"No." Zaire swallows, then says, "Kei was attracted to the public persona that is Zaire Kincaid. Once he saw the other side of me, he wasn't interested. In hindsight, I don't know why I thought we were a good match. We talked about getting married. That was the only reason I invited him to Sydney's wedding. I thought we were serious. For all India knew, I was madly in love with Kei. But it didn't matter to her. She saw him. She wanted him. She took him. And I haven't had a decent relationship since then."

"Not even with St. Barts guy?"

Zaire shakes her head quickly. Maybe too quickly, then she turns all her attention to her bottle of sparkling water like it's the most interesting thing in the world.

My jaw clenches as jealousy rages through me. Who is this guy that she spent her Thanksgiving holidays with? Why won't she ever talk about him? I'm like a dog with a bone, desperate to find out what happened between them. Does she still have feelings for him? Is she over St. Barts guy? Or will he rear his ugly mug right when we're ready to explore what our relationship could truly be?

I shouldn't press the issue, but I can't help it. I need to know.

"But—"

"You've dated many people in Kimbell," Zaire says, cutting me off. "I remember Izzie and Brianna being the ones that lasted the longest. What happened with them?"

Classic deflection. Part of me wants to steer the conversation back to her last relationship, but a bigger part wants to reassure her that there's no one I've dated in the past or would date in the future that could come close to how she makes me feel.

"Izzie was my high school sweetheart. No matter how many times we broke up, we kept getting back together. But it was young and immature and not sustainable. I went to college, which wasn't her thing, and we grew apart."

"You couldn't tell by how she acted at our surprise engagement party," Zaire says, a hint of annoyance in her tone.

I'm strangely satisfied to pick up on a twinge of jealousy coming from her.

"And Brianna." I inhale sharply. "She was special. I cared about her, and we were close for so long. We dated for almost two years before things ended."

"But you weren't sure that you loved her?" Zaire asks, avoiding my gaze.

"Sometimes I thought I did. Other times, she frustrated me so much that I didn't want to be around her. She's a sweet person. Nice and very … content."

"Content. Why is that a bad thing?"

"It's not. Maybe I'm not attracted to that trait in a woman. I look at you, and you're always pushing the envelope, trying new things, challenging yourself. Kincaid Real Estate wasn't enough, so you started Kincaid Construction. When you conquered residential developments, you moved on to commercial and planned the new Lake Lasso Center. That's almost complete, and now you're tackling custom furniture. That's how I am, even if I'm not as successful as you," I admit. "I want my dating app to be the best in the world. I keep tinkering with the AI, marketing, or services offered to improve it."

"And you didn't see those traits in Brianna."

I shake my head. "She's been working at Elevation Cupcakes for years. Cupcakes have never been good at that shop, even though all the other desserts are divine."

"Their macaroons are my favorite."

"Well, get this. Brianna makes a killer cupcake. She made them for me all the time when we were dating. I kept telling her to offer the recipe and her services in exchange for an ownership percentage. She wouldn't do it because she was afraid to rock the boat. Her words."

"So, we have been suffering without good cupcakes because she doesn't want to upset the owner. That's a shame. She could quit and open a real cupcake shop. Both would survive in Kimbell. We love our sweets."

"I tried to tell her that, too, but it didn't work. I wanted her to want more for herself. When she didn't, I realized she couldn't be the life partner I needed. A woman who would push and inspire me as hard as I pushed myself."

"That's understandable."

"Only by you. I think you get me."

"And you get me."

"Are we doing the right thing by waiting, Buttercup?"

I'm not sure how much longer I can pretend that I'm pretending to have feelings for Zaire.

"If this is headed where I'm thinking, then we have plenty of time. There's no need to rush."

I know she's right, even though I hate her answer.

CHAPTER 31

ILEY

❦

"WHAT ARE YOU WORKING ON?" I ASK, LEANING BACK against the wall as I rub my belly, swollen from polishing off the BLT sandwich, onion rings, and apple pie a la mode. I tilt my head to the right and sneak a glance at Zaire, sitting on the floor next to me. Her laptop is perched on her lap. The screen is filled with a spreadsheet full of numbers on one side and graphs and charts on the right. Her reading glasses are perched on the tip of her nose as she glances from the screen, then back down again to a slew of papers surrounding us like an island.

Zaire holds one page in the air. A complex schema diagram of a dining room hutch takes up the entire page. She stretches her legs out, pushing the heels from her feet, then says, "Reviewing mockups for new products I'm considering for Kincaid Furnishings."

She groans under her breath as she wiggles her feet in the air and shimmies her toes.

Rolling over, I crawl down the length of her body and sit next to her feet. Lifting her legs into my lap, Zaire stiffens.

"Wiley, what are you doing?"

"I'm going to massage your feet, Buttercup," I say, resting one foot in the palm of my hand.

"You don't have to do that," she whispers.

She's been in heels all day. I can imagine her feet are screaming in pain. I respond, "I know." I stare at the red polish on her toes that match her dress. The contrast between the bold color and her deep, dark skin is mesmerizing. I swear she has the prettiest feet I've ever seen. I resist the urge to tickle her, especially when she's looking at me … like … that.

That look I've been hoping to see from her.

She's starting to want this. To want an "us."

I'm kicking myself for suggesting that we wait until vlog post with Heather and Persia's wedding is behind us before exploring what our feelings mean. Before deciding if we want to be an actual couple. I shouldn't have let my fears stop me from trusting the dating app results. Didn't I create it for this reason? To validate that the feelings I have are the real deal.

I caress her ankle, then apply firm pressure to the arch of her foot. Using my thumb and knuckles, I knead into her foot in slow, long strokes. Zaire hums in appreciation, her head tilting back as a sigh escapes her lips.

"That feels amazing," she says as her eyes close.

"Open your eyes and get back to work," I say, rubbing my palms against the top and bottom of her feet. The tension and knots loosen from my movements. "I promised Simona I wouldn't let you work late."

"Like you can stop me," Zaire says, then reaches over to grab a stack of printouts.

I yank on her toes, and she yelps.

"Wiley!"

"Don't make me into a liar. It's the holidays, and you're cooped up in this office pouring over drawings and spreadsheets instead of ..."

Squeezing and pulling on her toes more gently, I allow my words to trail off. I won't push her. It was my stupid idea to wait. I'll stick to my word, especially since Zaire has doubled down on it. Like she said, we have plenty of time. There's no need to rush.

"Instead of?"

"Nothing," I say, focusing my fingers on the tension in the balls of her feet. "What's on those papers?"

"Sales reports from the last week and forecasts from the program you created for me. Because of the pace that sales are coming in, I'm going to have the manufacturer produce some of the more popular items in advance. That way, all they have to do is apply the custom fabric, and we can get shipments out faster."

"That's smart."

"And risky," Zaire says.

"I've never known you to shy away from a risk. I remember a presentation you gave about taking strategic risks a year ago. I know you trust your instincts."

"Only in business."

"Not in matters of the heart?" I wonder if we suffer from the same ailment.

She tries to extract her foot from my hands. I don't let her. I've touched a nerve.

"Do we have to talk about this?"

"Nope. You always have a choice, Buttercup." I want her to be comfortable talking to me about anything. If she isn't, maybe that means slowing down my feelings is the right move.

Zaire sighs and leans back on her elbows. "How can I trust myself with matters of the heart when I was played for a fool? Kei and I had issues. Things were far from perfect, but I thought he loved me. I was dead wrong. Every instinct about picking the right guy for myself was destroyed when I caught him with India. How could I have been so blind? How can I ever trust myself to know when a man wants me again?"

The pain in her voice and anguish over what she went through break my heart. But I know she's wrong.

"It's not about when a man wants you, Buttercup. You need to focus on when you want the man," I say, hoping I can get through to her.

"What do you mean?"

"Every time you talk about what happened between you and Kei, you mention India's betrayal, your embarrassment, feeling like a fool. You talk about people pitying you and how much you hated feeling that way," I say, thinking back on everything she'd ever told me about that awful time in her life. "But not once." I let my words sink in. "Not once did you mention losing the man you love. Or being heartbroken."

Zaire looks away.

"Deep down, you didn't love Kei. You wanted to because you thought he loved you, but I don't believe you ever loved him."

"If you're right, that makes me a horrible person."

"No, it doesn't. It makes you human, that's all." I tug on her legs, sliding her across the floor until her thighs rest on my lap and her face is inches from mine. I lean in and brush her lips with a gentle kiss. "It's okay to be more torn up about losing your relationship with India than Kei. She's your sister, after all."

"I'm worried about what it'll be like to see them again. For years, I hated her for what she did. I don't want to hate her anymore. But I'm not sure if we can recover from what happened," Zaire says, leaning against my chest. "India has always had this weird competition thing with me. In her head, she's lived in my shadow. She wants to shine brighter than me."

"Well, you make that hard, I can tell you that. Not just because of your professional success, either."

"Why can't we both shine bright?"

"That's a question you should ask her when she gets to town."

"Part of me doesn't want to say anything to her. She has never apologized for what she did to me. Sydney says she hasn't shown a hint of remorse or regret. I want to show her and Kei that I've moved on. We don't have to avoid each other anymore. We can attend family gatherings and be in the same room without it being awkward."

"Did St. Barts guy help you move on?"

The words are out before I can stop them. It wasn't me. Zaire never gave me a second thought romantically until a week ago. Someone else helped her get to this place, and it's eating away at me.

"Why do you keep asking about him?"

"Because you refuse to talk about him. You won't tell me his name, how y'all met, what happened on the island during the week of Thanksgiving—"

"Whoa! That's a lot. How long has this been on your mind?"

"Too long."

"Are you jealous, Wiley Alexander?"

"Absolutely. One hundred percent."

"You don't need to be."

"Promise?"

Zaire places her hands on the sides of my face as she nods. I watch with anticipation as her face comes closer to mine. Her lips part ever so slightly before she kisses me. Like every time we've kissed before, this one is sensational. With kisses, we say everything we're not ready to express in words. My head spins as I lose myself in Zaire, gripping her body and maneuvering her on top of me. The intensity increases as I take control, kissing her deeper, longer, harder. It's insatiable and greedy, as I forget all restraint. This is where Zaire belongs. Right here with me in my arms, kissing the daylights out of me. Seconds stretch to minutes until I lose all track of time. Our kisses continue unchecked and untamed until I feel Zaire pressing against my chest. I fight in protest, not ready for this moment to end.

She pulls away, her gorgeous dark irises hooded and full of regret. "It's getting late. I need to get home and finish the work you distracted me from."

Scowling, I nod as she rolls off me and stands up. Ten minutes later, I've cleaned up all evidence of our late-night office picnic. I stretch my hand toward Zaire. She slips her hand in mine as she grabs her purse. We walk through the darkened halls of the office in comfortable silence and make our way out to the parking lot. I stand in the brisk cold air of the winter night as Zaire enables the security system and locks the door. Her heels dangle from her hands.

"Caveman, wedding or piggyback style?" I ask, glancing over at her convertible BMW near the back of the parking lot.

"I think wedding style would be the most appropriate, considering what I'm wearing."

"You are smoking hot in that dress. I can say that now."

"You could've said that before. I'd never turn down a compliment from you."

"Good to know," I say, lifting her into my arms. She clings to my neck, the intoxicating scent of her rose tea perfume soothing me as I cross the parking lot.

I slow my pace as we approach her car. Zaire picks up on the tension clawing up my body. She turns to look at what's caught my attention.

"Oh my God. My tires …" Zaire says, forcing herself out of my arms. "Somebody slashed my tires!"

I shake my head, a blaze of anger flowing through me.

Not somebody.

This has my crazy ex written all over it.

Amanda "Don't Call Me Mandy" Tucker.

CHAPTER 32

Z AIRE

~

"I THOUGHT YOU WERE TIRED." SYDNEY TUCKS A PILLOW under her neck and turns to face me in my California king bed. "You've been staring at the ceiling for the past hour instead of sleeping like you should be."

"I'm too wired to sleep." I reach for the remote control. I press a couple of buttons and activate the massage function of the mattress. The bed shakes a second later, soothing my frayed nerves and tense muscles.

Memories from last night are still etched in my mind. Walking around my convertible BMW to see all four tires with long gashes in the rubber had left me speechless and more than a little rattled. I was happy Wiley had been with me, or I'm not sure I could've made it through the shock.

Normally, I'm the take-charge type in a crisis.

But that's when the crisis doesn't feel ... personal.

Someone wanted to make sure I didn't make it home last night. Thinking what that person would've done if I were alone sent shivers up my spine. The area was deserted, and I would have been easy prey.

"What did the cops say?" Sydney asks, concern in her gaze.

"They dismissed the idea that this was a personal attack since it was unfathomable to them I had any enemies."

"You? Enemies? Everybody loves you, Zaire."

"Not sure about everybody."

My mind wanders to Troy. I don't want to mention how angry he was about his abrupt departure from Kincaid Furnishings. An exit that was more personal than professional. I thought he'd gone back home to Atlanta, but he took a job working with Jimbo Barnes at the furniture manufacturing facility. He's the new COO over there, so we'll be forced to continue working together. Maybe more than when he was employed by me. The thought is unsettling.

"I am," Sydney insists. "Do they think it was a prank or something?"

I nod my head. "I authorized the security company to send them footage from all cameras on the property. They'll pull footage from the handful of CCTV cameras leading to the area, but they didn't seem optimistic that they'd find anything on it." I rub my eyes with the back of my hand.

"There was no sign of a break-in?"

"Detective Jaxon Jones thinks it was one of those fake Good Samaritan robbery attempts. During the holidays, it's not unusual for criminals to travel far and wide to steal. He said I was lucky that Wiley was with me." I glance down at the gorgeous engagement ring on my finger. When did I stop noticing it there? When did it start feeling like it was meant to be on my finger? I shake the thoughts away.

"Some fool slashes your tires, watches from afar, then trots over to pretend to help you. You're all thankful for the help. Then he demands all your money and credit cards," Sydney says, growing irate. "Thank God Wiley was with you. I'm sure he scared the robber off."

I nod my head. Strangely, the idea of it being a random attack is comforting to me. I don't want to consider that my actions could've pushed a desperate and angry person to lash out at me.

Sydney says, "And I'm glad you didn't go into the office. It's no telling what you would've screwed up because you're sleep-deprived, honey."

"That's what Simona said. She forbade me from coming in or logging in on my computer until this afternoon," I say, then glance at the clock. It's nine in the morning.

Wiley is arriving at the fire station for his shift on fumes. He probably only got four or five hours of sleep. He'd been my rock the entire night, taking charge by calling the police and a wrecker truck for the car. After the cops surveyed the scene and took photographs, they asked if I wouldn't mind going to the police station to finish giving my statement and sign off on the required paperwork. Wiley drove and stayed with me the entire time, playing the role of the concerned and supportive fiancé. But I could tell from the look in his eyes and the taut tension of his muscles that none of his feelings were an act. He was worried and concerned about the incident.

"I'm surprised Wiley didn't insist on staying with you himself," Sydney says, a sly smile on her face.

"Trust me. He tried. But I won the battle."

Seeing Wiley's raw emotions rattled me. I knew we needed distance. It took forty-five minutes to convince him not to call out on his shift to stay with me and allow Sydney to take on babysitting duties until I got some rest.

I continue, "I didn't want him to since it's the holidays and a lot harder to switch shifts. It's already worked out great that he's not on shift for the wedding shower this Sunday or the Christmas Day wedding."

"I'm sure he wouldn't mind. Seems like he'd move heaven and earth for you."

"Maybe."

"What do you mean? Maybe?" Sydney shrieks and bolts up in the bed. "Wait, Zaire. Do not do this. Do not sabotage your wonderful relationship with Wiley because you're scared. I know it's been a long time since you let a man into your heart. I know that's why you kept this relationship with Wiley a secret, so you could let yourself be comfortable with the idea of love in your life again." Sydney points her finger at me. "That is the only reason I didn't slap you upside the head for keeping me in the dark."

"It's not that, Syd ..." I'm a breath away from coming clean to her about the fake engagement.

"The wedding," Sydney slumps. "The last time you brought a man you cared about to a family wedding, you lost him. Are you afraid that's going to happen to you and Wiley?"

"Maybe." It's the only thing I trust myself to say at the moment.

"You and Kei had talked about marriage, but the two of you weren't engaged."

I scowl at Sydney. "Are you about to make an excuse for how India betrayed me?"

"Of course not," Sydney responds. "I'm still pissed at her for breaking the sister code and stealing your man while he was still your man. That was all parts wrong, and I don't blame you for struggling to forgive her. Your relationship with Kei was different from what you have with Wiley."

"Because Wiley and I are engaged."

"And y'all are crazy about each other. Neither of you can hide that as much as y'all seem to try, which Persia and I still don't understand." Sydney rolls her eyes.

"It's difficult going from private to public with our relationship. You'd think we are celebrities."

"You are ... in Kimbell. Persia is so jealous of you right now. She was ranting to Mommy the other day about how people have forgotten she's the one getting married in two weeks. All the talk is about your wedding to Wiley and how they can't wait to see how grand it is."

I laugh.

"Grand? Really?"

"You know country folk." Sydney smiles. "Promise me you won't sneak off and elope."

That's not going to happen. Wiley and I won't make it down the aisle.

I yawn before I can respond, snuggling under my down comforter. I give her a small smile and whisper, "No chance of that," before falling asleep.

CHAPTER 33

ILEY

"WHAT HAPPENED LAST NIGHT?" DARREN DEMANDS AS I push through the door of the break room at the fire station. He's on me before I get a few feet inside. Nate, Ronan, and Luke are close behind, surrounding me.

"Is Zaire okay?" Nate asks.

"Are you okay?" Ronan barks.

"Why were y'all at the police station?" Luke asks.

I'm not surprised they've already heard snippets of the ordeal Zaire and I went through last night. The expressions on their faces match what I'm feeling inside—shock, concern, and ... anger. Since I left Zaire early in the morning, I couldn't sleep.

Rage boils within me at the thought that Amanda Tucker could be behind the slashed tires of Zaire's car. I'd never forgive myself if I was the reason she was being terrorized that way.

Pushing past the guys, I head to my unofficial spot and sink into the chair. My head drops low, and I close my eyes, debating whether to tell them my suspicions.

Footsteps clamor behind me, and I'm surrounded. Over the next hour, I fill them in on every detail, from when Zaire left the Kincaid Real Estate offices to the interactions with Kimbell police to taking her home and waiting for Sydney to arrive so I could get home and get some rest before the shift started.

"You could've called out." Ronan grips my shoulder and squeezes tight. "Plenty of guys would've been happy to fill in for you, knowing what you'd been through."

I shrug, ignoring the sting of Zaire pushing me away last night. We're not faking our feelings anymore, but still too far away from the closeness that our fake engagement would suggest we have. My brain knows this, but my heart is struggling to accept it. Right now, I want to be in bed with Zaire, holding her as she drifts off to sleep. I want to be the one making sure she feels safe and protected. Not sitting in the middle of the fire station with my closest friends, wondering how she's doing.

I want to text her, but I resist. She should be asleep. If she isn't, knowing that will bother me all day, and I'm distracted enough. I hope it's a light day at the office and we don't get called into an emergency while I'm operating on fumes, worried about the woman who's captured my heart.

"Do you think the cops are right?" Nate asks, a pointed look in his gaze. "Some prank by some punks on a luxury car in the parking lot?"

"Doesn't make sense if you ask me," Luke chimes in. "Why slash the tires and not try to break in? Punks like that would want to joy ride in a BMW M8 convertible, not slash the tires and run away."

"Maybe the robbery angle is the answer," Ronan says. "The robber probably saw the lights on in the office, slashed the car's tires, and planned on stealing from whoever owned the vehicle when they left work. But Zaire wasn't alone, so they took off and abandoned their plans."

"Or the answer could be something entirely different." Nate's words are ominous.

"What are you getting at?" Darren glares at Nate.

"Slashed tires are a crime of passion. It's no secret that there are a lot of women upset that Zaire has what they've wanted for years—to be the woman Wiley wants to marry," Nate explains.

I'm quiet, wishing Nate would shut up about his theories. I still haven't decided what I'm going to do about Amanda. Or how to find out if she slashed Zaire's tires. She's not supposed to be in Kimbell.

When has Amanda ever done what she's supposed to?

Darren sits up straighter, his eyes trained on me. "You don't think that ... no, she wouldn't?"

"I'm not so sure," I admit.

"Who are y'all talking about?" Luke asks.

Ronan curses under his breath. "The last woman who vandalized a car in the name of loving Wiley Alexander."

In unison, they all mutter her name.

Amanda Tucker.

"She broke into our locked parking lot and set my Mustang on fire," I explain to Luke, who moved to town after Amanda and I broke up.

"An explosion woke us up in the middle of the night. We rushed outside to see Wiley's prized car engulfed in a huge ball of flames." Darren shakes his head. "When Wiley tried to stop her from getting away, she stabbed him with a knife she'd been hiding."

"All because Wiley gave her the pet name Mandy. The crazy psycho thought he was cheating on her with someone else and had called her the wrong name by mistake," Nate says.

Ronan says, "There's the restraining order keeping her out of Lasso County, though."

Darren interrupts, "No piece of paper will stop that kook. The question is, could she have found out about Wiley's engagement in Oklahoma? Who around here still talks to her?"

"Brianna." I stand and pace around the table. "After things ended with Amanda, Brianna reached out to her on social media because she sympathized with her crazy actions. Brianna told me people do stupid things when they are in love. She claims it helped both of them to deal with losing me by talking to each other. "

"There's only one way to find out if Amanda is down here." Nate pounds a finger against the table. "You've got to call her dad. The man was on your side when she lost her mind. He was the one who convinced her to leave you alone. If she's been here, he'll tell you."

"You think I should call Mr. Tucker?" I ask, even though that's what I'd been pondering.

"What other choice do you have?" Darren asks.

"You're not dating someone new. You are engaged to Zaire. That could be the thing to push Amanda over the edge," Ronan adds. "Call Mr. Tucker. You need to find out if Amanda is a threat to worry about."

That's all the encouragement I need.

Pulling my phone out of my pocket, I scroll through the contacts until I find Mr. Tucker's number. I press the green button to dial and put the phone on speaker.

Amanda's father answers after one ring. "Wiley, what a surprise." The man sounds genuinely surprised. "How are you doing, son?"

"I'm good, Mr. Tucker." I swallow hard and choose my words carefully. "I was calling to see if you heard I got engaged a couple of weeks ago?"

"No, I hadn't heard about that at all. Congratulations!" Mr. Tucker's voice lifts with excitement. "That's one lucky lady to catch you. I'm glad you found someone to give your heart to again. I know what Amanda put you through soured your views on relationships for a while."

He wasn't wrong. I avoided relationships and turned all my attention toward my dating app business.

"Do you think Amanda knows about my engagement?"

"No, she would've told me if she did. She doesn't keep up with anyone from Kimbell anymore. One girl kept reaching out to her on social media, but Amanda blocked her after a few weeks. She doesn't like to think about everything she did during that time in her life."

Nate scoffs, then throws his hands in the air. Darren presses his fingers to his lips and glares at him.

"How is Amanda doing? She still living with you?"

"She's good. Still seeing her therapist and back involved in softball. She's manager of one of the best youth teams in the state. In fact, they had a game last night and beat their biggest rival. We were up to the early hours in the morning celebrating."

I breathe a sigh of relief. No way Amanda could be in two places at the same time. "That's good. Well, I'll leave it up to you if you want to tell her about my engagement or not."

"Better that I don't, son," Mr. Tucker says with finality. "But thanks for giving me a heads up in case she hears about it from someone."

The call ends, and I lean back in the chair, balancing it on the back two legs.

"That's good news." Ronan rises from his chair. "Why don't you go get some rest? We'll split up your tasks and knock them out for you."

I glance at the guys, and they're all nodding in agreement.

Rubbing a hand on the back of my neck, I reluctantly agree. As I walk down the empty hallway to the sleeping quarters, I don't feel any relief from Mr. Tucker's call. Amanda may not have come after Zaire, but that doesn't mean Zaire is out of danger. That anyone would try to hurt her has my nerves on edge. I won't rest easy until I'm off work and able to see that Buttercup is okay.

CHAPTER 34

Z AIRE

~

"Do you know why Yves bailed on coming?" Extending my hands toward the fire pit, I warm my numb fingers over the soothing heat.

Sydney shrugs and tightens her leather coat around her body. "She's not talking. Mommy said things have been tense between them this whole week."

I glance over to see Persia with her fourth or fifth beer, twirling around to the rendition of Elvis Presley's Jingle Bell Rock by a band on the main stage at Santa's Wonderland. The impromptu outing to the holiday-themed amusement park in College Station was supposed to be a triple date for the Kincaid sisters—Wiley and me, Sydney and Matthieu, and Persia and Yves. Except Persia showed up tipsy, belligerent, and without her husband-to-be.

Despite our attempts to reschedule, Persia insisted that her party pooper fiancé wouldn't stop her from having fun. None of us wanted to leave her alone, so we bought tickets and entered the festive wonderland.

"Could be cold feet with the Jack and Jill wedding shower coming up on Sunday." I involuntarily shiver as I realize in one week, I'll be in the same room with India for the first time since Sydney's wedding five years ago. I glance over at Wiley and feel a sense of peace. He's huddled near an oak barrel, drinking a beer with Matthieu as Persia twerks to the live music near them.

Since my car was vandalized, Wiley has done everything to make me feel safe and secure. We've been inseparable over the past few days, with him chauffeuring me to and from work, grabbing dinner from local restaurants, and sleeping on the chaise lounge across from my bed. Working long hours became harder as the anticipation of being near Wiley grew stronger.

I thought being alone and in close proximity to a man as gorgeous and sexy as Wiley would be my undoing. But he's been the perfect gentleman. It's like we both don't want to rush anything, especially while the cloud of our fake engagement is casting shadows over our intentions to explore the feelings between us. Not that the flirting has stopped. It's more incessant than ever, even if neither of us is ready to cross the lines into physical intimacy.

"Or it could be our baby sister being the spoiled brat she always is. I'm sure Yves didn't jump at one of her demands, and she decided to pout and be difficult. She'll get over it. Marriage is about compromise, give and take. She'll learn that to be happy, she can't be the one taking all the time." Sydney reaches to the ground and picks up her cup of hot chocolate. She takes a sip, then gives me a strange look as she swallows.

"What is it?" I ask.

"Mommy heard from India this morning ..."

"Does she plan to skip the wedding?"

Sydney gives me a sheepish frown. "The opposite. She's coming early to attend the wedding shower this weekend. I don't think Kei is coming with her. He's going to show up closer to Christmas Eve."

I let her words settle within me, waiting for the rush of dread or anger to come. But it doesn't. I won't pretend that I'm looking forward to this dysfunctional reunion, but its importance to my life has waned since everyone found out about my fake engagement with Wiley.

No, that's not true.

The change happened when I discovered we're a ninety-eight percent love match on his dating app. All the feelings building within me for Wiley and the feelings I sensed were coming from him took on a new meaning. Deep down, we were compatible at a level neither of us realized. Drawn to each other in a way that surprised us both. I fight back a smile. It's sweet torture to wait until we get past Persia's wedding and the Valentine's Day post on Heather's vlog before we turn all of our attention to what the future might hold for us as a real couple. But I know Wiley will be worth the wait.

I glance down at the engagement ring sparkling on my finger.

"I'm proud of you," Sydney says, interrupting my thoughts. "You're not phased anymore about seeing India and Kei."

"I wouldn't go that far," I admit, thinking back on Wiley's suggestion that I was never in love with Kei. "But I realize it's not the big deal I made it out to be in my head. Life goes on, and holding onto past hurts is a waste of my time."

"Especially when you have so much good to look forward to. Once you're married to Wiley, we can get back on track with the proper order of things," Sydney says, cackling with laughter.

"What are you talking about?"

"Mommy wants grandbabies, and since you're the oldest and will finally be married, you need to be the first to get pregnant!"

"Whoa! Slow down. I'm not having a child any time soon. Wiley and I—" I pause. The lie that Wiley and I planned to tell everyone as the reason for our break-up floats through my mind. Is that still the plan now that we've discovered that our feelings for each other aren't fake? How are we going to pull off the end of this engagement yet still give ourselves a fair shot at a real relationship with each other?

"Y'all what?"

"Haven't talked about kids or anything yet."

"Don't you think you should?"

"Of course. We will. But we've only been engaged for a couple of weeks. Can't we get used to that first?"

Sydney gives me a shrewd stare. "You're hiding something, but I'll let you keep it for now. Especially since our baby sister is twerking all up on your man."

I jerk my head to the right and watch in horror as Persia is almost assaulting Wiley with her stripper-style dance moves. My blood runs cold as I notice the expression on Wiley's face.

He's not appalled. Or repulsed. Or trying to stop her.

He looks like he's enjoying the show ... too much.

"Honey, go stop that train wreck," Sydney says, shaking her head.

"Why should I? Looks like they're having a great time," I say, unable to hide the edge in my voice.

"Zaire, come on. He's being nice to her—"

"Whatever. I'm going to get a glass of wine. I'll be back."

I bolt up from the wooden bench and push through the crowd. The sounds of the live band grow distant as I meander along the sidewalk and gaze at the millions of twinkling lights arranged to create a stunning landscape of Christmas motifs along the manicured lawns— Santa in his sleigh led by reindeer, a giant cowboy boot with gingerbread men dancing around it, trumpeting angels that appear to float in the air. The beauty of the decorations does nothing to calm the roar of blood rushing through my ears or the pounding of my heart.

Wiley should not have put me in a position to feel jealous of another one of my sisters.

It would be fine if this fake engagement was ... fake. If we were lying about our feelings for each other, I wouldn't care if Wiley got a quasi-lap dance in the middle of a family-friendly holiday theme park. He could do what he wanted, and so would I.

But we aren't pretending to be into each other.

We haven't said the words. Not exactly. More implied.

But our actions speak volumes. Our kisses tell the real story of what's going on between us. After this fake engagement is over, our real relationship can begin. We've danced around the subject so many times. I know I wasn't misreading things.

So why would he let Persia pounce on him with me sitting a few feet away? It's like he forgot that I'm his fiancée, not her. I'm the one he texts nonstop during the day. I'm the one he insisted on spending time when he gets off work, even though there's no one around for us to put on a show.

It was me and him sharing meals, talking about everything and nothing, cuddling in my movie room watching holiday movie classics.

When I called him this afternoon about coming out to Santa's Wonderland with Sydney, Persia, and me, he didn't hesitate. In fact, he said he'd been waiting on my call, hoping I'd be free to spend the evening with him doing something or nothing at all.

I stifle a scream.

I'm falling in love with Wiley.

Wiley is making me fall in love with him.

Like he's made so many other women do the same thing.

I sigh in disgust.

"Trouble in paradise?"

I stop walking and turn to see Wiley's ex-girlfriend, Brianna.

Her face is a mask of pity and sympathy as if she knows a truth I can't see yet.

"Why would you say that?" I ask, hoping she didn't see Persia and Wiley dancing near the main stage.

"This is a romantic spot. Strange to see you walking through these beautiful lights alone without your fiancé."

Her voice is sweet and without a hint of malice that would make me justified in giving her a snarky response. Instead, I remind myself that I have a role to play as the happy fiancée of Wiley Alexander.

"I wanted to take a few pictures now that the crowds have died down," I lie, then wave my cell phone at her. "Did you come with friends?"

Brianna shakes her head. "I pick up hours here during the holidays to make extra money when I'm not on the schedule at Elevation. It pays a lot better even though it's further away."

"Well, that's wonderful. If you have to work, you might as well do it in a great atmosphere like this," I say, growing uneasy with the awkward conversation.

"My break is almost up, so I better get back. I'm working in Maw's Bakery, and they have wonderful cupcakes if you and Wiley want to stop by and get some."

"Sure, we'll do that." Although I'm not sure I'll be speaking to Wiley for the rest of the night. Lucky for me, he's on shift at the fire station tomorrow. I need time to sort through my chaotic emotions without him around.

"I hope things work out for y'all," Brianna says, fumbling with the sleeves of her flimsy windbreaker as a gust of cold, blistery wind blows past us. "He falls in love fast and falls out of love faster. So, take it slow and guard your heart until you know for sure he's in it for the long haul."

Her words hit me like a sledgehammer.

I plaster a smile on my face and raise my left hand to show off the stunning diamond engagement ring.

"Thanks, but I think Wiley has made his feelings for me crystal clear."

Brianna gives me a smile and a quick nod, then walks away.

I wish I believed what I told her.

CHAPTER 35

WILEY

~

Stuffing my hands in my pockets, I cross the packed parking lot of Thorn Restaurant as the frigid cold seeps into my bones. The temperature took an unexpected turn into the high twenties this morning, casting a miserable cloak of weather on Lasso County.

A perfect match for my mood.

I glance ahead at Zaire, walking with confident strides toward the entrance of the restaurant. It's closed on Sundays, making it the ideal venue for today's wedding shower. It helps that Zaire is close friends with the owner and finagled the booking at the last minute.

Based on Zaire's assessment, we're fashionably late, but I know she's dreading the Jack and Jill wedding shower. She's only minutes away from being face to face with India and Kei again for the first time in five years.

I noticed the shift in her mood on Friday when we were at Santa's Wonderland in College Station. The night started fine, but she was quiet and distant by the end. Talkative enough to not draw attention, yet withdrawn.

If I hadn't had to work on Saturday, I could've spent more time with her before the wedding shower to help calm her frayed nerves. I hope she feels the support I'm sending her without being too overbearing. Zaire can handle this. She can handle anything. Doesn't mean I shouldn't do everything I can to let her know I'm in her corner, cheering her on.

Picking up my pace, I pass her up in time to open the door to the restaurant for her.

She looks at me as if noticing I'm here for the first time, even though we've been together all morning. We didn't talk much as I waited for her to get dressed for the party. When she walked into the living room, my heart raced at the sight of her. Per Persia's instructions, guests were supposed to wear winter white. Zaire doesn't disappoint in a white sweater dress that hugs every delicious curve of her body. Her makeup is flawless. Long dark lashes frame her vibrant brown eyes, and dark red lipstick gives her an air of refined sophistication with a hint of playful fun.

The swell of longing building inside me can't be denied. I want to pull her into my arms and kiss the lipstick off her mouth. Rattle her out of the daze she seems to be in, consumed with thoughts of seeing the sister who betrayed her five years ago.

My eyes shift to the swaying of her hips as she enters the restaurant, and I let out a low whistle. Her head whips around to look at me. The slight curve of a smile on her lips is the first sign I've had of the Zaire I love all day.

Wait.

Zaire, I ... love?

Did I really think that?

"I was wondering if you noticed," Zaire says, handing her wool coat to the attendant.

"How could I not? You take my breath away." I reach for her hand. It's limp. She doesn't hold mine back. "Everything okay?"

She nods, then pulls her hand away.

Of course, everything isn't okay. She's gearing up for a battle with her sister. What should be a pleasant and enjoyable party to celebrate Persia and Yves has an edge of tension with everyone anticipating what will happen when Zaire and India see each other again.

I slip an arm around her, stopping her. I pull her close to me, wrapping both arms around her waist. We stand there for a long moment, my chest pressed against her back, as I lean down to kiss her on the ear.

"You got this. It's going to be alright. I promise," I whisper in her ear. She relaxes in my arms but doesn't respond. "No matter what happens, I'll help you get through it."

She pats my arms, then eases from my grasp. Turning toward me, she says, "There's Sydney and Matthieu."

I look past her to see her sister and brother-in-law standing near a table close to the windows that look out onto the lake. Pale gray clouds blanket the sky, casting a gloomy shadow over the area. They are far away from the pageantry surrounding Persia and Yves as they bask in the attention of their guests. Sydney waves an arm wide through the air, beckoning us to come over.

Before I can react, Zaire is across the room, hugging her sister. I knew today would be hard for Zaire, but I can't ignore the nagging feeling in the pit of my stomach that something's wrong … between us. This distance feels personal. Like she's separating herself from me. From what she feels for me and what I feel for her.

I just don't know why.

Walking over, I extend my hand to shake Matthieu's.

"Long time no see, my friend," Matthieu laughs, then gives me a half-hug. "Hope you weren't too buzzed at work from all the drinking we did on Friday night."

I grin, knowing I did a lot less drinking than any of them realize. I nursed one gin and tonic all night. I never indulge when I have work the next day. I might be a goofball, but I take being a firefighter seriously.

"All good. And it was a boring day. No calls. We stayed in doing paperwork and cleaning up the fire station," I say.

"Well, I want to warn you I might have to give you the cold shoulder while we're here. Persia invited my brother, and I can't let him see that I'm making friends with the enemy." Matthieu chuckles under his breath.

"Stop that! Wiley is not the enemy," Sydney says, laughing.

"You know Troy had his heart set on being with Zaire. It's the only reason he moved from the ATL to this tiny town," Matthieu says.

Sydney crosses her arms over her chest and steps toward me, giving her husband a glare. "You see, Wiley, Atlanta people have an arrogance that borders on rudeness. My husband doesn't see the charm of growing up in a small town like we do."

"Yeah, but you like my arrogance. You said it was sexy." Matthieu gives his wife a seductive wink.

"Not when you're bashing the place that will always be my home," Sydney says.

"Stick around," I say, easily taking sides. "You'll fall in love with Kimbell, like every other city slicker that comes through here."

"I don't doubt it," Matthieu says. "My brother definitely has. I thought he'd be on the next plane back to Atlanta after he quit working for Zaire, but he took a job at the furniture manufacturer she uses instead."

My jaw clenches. I look at Zaire as she swipes a flute of champagne from a passing waiter. She takes a long sip and avoids my gaze. "Guess he couldn't give up working side-by-side with Zaire after all." I try to keep the tension from my voice, but from the looks on Sydney's and Matthieu's faces, I fail miserably.

"Honey, you have nothing to worry about. My sister only has eyes for you, and you know it," Sydney reassures me.

But I don't feel reassured.

I want to hear Zaire tell me I have nothing to worry about. Not her sister.

I feel like Zaire and I are walking a tightrope and could fall off anytime, sending our bodies hurtling far away from each other. The thought of not having her in my life fills me with dread. I'm tired of pretending to be something we're not and ready to become what we are supposed to be. Whatever that will look like. In my heart, I don't doubt we'll end up in this same place, with her wearing my grandmother's ring. My dating app is batting a thousand with couples matched at our level—ninety-eight percent love match.

Still, the app's results are no substitute for our real-life experiences. I know Zaire and I need time to have more of those. I hope she's not changing her mind about that.

Sydney continues, "You should have heard how she talked about you when y'all were in St. Barts. She was gushing."

"Is that so?" I force a smile on my face.

"There was so much speculation about who you were when we were all in the dark," Matthieu says, nodding at his wife. "For most of that week, Syd and I were convinced Zaire was with my brother, Troy."

"You never told me that." Zaire sounds strained and tense.

"Well, it was after you'd arrived, and you told me that the mystery guy was still on the way to the island, and his plane hadn't landed yet," Sydney says.

"My brother called at the same time, and I heard airport noise in the background. I thought he was there to board his flight to Atlanta, but he told me his flight was overbooked, and he couldn't find another one that would get him home in time. So, he was going to stay put. But in the background, I heard the announcement for the last call for boarding a flight going to St. Barts—"

"You weren't sure it was St. Barts." Sydney jumps in to correct him. "You knew it was saint something, but we weren't for certain that's what Matthieu heard."

"That didn't stop you from assuming that Zaire and Troy were sneaking off on a romantic holiday getaway. Then you told your Mom and Persia, and all of you were convinced," Matthieu says.

Sydney says, "Well, I'm glad that I was wrong because Wiley is a better fit for my sister than your brother."

"I can see that." Matthieu bumps me with his shoulder. "Don't tell Troy I said it."

"Of course not," I say. Zaire is strangely quiet. She finishes the glass of Champagne and grabs another.

"Anyway, I'm surprised our daily calls didn't put a crimp in y'alls vacation. Zaire, do you remember when I called and you and Wiley were on that private beach? You were trying so hard to rush me off the phone!"

"Yes, I remember Sydney. I don't think you need to tell Wiley about our sister talks. It might go to his head." Zaire places another empty flute of Champagne on a passing waiter's tray. She fidgets with her engagement ring, twisting it around and around her finger.

"Keep talking. I'd love to hear what Zaire said about *me*," I say.

All the pieces are coming together in my head at breakneck speed, leaving me with a pounding headache.

I always thought Troy's reaction to finding out Zaire and I are engaged was extreme. He lashed out at her and quit his job at Kincaid Furnishings. Why would he do all of that?

There's only one reason.

Because he's St. Barts Guy.

And Zaire never told me.

My muscles tense, and I clench my fists at my side.

No wonder he was so pissed when he found out about our fake engagement. He'd spent the week before with Zaire on a romantic Caribbean island and then was blindsided by the fact she was engaged to another man. Did he think she was seeing both of us at the same time?

Zaire was adamant that things were over between her and St. Barts Guy. I'm not so sure that's true. She didn't agree to be fake engaged to me. When her mom and sisters came over unexpectedly and jumped to that conclusion, she didn't correct them. The decision to be my fake fiancée was taken from her. She didn't do it willingly.

Then she finds out Troy is staying in Kimbell.

That's one declaration of true love she can't deny. There's nothing and no one else keeping him in town but Zaire. Did that change her mind about him? Did she realize Troy is the man she wants to be with? Not me?

Sydney beams. "She said so many wonderful things. It was like as each day passed, y'all were growing closer and closer. But you know that. It's no surprise you proposed when y'all got back to town. It was inevitable."

Zaire frowns, then rubs a hand along the back of her neck.

"The one thing she said that stuck with me the most, and I know she won't mind me telling you this, is that you were everything she didn't realize she wanted or needed in a man." Sydney rests a hand over her heart and closes her eyes dramatically as she sways. "She said she could be herself with you, and you made her deliriously happy."

I swallow past the massive lump in my throat and force the words from my mouth. "I hope she always feels that way about *me*."

Zaire and I lock gazes for a long moment.

I see the panic in her eyes.

She knows I've put all the pieces together.

I'm not misreading her feelings for me, but it doesn't mean this pull she has toward me overshadows the love she has for Troy. And no doubt from what Sydney is implying, Zaire was falling in love with St. Barts Guy.

Zaire loves Troy.

The thought hits me like a sucker punch. I stop a passing waiter and ask for a whisky neat. I'm going to need it to make it through this party.

She could've saved me the heartbreak by coming clean long ago. Troy would only stick around Kimbell if Zaire asked him to. She's made her choice.

While I was becoming more attached to Zaire, she and Troy

rekindled their romance. She probably told him the truth—that this engagement is a lie and will be over in a couple of months. If he cares about her as much as I do, then he'd never do anything to hurt her. Even if that meant watching her pretend to be in love with and engaged to another man.

Pretend.

That's what she's doing with me.

The connection we feel for each other isn't strong enough to erase the love she has for Troy—the man who is everything she never realized she wanted or needed in a man. The results of my stupid dating app are no match for her history with him.

And from the looks of things, he's the man she wants.

Zaire takes a step back. "Looks like I've had too much Champagne. I need to sneak off to the ladies' room. Be right back."

CHAPTER 36

Z AIRE

~

I BLINK BACK TEARS AS I MAKE A BEELINE FOR THE LADIES' restroom near the front of the restaurant. The sweater dress has me sweltering as my body temperature has ratcheted to fever status. Sydney's words ring in my ears.

You were everything she didn't realize she wanted or needed in a man.

You made her deliriously happy.

The words haunt me as memories flood my mind of the week in St. Barts. Every time Sydney called me and asked how things were going with my secret man, I would think about something Wiley and I had done when he was working on my e-commerce website months ago and feed that to her in response.

Those were my words.

Have I been blind?

All this time, I thought these feelings I have for Wiley had sprung up on me out of the blue after we pretended to be engaged.

But is that true?

Did the time we spent together plant this seed months ago?

And being with Wiley again watered it, making it blossom and grow faster than I ever expected?

I push past Yves and Persia as they greet more guests milling about the room. The crowd is suffocating me, and I need to get away and think.

Think about what all of this means.

I doubted the results of the dating app.

I conjured up dozens of scenarios about how it could be wrong.

That Wiley and I might not be a ninety-eight percent love match.

But the dating app isn't wrong.

Wiley is my future, and I was too preoccupied to see it.

My hands shake as I push through the restroom door, barreling into a woman standing on the other side. Our bodies crash into each other, and I stumble, gripping her tightly as I fight to stop us from falling to the floor. Getting my bearings, I'm able to keep us upright.

"I am so sorry." I take a step back and freeze.

My mouth gapes open as I stare at my sister.

India Kincaid-Yamamoto.

She's wearing an elegant white A-line dress, and she's ... huge.

"You're pregnant?" I ask, noticing her tear-stained face.

India swipes at her cheeks, smearing her makeup worse than it was. She looks down as if only now realizing her state.

Her gaze lingers on my left hand, then jerks back to my face. A flash of anger and pain reflects at me.

She says, "And you're engaged. I suppose the first words we've said to each other in five years should've been congratulations. Too late for that."

I glance around the bright modern restroom and realize we're alone. "It's not too late. Congratulations. I'm happy for you and Kei."

India scoffs, crossing her arms over her chest. "Liar. You're about as

223

happy for me as I am for finding out that you snagged Kimbell's hottest bachelor to be your husband."

"You heard about Wiley and me?" Unease settles within me, making me nauseous. In the weeks leading up to this encounter, all I wanted was to flaunt my fake relationship with Wiley to India and Kei. Now that the lines have blurred from fake to real, I feel fiercely protective of Wiley and whatever our relationship will be in the future. I can't let India do anything to sabotage or ruin what I could have with him.

"Kind of hard not to. You're Kimbell's version of royalty. Everyone is losing their minds over your wedding and salivating to know when it will be. Everybody except me." The harsh disdain in India's voice is hard to ignore.

"Is this how it's going to always be between us?" I take a deep breath to calm the anger threatening to overtake me. "Or do you think, for the sake of your unborn child, we could let bygones be bygones?"

India rubs her belly. "Not when you always come out on top, Zaire. You have to best everyone in every situation. You're the smartest. The most successful. The richest. The sister who always had her act together. Your life is, and has always been, perfection while my life is a train wreck."

"No one told you to disappear from our family after you and Kei got married." I struggle to keep my composure. "I won't pretend I wanted to be around you or Kei back then. I needed distance from the whole situation. But Mommy and Daddy love you unconditionally. They were so hurt that you vanished from their lives."

"I had no choice. They were all on your side!" India snaps. "I was a pariah for falling in love with a man you barely liked. Deep in your heart, you knew you'd never marry Kei. You hated that for once, you weren't winning. Someone picked me over you. It ate you up inside that I wasn't coming in second place to you."

"Are you hearing yourself? You think those depraved thoughts were going through my mind? News flash, India. They were not!" I storm past her toward the opposite end of the restroom, then turn back to face her. "There isn't a competition between us. There never was. We're family. But you can't see that, can you?"

"Says the sister who has it all." India presses her hands on her hips as a fresh wave of tears floods her face. "I should have known that you'd still come out on top in the end. My happiness was only temporary."

"Temporary? What are you talking about? You're about to be a mother. That's amazing. You have a husband who adores you—"

"No. I have a husband who cheated on me with dozens of women from the moment we said 'I do.' I did everything to keep him happy and interested, but it didn't work. My last ditch effort was to lure him with this baby." She points at her stomach. "Do you know what happened? My pregnancy was the ultimate thing that caused him to leave me for good."

"Your marriage with Kei is over?"

"Divorce was finalized last week."

"India, I'm sorry." I move toward her, but she raises a hand to stop me.

"I don't need comfort from you. This is all your fault. You know that, right?"

"How are you going to twist the story to make me the villain? Please, go ahead. Tell me."

"You brought Kei into our lives," India replies, unfazed and convinced of her perspective.

"No." I wag a finger at her. "I didn't make you fall for him, and I definitely didn't orchestrate you making a fool of me in front of our family and friends by having sex with him in the utility closet of the hotel at Sydney's reception."

My sister looks pained by my statement. She slumps, resting against the basin of the sink.

"Not once did you ever apologize for embarrassing me. For the record, I love you, and I've always wanted you to be happy. I would never have stood in the way of you and Kei, but you owed me a sliver of respect as my sister to have handled it differently. You could've talked to me instead of flaunting it in front of everyone at the wedding. But despite all that, I'm not happy that Kei cheated on you. It brings me no joy that you've gone through what I'm sure was a painful divorce without the support of your family. You've been pregnant and alone this whole time, and you didn't need to be."

"While my life was imploding, yours got better and better." India's voice is hard and cold. "How do you do it, Zaire? Wiley Alexander is more than you deserve. He's drop-dead gorgeous, a bona fide hero, risking his life to save people as a firefighter, and head over heels in love with you."

I close my eyes and wonder if India and the whole town are right. Is Wiley falling head over heels in love with me? Like I am with him. I can only hope that's true. But there's no time to think about it as I suffer through India's verbal assault.

India says, "If that wasn't enough, you launched your third business to massive success a couple of weeks ago. For once, I wish you could experience the misery that the rest of us feel—"

"I'm done with this conversation. I'm done trying to mend fences with you." I swipe my clutch purse from the basin and walk toward the door. Pulling it open, I pause and look back at India. "I wish you the best, but there's no reason for us to talk again. You are toxic, and I hope you get your act together before you poison your child with that misguided and pathetic mindset."

"Shut up!" India screams at me. "I hate you. Go! Me and my little girl don't need you! We don't need anybody!"

I walk out of the restroom, allowing the door to slam behind me. The sounds of India's pained cries filter through the walls. I head to the coat check room, give them my ticket, and grab my phone from my purse.

I order a ride share, then open my texting app. Pressing Wiley's number, I type:

I saw India. It was horrible. Going home. I kinda need to be alone tonight. Please don't worry. I'll be better tomorrow in time for the interview with Heather. I promise.

CHAPTER 37

Z AIRE

~

MY CELL PHONE HAS BEEN QUIET FOR THE PAST TWENTY-four hours. After I abandoned the wedding shower and texted Wiley, the only response I received was a simple "ok." Nothing else. Part of me thought he'd check in with me throughout the rest of the evening or this morning, but there've been no other texts from him.

He's giving me space when I'm not sure I want him to.

"You shouldn't keep eating this cake." Mommy caresses my arm as she eases into the chair next to me. "Are you feeling better? We were worried when Wiley said you left because you weren't feeling well."

"I'm fine now." I stare at the table filled with thirteen different flavors of wedding cakes delivered to Kimbell by one of the top cake makers in the Hill Country. Gwen Paul, owner of Gwen's Country Cafe, graciously allowed us to take over part of her private dining room for the tasting.

Persia goes back and forth, tasting and re-tasting each piece of cake. My head is swimming, and my body is shaky from the sugar rush of the cake tasting. It's worse than drinking a quadruple espresso shot, which I'm prone to do once or twice a week.

"Sydney thinks you faked being sick so you wouldn't have to see India." Persia licks almond buttercream from her fingers. "Turns out it was a good move. I imagine things would've been tense with her pregnant and divorced while you and Wiley are engaged and happy. Not that I wanted you to miss my shower or anything."

I frown and glance at Mommy, who is rolling her eyes at Persia. "What your sister is trying to say is that there was enough drama at the shower when India showed up. She was already overwhelmed by breaking the bad news to us, and it helped that she didn't have to face you as well."

"Sydney filled me in," I say, wishing we could change the subject. India kept our restroom run-in to herself, and I don't see a reason to tell anyone about it either. "Is she sticking around for the wedding?"

"Of course. I made her promise not to make a scene when she sees you there. I'll be stressed enough. I don't need to be worried about the two of you going at it," Persia says.

"I wanted India to come to Paris with your father and me after the wedding, but she didn't want to. So, I offered to stay with her in D.C. until the baby is born, and she agreed," Mommy says.

"I'm glad she's not being too stubborn and accepting help from you."

"She's going to need it," Persia says. "Can you imagine what kind of mother she's going to be? I'm scared for her little girl."

"Persia! Can you hurry and pick a cake or at least narrow down the options," Mommy demands, glancing at her watch. "We've been here too long, and you know Zaire is planning to meet up with Wiley this afternoon."

"What time is it?" I ask.

"You have plenty of time. I'll let you know when you need to leave. It's not like Bell Park is very far from here," Mommy says.

Leaving early from the cake selection is not an option, but I'm eager to see Wiley. Even though I bailed on the wedding shower, having him with me means more than he could ever know. I want to support him at the meeting with Heather Grimley like he supported me. There's no way I'm going to let him down. We would never have gotten to this place in our real relationship if he hadn't needed a fake engagement to convince the love guru to feature the Ladies Love Country Boys app on her blog.

A couple of weeks ago, I thought I'd need to give the acting performance of my life.

Now, there's no acting necessary.

I can be myself.

I can let out the feelings I have for Wiley without worrying about anyone thinking that this isn't real.

Because it is … real.

Ninety-eight percent love match real.

"This one is my favorite." Persia pushes one plate of cake toward the center of the table. It's a six-tier red velvet cake adorned with white roses made of frosting and silver beads. The colors are bright and vibrant, a suitable choice for a Christmas Day wedding.

"It will blend beautifully with the theme and colors," I say, thinking of the sleeveless column ruby red dresses Sydney and I will be wearing.

Mommy tsks, then says, "Yves is allergic to chocolate."

"Red velvet cake only has a dash of cocoa powder. That's not enough to trigger his hives," Persia says, looking at me for agreement.

"Do you want to take that chance?" I balk. For the life of me, I can't understand my youngest sister.

"Fine, I'll ask them to exclude the cocoa powder." Persia purses her lips, upset about having to make the modification for her future husband. "But if anybody complains about the taste of the cake, I'm going to tell them it's your fault." She points her finger at me.

"Red velvet it is." Mommy gets up to finalize the order with the baker. "Zaire, you better head out now. You're already late."

"What?" I glance at my wrist, devoid of a watch, then fumble for my phone. It's ten minutes past three o'clock when I'm supposed to meet Wiley and Heather at the gazebo in Bell Park.

It's not worth complaining to Mommy and Persia. Both would be oblivious to their roles in making me late for the most important interview of Wiley's entrepreneurial career.

Grabbing my Dior crossbody, I race out of the restaurant and break into a sprint toward the park. It's only a few blocks away, but it feels like I'm running to Houston. The one thing Wiley needs from me, and I'm late. What is Heather going to think about that? It doesn't matter. I'll make her understand.

Minutes later, I'm rounding the corner toward the back of the park. The glossy white painted fence comes into view. The gazebo is majestic in the distance, decorated for the holidays. It's a beacon of our town revered by all the citizens. One of the spots Kimbell is known for, in addition to the Elm Street Brewery, which is still being renovated from the fire months ago, and Bakers Bros BBQ.

I can barely make out Wiley sitting on the wooden benches that line the interior of the octagon ... and he's alone. I slow my pace. Maybe Heather is running late, too.

Swiping at the sweat beads sliding down the side of my face, I grab a mirror from my purse and make sure I still look presentable. Pleased with what I see, I catch my breath, then head to the gazebo.

When I reach the three steps that lead into the structure, I look at Wiley and know something is ... horribly wrong.

CHAPTER 38

ILEY

~

"WILEY ..."

I don't need to look up to know Zaire is here.

She walks up the steps into the gazebo and stops.

I'm a wreck, but that's not enough for her to come to me.

To comfort me.

Because her heart belongs to Troy. Not me.

No point in being pissed off about it anymore.

It doesn't matter.

"You're late," I say, a hard edge in my tone I can't hide.

"I know. I'm sorry. The cake tasting ran over, and I lost track of time." She eases down onto the bench. The distance between us feels like a mile instead of a couple of feet.

I stiffen. My body rigid with anger.

Everything I thought was within my grasp has disappeared in the past twenty-four hours. I should've known none of this would work out for me. After all the hearts I've broken over the past decade, do I deserve to have a happy ending? Despite ending on good terms, I don't think any of my exes will feel bad that the one woman I want more than anything doesn't want me back.

Some kind of sick, twisted poetic justice, I suppose.

"Is Heather running late?" Zaire asks.

"She's not coming."

"Was her flight delayed?"

"No."

"What happened? Did you talk to her?"

"She called at three on the dot to tell me I've been eliminated from the feature and that she'd changed her flights to visit another owner of a dating app in Dallas." I lean back and drag a hand down my face.

"What? Why? Did she find out the truth about … our engagement?"

A sarcastic laugh slips through my lips.

I was the one that found out the truth. Not Heather. I got a dose of cold reality that my feelings for Zaire weren't reciprocated. At least not in the way I wanted them to be.

"I wish that's what she found out." I shake my head. "It's much worse."

Zaire inches closer. The smell of her intoxicating perfume is torture. "What happened? Tell me."

"Why? Can't you see none of it matters anymore? My chance to increase exposure for my app blew right out of town, and there's nothing I can do about it."

"How do you know there's nothing you can do? If you tell me what happened, I'm sure we can develop a strategy. A way to convince Heather she's made a mistake. We can drive to Dallas and meet her there. Whatever you need."

"I can't have what I need." I pause and inhale a sharp breath. I do not want to make this personal. I can't blame Zaire for choosing Troy over me. I blew into her life unexpectedly. It was a long shot she'd go along with the fake engagement. I never should've gotten close to her. Fallen for her. I clear my throat. "My dating app is a fraud."

"I don't understand."

"The code. The AI. Everything I built the dating app on is flawed. My app failed the independent tests Heather's AI experts ran on it."

It's hard for me to admit the truth.

Hard because it means so much more than losing exposure for my business.

I've lost any hope of having Zaire, too.

"That's not possible," she says. "All those people who found love with your app can't be wrong."

"The app failed the most basic of tests. The experts created a profile and had five different people join my app with the same identical profile within the same hour. The test is simple. If the predictive analytics and AI are effective, the results should be the same."

"All five profiles should get the same matches with the same love match percentage. Makes sense."

"That's not what happened. All five tests resulted in five different matches. They did the test three times and concluded my app has no better likelihood of identifying love matches than a random sample."

I wait for her to respond, but she says nothing.

I look over at her.

Shock registers on her beautiful face. A cascade of emotions plays out as she processes what I'm saying.

Her voice shakes as she says, "That can't be right."

"All my research and everything I poured into the app didn't matter. The matches were random and not based on anything. A fluke that people found love through it. I might as well have marketed it like other dating apps where they show you profiles and let you make your own selections. In a couple of instances where the profile was matched with the same person, the percentages were all over the place—eighty, ninety-two, eighty-nine." I rake my hand through my hair. I give her the details, so she knows what this means. The depths of my disappointment are without limits. I'd give anything for my app to have been correct. And not for the people who found love from it. This time, I'm being selfish. I wanted the app to be right for me. But it wasn't.

I say, "I don't understand how this could've happened. I was so sure it worked. Convinced. But it was all a lie."

"A lie? All of it was ... a lie?"

She's not saying the words. She doesn't have to. I don't, either.

The ninety-eight percent love match between the two of us is a lie. Random.

Nothing exists between us that makes us more compatible with each other than any other guy or girl on the app.

"None of the results can be trusted. Heather implied I should have my app checked and correct things, so I won't be sued for false advertising and unethical business practices." I stand and pace to the other side of the gazebo. It hurts to be so close to Zaire, knowing there's no chance for us. In the back of my mind, I'd held on to the results of the dating app as a beacon of hope that I might convince her to choose me over Troy. To look past her love for Troy and focus more on her strong connection with me. A connection I believed would lead to love. But there's no chance of that anymore.

"She thinks you misled people on purpose? You would never trick people like that," Zaire says. Her faith in me after everything that's happened surprises me.

"I thought she was going to change the focus of her feature to expose my app as a lie to manipulate and steal money from innocent people who want to find love."

"I don't know what to say," Zaire admits.

"You don't need to say anything. This is my screw-up. I wasted your time for weeks ... for nothing." I shove my hands into my pockets.

She glances down at my grandmother's diamond ring on her finger.

I know what comes next, and it feels like someone has taken a dagger to my heart and ripped it to shreds.

"What's your next move?"

I shrug. "I spend every waking moment I'm not working at the fire station to figure out what went wrong. Understand why the AI stopped working if it ever did. If I don't figure it out, it's a matter of time before the truth gets out and I lose everything. I can't let that happen."

Zaire's face is blank. She stands and takes a step toward me. "I know we had a deal. But none of that matters anymore. I don't need you to go to the wedding with me."

"You don't." It's a statement. Not a question. Of course, she doesn't. She's free to speed up her reunion with Troy. He can be her date to the wedding. He can be her man. He can be her future husband. Not me.

"What are you going to tell your family?"

"I'll tell them what we planned from the beginning. We had a deal-breaker argument. You don't want kids. I do, and we couldn't see a way around it. So, we let each other go." She says the words with a finality that crushes me.

"You think that's the right thing to do?" I'm clinging to a hope that is long gone. Desperate to hang on to Zaire in any way I can. I don't want her to walk out of my life, but there's nothing I can do to stop her.

She looks down at my grandmother's ring one last time. Twisting it, she slips the ring off her finger.

I suck in a breath.

"Yes, I do." She extends her hand toward me, dropping the ring in the center of my outstretched palm. "Don't you?"

I stare at the ring for a long moment, then shove it into my pocket.

"As you wish," I say, then turn and walk out of the gazebo.

CHAPTER 39

ILEY

MY BODY SLAMS AGAINST THE BRICK WALL, CAUSING MY teeth to clamp down on my tongue. The taste of blood fills my mouth as pain radiates through my core.

"What were you doing back there?" Ronan's eyes are wild with rage as his hands have a death grip on my shoulders. "Burning to death is one of the worst ways of dying."

"I know," I force the words out of my mouth, regret rushing over me.

"You know? You know? Then why did you put our entire crew in danger with your reckless actions? Why did you put yourself in the line of fire, going off without backup into that house?" Ronan demands, his words like rapid fire pelting into me. "I told you to stand down. You ignored a direct order."

"The rabbit was ... trapped," I fumble with an excuse.

A wry laugh escapes Ronan's lips as he releases his grip. "You think that rabbit is worth your life? How about the lives of Nate and Luke, who barreled in after you to make sure you didn't get trapped in that inferno? Was the rabbit worth that?"

"I made a mistake," I say, raking a hand through my hair.

"That's an understatement. Especially since the rabbit was safe and sound, hiding behind the tree in the backyard. You would've died for nothing because you didn't follow protocol."

"It won't happen again. I swear," I say, sinking down to the ground. My body shakes from relief as the realization of what I'd done, the risk I took, overwhelms me. I wasn't thinking straight.

I wasn't thinking at all.

I was trying not to think about how everything I wanted had slipped through my fingers in one afternoon. My dating app was on the verge of being unfairly exposed as unethical. All my hard work and the business I was trying to build would be ruined.

And the one person I wanted, no needed, to be by my side as I dealt with that disaster had walked out on me.

Zaire didn't believe in us.

She gave the ring back and walked out of my life.

From that moment, my thoughts were a jumbled mess. I struggled to focus on what I was supposed to be doing. I shouldn't have come to work, but I wanted the distraction. I wanted an escape from the misery I was stuck in.

But instead of getting free, I made more mistakes, putting my life and the lives of my crew in danger.

Ronan looks down at me with disgust.

It hurts to see how much I disappointed him with my actions.

I can't seem to do anything right anymore.

"Get your act together. We trust you to be focused and on top of your game every second you're working with us. If you're incapable of doing that, you don't need to be here. You hear me?"

"Yes," I say, but I can't force myself to meet his gaze.

"Go to the truck. We'll wrap up without you."

Ronan turns and walks away. In the distance, Nate, Luke, and Darren huddle near each other watching the confrontation. Ronan barks an order at them, and they disperse.

An hour later, I'm the last to exit the fire engine as it sits idle in the garage at the fire station. My body is numb from the uncomfortable silence on the ride from the burned house. None of us dared to speak as Ronan's anger cast a gloomy pall over us.

Taking off my equipment and gear, I stumble into the building and head toward the shower.

"You shouldn't go in there yet," Darren says, emerging from the room. "Don't want Ronan to rip your head off again."

"I never should have gone back into the house," I say, bypassing the bathroom to head to the break room.

Darren follows me inside. I cross the room and collapse on the couch.

"It happens. We've all had those moments when we've done something we shouldn't have. No matter what, we always have each other's back. That won't change," Darren says. He walks over to the refrigerator and grabs two ice cream bars. Tossing one toward me, the cold treat lands on my lap.

"Luke and Nate pissed at me?"

"Not at all. Ronan came down too hard on you. You've been dealing with a lot, but we all understood why you tried to save the little girl's rabbit. None of us thought you were being reckless," Darren says.

I tear the paper from the ice cream bar and take a bite. "I ignored an order."

"Haven't we all? Name a time when one of us hasn't gone against Ronan and gotten chewed out about it," Darren says, slumping down in a chair across from me. "How are you? Really?"

I drag a hand down my face and think about the answer to his question. There's no point in lying to Darren. He'll see through any attempt to pretend to be something I'm not.

I reach into my pocket and remove Zaire's engagement ring.

I squeeze my eyes shut, forcing myself to face reality. It's my grandmother's ring. Not Zaire's.

Holding the ring up to the light, I wave it at Darren. His eyes widen.

"Why do you have that?"

"She left me."

"Zaire broke things off with you? I don't believe it."

"Right after I got the news from Heather Grimley about my AI dating app being a sham, Zaire showed up. When I told her, she could only focus on one thing."

"She didn't believe y'all were a match anymore," Darren says, realization dawning on him.

"Nope. Told me there was no point in continuing to pretend, released me from going to Persia's wedding, and handed me the ring back," I say, feeling more miserable sharing the story than when it happened. It's like telling Darren makes it more true. More real. More … final.

"But what about everything y'all feel for each other—"

"She didn't care about any of that. It didn't matter. All that mattered was that the ninety-eight percent love match was a lie. To her, that meant everything else we felt was a lie, too."

"You believe she feels that way?"

"What else am I supposed to believe? If she had feelings for me, she wouldn't have walked away. She wouldn't have ripped my heart out of my chest right when I was already at my lowest and needed her more than ever …"

My words trail off as a smile spreads across Darren's face.

I throw my half-eaten ice cream bar at him. He tries to duck, but it crashes into the side of his neck and oozes down his shirt.

"What are you smiling at? This is not a good situation. My life is falling apart, and you're grinning at me?" I push up from the couch. "What kind of best friend are you?"

Darren stands up and steps in my path, stopping me from going around him. "The kind of best friend who is happy to see you find a woman to love."

"Love." I scoff. "You're crazy."

"Trust me. You wouldn't feel this crappy and act so out of sorts if you weren't in love with your fake fiancée."

I glare at Darren, unable to deny the ache in my heart from the moment I walked away from Zaire. Or that I've wanted to call her, started texts to her I didn't finish, and dreamed about seeing her again almost nonstop since we were at the gazebo.

All these emotions and thoughts are unfamiliar territory for me.

No woman has ever made me feel like this.

But I can't believe I'm already … in love.

Did I suspect that Zaire and I would fall in love after the terms of the fake engagement had passed and we could discuss being a real couple? Absolutely.

That was supposed to happen in the future.

Not right now.

Not already.

"I thought being in love was supposed to make you feel good. This ain't fun." I push past Darren and head toward the sink. Grabbing a dish towel, I turn on the faucet to wet the fabric, then wring it out before tossing it at Darren. "Clean yourself up."

"Trust me, I know a lot about love that doesn't always feel good. I've been living that every day for years," Darren admits.

"I don't know how you do it. How do you not tell Jasmine how you feel about her?"

"Because I can't lose her. I can't take the chance that finding out that I love her might make her uncomfortable and put distance between us. She's too much a part of my life to live without her, so I stay quiet," Darren says. I hear the pain and longing in his voice. "But my situation differs from yours."

"Ironic, isn't it? Of all the women who've loved me and I didn't love back, I fall in love with the one woman who doesn't feel the same about me. One minute, we were planning to explore what a real relationship could be like between us. The next, she's giving me a hard pass," I say, leaning against the counter. A jolt flushes through my body. "You think I'm in love with Zaire?"

"It's obvious. Has been for a while. We all can see it. I was the only one who knew you weren't supposed to be in love with her because the engagement was fake."

"That explains a lot."

"Like what?"

"Like how I think about her all the time, and not only because she's beautiful and a fantastic kisser. Zaire is one of the smartest people I've ever met. She's generous with her time and experience, even though she's super busy running three companies. No matter how down I would get about anything, she was there, encouraging and uplifting me. When my belief in myself waned, she was there to believe in me and force me to believe in myself. To keep trying and to keep pushing."

"She brings out the best in you. That's more than anyone could ever dream of for the person they give their heart to," Darren says, taking a deep breath.

"Jasmine does that for you too—"

"We're not talking about Jasmine and … me. Stay focused. You and Zaire are a great fit."

"Because I can be myself with her. She saw every part of me—the flirty, the jokey, the nerdy, the serious—and she liked all of them. She enjoyed being with me."

"Yes, she … does. Wiley, it's not past tense. Zaire was blindsided by the flaws in the dating app. She had a knee-jerk reaction to it. That may not be her final thoughts on the situation or y'alls relationship. Don't you owe it to yourself to talk to her after both of you have processed things?" Darren asks.

I want to tell Darren the whole truth, but it hurts too much.

Troy is the man Zaire wants, no matter how much she may be attracted to me. He's St. Barts Guy. The guy who was everything she didn't realize she wanted or needed in a man. The one who made her deliriously happy.

Not me.

"I owe it to myself and Zaire to not make this more awkward than it already is. She made her choice when she gave this ring back to me and ended our fake engagement early," I say, dismissing Darren's suggestion.

"Come on, man. The fake engagement was going to end at some point, and the two of you were always going to hit a crossroad—should y'all continue to be a couple or not? Who cares if she ended things early? Doesn't change the decision the two of you need to make."

"You weren't there, Darren. Any hope I had of her having feelings for me ended when I told her the app was wrong." I sigh and rub my throbbing temples. "It's my fault for picking the wrong woman to love. I knew this situation was fake from the beginning. Thinking it could be something more was foolish. I won't make things worse by forcing her to say that to my face. It's time I move on. I have enough to do to salvage the one thing I control—my dating app."

"You need to talk to Zaire," Darren insists.

"And you need to take your own stupid advice and talk to Jasmine," I slam back at him. "I'll talk to Zaire after you tell Jasmine you've been in love with her since y'all were six years old."

Darren flinches, and I know I've pushed too far.

But I don't care.

"Where are you going?" Darren asks as I walk toward the door.

"To the park to clear my head."

CHAPTER 40

Z AIRE

~

WARM WATER CASCADES PAST MY LEGS AS THEY DANGLE over the edge of the outdoor pool. I reach over and skim my hand over the surface, trying and failing to block the last memories I have of being out here. Memories of Wiley, giddy like a kid, as he splashed around in the water beckoning for me, fully clothed, to join him.

Tears spring to my eyes, but I blink them away.

There's no reason to cry.

Sure, I miss Wiley more than I ever thought, but the memories I have of spending time with him are precious. They are times of fun and fondness that should lift my spirits, not bring me down. I always knew that our relationship was temporary. For a moment, I thought Wiley could've been that epic love I'd always wanted that eluded me for years. Turns out I was wrong like all the times before. It was a bitter pill but not one I wasn't used to swallowing.

"Zaire! Are you okay?"

I jump, jerking around to see Persia barreling toward me, followed by Sydney, holding a paper bag labeled Gwen's Country Cafe, and Harlow-Rose, carrying two bottles of what I can only hope is her award-winning Cabernet Sauvignon.

"What are y'all doing here?" I wrack my brain to figure out how they could've gotten into my house without me knowing it.

Persia says, "I was worried about you. Simona said you called in unexpectedly and worked from home today. She could tell something was wrong because you were off and a step behind in all your meetings, which is very unusual."

"I was not a step behind." Sure, I found my mind wandering during the day, but I was still productive. I swing my legs out of the water and stand up.

"That's not what Simona says, and she would know. I called Sydney to see if she knew what was up with you," Persia continues.

"And I told her I hadn't talked to you since the Jack and Jill wedding shower." Sydney gives me a shrewd look. "So, I hung up with her and called Harlow-Rose."

"And I also hadn't heard from you since last week." Harlow-Rose raises a questioning eyebrow. "That's when we knew it was time to come check on you."

"All three of you?" I ask.

"If anyone of us had come alone, you would've weaseled your way out of telling us what is going on," Persia says, plopping down on one of the lounge chairs near the pool. "There's no way you can do that with the three of us here."

"Strength in numbers," Harlow-Rose agrees. She walks to a side table and places the wine bottles on the surface. "Plus, we brought food. I know you haven't eaten dinner if you worked from home."

My stomach growls in response. "What's in there?" I walk over to Sydney and peer down into the bag. Wonderful smells greet my nose, soothing my annoyance from having my solitude interrupted.

"Chicken fried steak, of course," Sydney says.

"Garlic mashed potatoes and fried green beans, too?" I ask, hoping she didn't forget.

"Yes, Zaire. I know what to order from Gwen's." Sydney shakes her head, then pushes past me. She lifts the to-go containers from the bag and places them on the table.

"I'll go grab some wine glasses—"

"Zaire, where's your ring?" Persia screeches, tumbling out of the chair. In three quick steps, she's next to me, holding my left hand in the air.

I suck in a deep breath, not ready to tell the world the pre-planned lie about Wiley and me ending our engagement. We hadn't planned on doing this for another couple of months. Now that the timing has accelerated, I'm not ready to do it. I don't want our family, friends, and the whole town to know that we aren't ... together anymore.

But we were never together.

It was all a lie.

A lie that will end tonight as soon as I tell my sisters that the engagement is off.

"Why aren't you wearing your ring?" Persia peppers me with questions.

"I don't want to talk about it. Not yet." I stall for time when I shouldn't.

"Too bad, sister, because you need to spill. Now!" Sydney grabs my other arm and pulls me toward the table. I sit in one of the high chairs as Persia, Sydney, and Harlow-Rose join me. Their eyes are full of concern as all attention settles on me.

Still, I can't seem to force myself to say the words.

"We saw that something was off between y'all at the shower. We talked about it with Mommy, but none of us could figure out what happened," Sydney says.

Persia says, "The two of you seemed so perfect for each other. How could it all fall apart so fast? You're not wearing your engagement ring anymore. Does that mean the two of you have broken up for good?"

"Yes."

"Oh. Wiley is single again. A lot of ladies around town will be happy about that," Persia says. "But why?"

"I think I know why," Sydney pipes up.

I'm almost afraid to hear what she thinks this is about.

Sydney continues, "You were blindsided by India's pregnancy—"

"India is pregnant?" Harlow-Rose leans forward. "She and Kei are having a baby?" My bestie looks at me, her eyes searching my face.

I keep my expression passive.

"India is having a baby alone. Kei had been cheating on her for years and divorced her when he found out she was pregnant. He made it clear a child wouldn't force him to stick around." Sydney looks miserable as she grabs my hand. "You've spent years thinking that India stole a good man from you and robbed you of a chance to have your own happily ever after. Now you find out Kei was a despicable ho that didn't deserve your love or India's."

"None of that should matter anymore since Zaire has Wiley. Why would she care if Kei turned out to be a douche?" Persia asks.

"Because it makes her feel like she can't trust her heart in choosing men to love," Sydney says. "Like she's destined to always pick the wrong guy. Wiley is a sweetheart, but he's not known as the Playboy of Kimbell for nothing."

"You panicked and pushed Wiley away, didn't you?" Harlow-Rose asks, staring intently into my eyes. She's the only one who knows the truth about my fake engagement with Wiley. Her question has so many layers that my sisters don't realize.

"No, I didn't," I say, my voice trembling. I'm wilting under Harlow-Rose's scrutiny, but I can't tell her the truth. Even if my sisters weren't here, I'm not sure I could admit to her what happened between Wiley and me. Instead, I focus on the pre-planned break-up story. "Sydney is right that this relates to India's pregnancy, but not in the way y'all think."

"Then in what way?" Persia asks.

"Wiley and I talked about how Kei abandoned her and his unborn child. That's when he told me he doesn't want kids and hopes that wouldn't be a deal breaker for me."

"What?!" Sydney and Persia scream at the same time.

Harlow-Rose gives me a look of disappointment and turns her back to me. She knows more is going on and that this is a ruse. I'm thankful she doesn't push me to tell the truth or blow my cover with my sisters.

"How could he not want children?" Persia asks, dumbfounded.

"Zaire, you remember we talked about this? I told you to find out where he stood on the important things, like kids, and you brushed me off. Honey, I'm so sorry." Sydney pulls me into a tight hug.

Persia joins her. "Of course, you can't marry him now. I understand some women don't want kids, but we always dreamed of having them."

I pull away from my sisters. "That's why we had to end things now before …"

"We understand," Sydney says, nodding as she squeezes my hands for support.

Persia looks away, staring off into the distance at the rippling waters of the lake reflecting the night sky. She says, "I'm so proud of you for having the courage to walk away. I'm not sure I could do the same thing."

"We're Kincaid girls. Of course, you could." Sydney rolls her eyes. "But this isn't about you, Persia. We need to support Zaire right now."

Harlow-Rose is conspicuously quiet.

"Maybe he'll change his mind after he has time to think about it more," Persia says. "The two of you fit. I've never seen a couple more compatible and in sync than you and Wiley. I can't believe he'd lose you over this."

"Well, he can't expect Zaire to take that risk and end up devastated if he doesn't," Sydney says. "It's not fair to her. What do you think, Harlow-Rose?"

I turn to look at my best friend.

Harlow-Rose leans back in her chair and studies me for a long moment.

"I think," Harlow-Rose starts, then leans closer to me. "You should fight for the man you love. Convince him that the two of you are worth saving, despite your differences."

My mouth gapes open.

Fight for the man ... I love?

Persia sticks her tongue out at Sydney. "See, Harlow-Rose is on my side. You're wrong, Syd."

Before I can respond, my cell phone rings.

I glance at the screen and see Sally Alexander's name.

"Excuse me, I need to take this," I say, then snatch the phone and rush back inside the house. Once I'm inside, I answer the call.

"I'm sorry to call you so late. Did you hear about the fire at Jimbo Barnes's house?"

"Fire? Tonight?" I say, feeling all the air rush from my lungs. Wiley is on shift tonight. "Is Wiley okay?" Please, God, don't let him be hurt.

"Yes, well, physically, yes. Mr. Barnes called me to thank me for raising a wonderful son. After saving his little girl from her upstairs bedroom where she was trapped, Wiley went back inside the burning building to save the child's pet rabbit."

"He did what? Why would he risk his life like that?"

"I don't know. Mr. Barnes said Ronan told Wiley not to go back into the house. The family begged him not to go, but he went anyway," Sally says, her voice shaking. "Luke and Nate had to go in after him and make sure he got out alive. The rabbit is safe, though."

"Okay. Well, I'm glad he's okay ..."

"It was a rough night. He won't call you, but it would mean the world to him if his fiancée stopped by the fire station to check on him," Sally says.

His fiancée?

Wiley hasn't told his mom that our engagement is over.

Why hasn't he told her?

I take a deep breath. "Of course. Yes, I'll head right over there."

"Thank you, dear. I'm so glad Wiley has you in his life."

CHAPTER 41

Z AIRE

~

THE DRIVE TO DOWNTOWN KIMBELL PASSES IN A BLUR. MY head is full of confused, jumbled thoughts. I could feel myself falling hard for Wiley, but I didn't think I'd crossed the threshold. Not yet.

Am I already in love with Wiley?

My bestie knows me better than anybody, and it wouldn't be the first time she saw something in me I hadn't realized yet. Especially since she's the only one who knows my relationship with Wiley is fake. Had she noticed a change between Wiley and me? Something that made her believe I'd stopped pretending?

Of course, she had.

Because of the results of his dating app, I believed there could be something more between us. But the results were wrong.

We were not a ninety-eight percent love match.

I'm not sure we would have explored more between us if it hadn't been for that result. Maybe we tricked ourselves into agreeing with the app when there were no underlying feelings.

Is that what Harlow-Rose had picked up on?

And if there aren't any real feelings between Wiley and me, why am I driving to see him at the fire station to see that he's okay?

Sure, his mom asked me to, but I could've declined.

Or texted him.

Or called him.

I didn't have to bolt from my house, leaving my sisters and Harlow-Rose behind, wondering what emergency was so important that I dropped everything to check on it.

"I'm getting nowhere with these crazy thoughts," I mumble as I pull my car to a stop outside the Kimbell Fire Station. My heart thuds at seeing Wiley again for the first time since I gave back his grandmother's engagement ring. I'm anxious and jittery, nervous and ... excited. I've missed him, and I want to see him. There's no denying that.

What does that mean in the grand scheme of our ... relationship?

I have no clue and now is not the time to figure that out.

Exiting the car, I head up the walkway as the door swings open.

Darren Manning stops and stares at me. A slight smile curves on his lips as he comes a few steps closer.

"He's at Bell Park." Darren stuffs his hands in his pocket.

"I heard y'all had a rough night putting out the fire at Jimbo Barnes's house." I'm stalling for time for some insane reason.

Darren nods. "No matter how many warnings we give about proper care of Christmas trees in the home, it doesn't seem to sink in."

"And Wiley almost got trapped in the fire?"

"I'll let him tell you that part of the story."

"Is he okay?" I ask, unsure what I'll intrude on when I see him in the park.

Darren glances toward the park for a long moment. "He will be."

Not sure how to interpret that cryptic statement, I give Darren a smile, then head toward Bell Park. In the distance, the swings creak through the air. The cold front is long gone, and the atmosphere has a tinge of brisk coolness that doesn't require a coat.

The eighteen-foot tall, town Christmas tree sparkles with thousands of lights against the darkness. As I approach, Wiley comes into view. He's perched on the middle swing, kicking his legs against the ground to propel himself only a few feet into the air. His hands grip the steel ropes as he stares into the distance.

Taking a deep breath, I head straight for him. I don't want to scare him at a time like this. Better that he sees me coming. He stops swinging and stares at me when I'm within a few feet of him. I can't read his expression. I'm not sure what he's thinking. I'm not sure he wants me here.

I press my hands on my hips. "I hear you tried to get yourself burned up. What's up with that?"

Wiley's laugh cuts through the night air, sending a flurry of butterflies scurrying through me. "Not my wisest decision, that's true." He glances over at the swing next to him.

I sit on it and twist to face him. "What happened?"

"It was like in our training. Jimbo Barnes and his wife had tucked their daughter into bed and turned in without turning off the lights on their Christmas tree. They admitted they didn't pay attention to whether they were watering the tree sufficiently. The heat likely got to some drier branches and started the fire. By the time we showed up, the entire downstairs was in flames, and they were trapped upstairs."

"That's horrible. So, y'all had to go in and get them out?"

"Luke and I went in, got everybody out." Wiley rakes a hand through his hair. He gives me a sheepish grin.

"Spill it. What did you do?"

"Ronan told us to stand down because the fire had breached the second floor." Wiley shakes his head. "But then I saw Jimbo's daughter crying, and she kept saying over and over, 'Poor Princess Carrot.' So I dropped to one knee and asked her about it. It was her pet rabbit, trapped in a cage in her bedroom, that she knew would get burned in the fire."

I frown. "Tell me you didn't go back in after a rabbit. You risked your life for a rabbit?"

"I couldn't watch another person lose something they loved. I'd been doing too much of that lately, and I reacted. It was like Dante's Inferno when I raced back inside. But the door to the cage was open, and the rabbit had already gotten out. I looked around for her but couldn't find the darn thing. I was about to leave when the floor collapsed—"

"Wiley!" I grab his arm.

He looks down at my hand resting against his skin and takes a slow breath. His hands move to cover mine. "I'm here. I made it out okay. Nate and Luke wouldn't let me die in that house. You don't have to worry."

"I do if you're breaking protocols to go in and save a rabbit."

Wiley gives me that devastatingly gorgeous smile. "Both Princess Carrot and I are safe and sound. We found the rabbit in the backyard behind a tree, slightly burned but alive. All is right with the world, except Ronan ripped me a new one for what I did. He's going to write me up over it."

"Good. Serves you right. We kinda like having you in this town, so I need you to focus on not putting yourself in harm's way when you don't need to. Can you do that?"

"For you? Yeah," Wiley says, then looks away. "Can't believe you came all this way to check on me. Who told you about the fire?"

"Your mom. Mr. Barnes called her and gave her all the details. She thought you'd rather have me check on you than her." I swallow past the lump in my throat. "She didn't seem to know that our engagement is over."

"I haven't told her. I haven't told anybody. You saw the mania that this town went through when they found out we were engaged. I can imagine it's going to be ten times worse when they find out we split up," Wiley says, slumping over. "I figured it would be better for you if we waited until after Persia's wedding to spread the news."

"Much better. I don't want to think about all the ladies who'll be celebrating now that you're back on the market," I say, unable to ignore the sourness flooding my stomach. "Your phone is going to be blowing up."

I'm trying to add humor to the situation, but my voice contains no mirth.

Wiley scratches the side of his face. "I guess it's time for me to get a new phone number."

"You are so silly. But make sure you give the new number to your real friends. We still want a way to reach you."

He twists in the swing to face me. I stare into his sparkling aqua eyes and feel my heart soar.

"We're friends now? No longer acquaintances?"

"You've been promoted to friend status." He's been promoted to much more, but I'm not sure now is the time to broach the subject.

"Yes!" Wiley pumps a fist in the air. "Even though you have a zillion friends, so I'm not sure that's much of a change for me."

"So do you," I remind him. "How about you've been promoted to a close friend. Part of my inner circle."

"That sounds like a good place to be. I'm sure I'll get more perks as part of the inner circle. Like late night visits to make sure I'm doing okay after a tough night fighting fires," Wiley teases.

I giggle. "Yes, like that. Anyone who can get me to leave my house after ten at night is in the inner circle."

"And maybe we could still text each other."

"Yep, we can do that."

"And talk on the phone."

"That too."

"And hang out from time to time."

"I'd like that." Emotions creep into my voice despite my attempts to hide what I'm feeling. "Wiley, I don't regret any of the time we spent together. I'm glad I got to know the real you. You're an amazing person." I bite my bottom lip as tears spring to my eyes.

"It's about time you realized that," Wiley says, winking at me.

"These next few weeks will be hard to get through, but we can do it, right?"

"Absolutely. My sisters bought the story about our different views on kids, and it makes sense to them we could break up over that." I turn away from him and push against the packed earth, propelling my body forward and backward a few feet on the swing. "Sydney's pissed at you, but Persia thinks I can change your mind about things. Who knows what everybody else will say? But those are the two people I was worried most about. How will your mom and sis take it?"

"Ma is going to be devastated. She wanted me to become a Kincaid," Wiley says, laughing.

"How would you become a Kincaid?"

"She told me to take your last name after we married because it has more weight and respect, which she thought I needed."

"You're joking!"

"Dead serious. Hayley will be pissed at you. She's very protective of me. Kinda like my second mom since she's fifteen years older. I'll have to convince her not to drive down from Houston and claw your eyes out for breaking my heart."

"But I didn't break your heart. We mutually parted ways, remember?"

Wiley is quiet, and I swear I can hear his heart pounding.

"Right," he says finally.

Trying to ease the tension between us, I say, "I forgot to tell you. I talked to Lance about the situation with Heather Grimley. He was confident that you'd have grounds to sue if she changes the focus of her feature to an exposé on the results of their test of your dating app. So, if you hear from her and think she might try something like that for one second, tell her you'll have your attorney call her. That should stop her in her tracks."

"Wait. You did all of that … for me?"

I shrug. "You didn't have to say the words for me to know that was one of your concerns. Especially after you had a front-row seat to everything Darren went through with the media twisting his situation into something it wasn't. I wanted you to have some security and a game plan, just in case."

"Thanks, but none of that will matter in a couple of weeks. I'm planning to shut the site down at the end of the year."

"Why would you walk away from your life's work because of some unsubstantiated claim from that vlogger? She hasn't given you the details of their test so that you can analyze what they did," I say, jumping from the swing. I step in front of Wiley. "You can't give it all up because of one person's claims. Too many people have found love through your app."

Wiley stands, and I take a step back, still affected by his glorious sensuality.

"I appreciate your belief in me." Wiley closes the distance between us. "It means more than you'll ever know. But I got all the documentation on their tests, and I've poured over the results and can't figure out where things are going wrong. I don't have the energy anymore to figure it out. The AI is broken. I failed."

"Do you know how often I've failed since starting my first business? I don't have enough fingers or toes to count them all."

Wiley's eyes go wide with shock. "What are you talking about? You have the Midas touch for building businesses."

"It only seems that way in hindsight. I'm a ten-year overnight success," I say. "I built my businesses by failing fast and learning from the failures faster. That's what you have to do. You can't throw in the towel on all the research and hard work you put into your dating app."

"This isn't a small failure, Zaire. It's massive, and I can't figure it out."

"You're right. This is a catastrophe in the making, but you can figure out how to fix this. Do you think I wanted to start a construction company? Real estate was my game, not construction. I bought land and worked with the best construction companies in the Hill Country. I was driven and demanding, and I made a lot of enemies. So many enemies that all the companies refused to work with me anymore. I was blackballed after buying up tons of property," I say, shaking my head at the memories.

"I never knew that. How did you get out of it?"

"One, I had to tear down everything I'd tried and start fresh with a clean slate. I re-crafted my business from the ground up. I found some disgruntled construction workers looking for a fresh start and learned how to be a better business *partner* with them. They weren't peons who worked for me. If I wanted to be successful, I had to view them as co-owners in every endeavor, whether that was reality or perception. That's how I turned things around and became the owner of Kincaid Construction."

"You think I need to go back to the drawing board? Reconstruct my AI from the ground up and ..."

"Make it better than before. You know how they tested your dating app. You can run those tests before you go live with the new and improved version. You can do this, Wiley." I grab his hands in mine.

"It's hard not to believe when I have a motivator like you by my side."

"Does that mean you won't throw in the towel?" I hope I got through to him.

Wiley stares at me. I see a shift in him. As if a light bulb has turned on, and he's infused with a new motivation.

"I'm going to do what you said. I'll rebuild the app and prove to ... everyone ... that it works."

CHAPTER 42

ILEY

WITH BLEARY EYES, I STARE AT THE LINES OF CODING AS IT fills the screen. My fingers move across the keyboard as Mariah Carey's "All I Want for Christmas is You" blasts from the speakers mounted on my wall. The song has been on repeat since the clock struck midnight on Christmas day. A reminder of why I'm skipping the drive to Houston to spend Christmas with my sister and her family. I'm pouring every ounce of energy into fixing the dating app, so I can get what I want for Christmas—Zaire.

Zaire encouraged me to fix the AI design and not give up on my dating app business.

But all I want is a way to convince Zaire to give a relationship with me a chance. She lost faith in the feelings between us because

Heather's test revealed my app was randomly matching people with no connection to the research I'd based the algorithm on.

In hindsight, I shouldn't have given up on Zaire and myself. If Troy was the man she wanted, without a doubt, she wouldn't have played the role of my fake fiancée for weeks. She resisted him because a part of her didn't belong with him. She belonged with me instead.

But the end of her relationship with Kei and the other relationships that followed and failed had worked a number on her confidence in love. She didn't trust herself to choose the right man. That's why the results from the dating app had been so important to her. It was a way to validate that what she felt for me was real and safe, like I thought I needed it to validate that I'd found "the one."

I thought I wouldn't recognize when I'd found true love. Now that I know without a doubt that I love Zaire and what that feels like, it's obvious I haven't loved anyone before. None of what I had with my exes comes close to my love for her.

I must convince her she can trust her feelings for me, too. She doesn't need to settle for Troy.

I'm starting with a clean slate and rebuilding the AI, ensuring it uses my research. The algorithms will be redesigned and taken through rigorous tests for consistency and accuracy of results. When I re-run our profiles, there will be no doubt about the results. No experts will find a flaw in my method. Zaire will know we are meant to be together.

An elbow shoves against my arm, jarring me from my thoughts. I pitch forward, sending the bowl of red, green, and white plain M&M's flying across my desk.

"Ma!"

"I'll get that." She looks innocent as she leans over to pick up discarded scraps of balled-up pages, empty food wrappers, and a stack of dishes from the past three days.

"Weren't you leaving to go to Hayley's an hour ago? I'm sure they're waiting for you to get there before opening presents. I don't want Lydia, Peter, and Patrick calling me upset because you're not there," I say, wishing she'd get on the road and leave me in peace.

"The grandkids can wait. I'm not leaving my beautiful son behind in this mess of an apartment on Christmas Day. It's my gift to you since you won't let me buy you anything," Ma says, filling her arms with the items. "I don't know how you can focus in this hog pen. How in the world will you fix the app and convince Zaire that y'all are perfect for each other with all this clutter around?"

What seemed like an innocent request to stop by my apartment to grab the Christmas gift I bought for her has turned into a smother fest. As I gave her the envelope with a gift certificate to a luxurious spa in Houston, she caught sight of the jewelry box on my kitchen table. The one that I returned my grandmother's ring to after Zaire gave it back.

Ma burst into tears and demanded to know what I'd done wrong. I had no choice but to come clean about the whole fake engagement. A couple hours later, I'd taken her through more details than I should have, and she was up to speed on the most important fact—I'm in love with Zaire.

"Ma! First, do not spill one word of what I told you to Hayley," I say, giving her a stern look. "Second, fixing the app will take months, not hours. It's going to be a while before I can prove to Zaire that we are perfect for each other."

I'm hoping it only takes months, not years, like the first generation of the app. I don't think I could handle being apart from Zaire for that long. I need her to trust me. I need her to believe that my love for her is authentic, genuine, and the most real thing I've ever felt for any woman in my life.

"But the wedding is today," Ma says, swiping at the desk with a dish towel to gather the food crumbs.

"She's done with pretending we're a couple. She doesn't believe we have a future. She gave the ring back, remember? If I push her on this before having the dating app results to back me up, it could backfire."

I should be with Zaire today when she comes face to face with India and Kei at the wedding and reception. She had a nasty run-in with India at the Jack and Jill shower and left early, but fleeing the wedding if things get rough won't be an option. She'll have to stick it out, suffering through the awkwardness and anger alone. She's strong enough to handle it, but it doesn't stop me from wanting to be by her side.

"Stop being foolish. The whole town bought into y'alls lie because the two of you weren't lying about the attraction you felt to each other. Y'all weren't lying about the compatibility and closeness you shared. The only lie was that you had been secretly dating for the past six months. Everything else was one hundred percent real. You know that, and trust me, so does Zaire," Ma insists.

One look at the sureness in her eyes, and I can't help but be convinced.

"But Ma—"

"No, you listen to me. This Troy fella will be at that wedding, ready to swoop in and support Zaire if you're not there. You can't let that happen," Ma says, pulling a chair and sitting down a few feet away from me. "Zaire is a strong woman, but she will need to see a face in the room that is on her side. And trust me, she wants that face to be yours." Ma hands me a wet wipe. "Clean your keyboard. I can see the crumbs and sticky spots from here."

I do as I'm told, forcing thoughts of Troy and Zaire from my mind.

"I thought about going but I can't. Today will be hard for Zaire, and if I show up, she'll have to pretend that things are great between us when they aren't. That's more stress for her to deal with, not less. I won't do that to her."

"My goodness, it's so clear that you don't know how to handle loving someone. I've spoiled you too much."

"What does that mean?"

"You say you love Zaire, and I believe you do. You know today will be difficult for her, which means it will be a rough day for you, too. When you love someone, you walk a tight line of doing what they need you to do and doing what *you need* to do for them." Ma pokes me in the chest. "Look at me. I should be in Houston now, helping my

261

grandkiddos open their Christmas presents. But I'm here with you because it's what I need to do for my son."

"And you think I need to be at the wedding for Zaire? To show her that no matter what happens between us, I love her enough to be in her corner, supporting her when she's facing a tough situation."

Ma shrugs and gives me a big smile. "Only you can answer that."

I grab my cell phone and open the magic eight ball app. Shaking it from side to side, I wait for the result.

Outlook not so good

But Ma said only I can answer that.

And both my head and my heart disagree with the magic eight ball.

I take a deep breath, then say, "I'm going to the wedding."

Ma squeals with excitement, clapping her hands.

"Your clothes are hanging on the bathroom door," Ma says, pointing behind her. My tuxedo hangs on the top ledge, and shiny black patent leather shoes rest against the wall.

When in the world had Ma done that without me noticing?

She stands and leans over to give me a kiss on the head.

"Where's Zaire's ring?" Ma asks.

I reach into my pocket and place it on the edge of the desk. I look up at Ma, frowning. She didn't call it her mom's or my grandmother's ring. She referred to it as Zaire's. Deep in my heart, I feel the same way.

Ma reaches behind her neck and unclasps the sparkling, thin platinum chain I bought her for her birthday a few years ago. She places it next to the ring. "It might be too soon for her to wear that on her finger again, but it belongs to her. Make sure she has it, you hear?"

I reach for the necklace and thread the ring onto it, then secure the clasp. Another glance toward the door with my tuxedo, and I know Ma is right. "I'll get you another one."

"Don't bother. I'd much rather a daughter-in-law instead."

"Yes, ma'am," I say. Smiling, I push up from the chair and wrap her in a big hug.

CHAPTER 43

Z AIRE

~

"WHAT ARE YOU DOING IN HERE? YOUR SISTER NEEDS YOU," Mommy says, storming into the restaurant near the back entrance of the Harlow-Rose Winery.

Twisting the wine opener into the cork of the bottle of Merlot, I don't turn around. I've been on a mission, hunting down Persia's favorite wine and luxury Belgian dark chocolates, which my baby sister insists she can't drink the wine without. Even though the restaurant is still under construction, Harlow-Rose's manager, Gina, whispered that the place was a treasure trove of goodies that might help me with Persia.

A hand rests on my shoulder as I wiggle the cork free.

"Grab a wineglass from the back counter, would you?" I ask, then scoop the chocolates wrapped in rose gold foil and turn to pour wine into the glass Mommy holds. "This is the only thing that might calm her nerves."

"Something has to," Mommy mutters under her breath. "I understand having wedding day jitters, but this is too much. Why does your sister always have to be so … extra?"

"No clue where she got it from," I say, placing the wine bottle back on the counter.

"I blame your father. He's the reason she's so spoiled," Mommy says, then loops a hand in mine. Her gaze lingers on my left ring finger. The one devoid of the engagement ring Wiley gave me weeks ago when we pretended to be engaged.

"Is Wiley coming to the wedding?" Mommy gives me a raised eyebrow.

"You know, he isn't. We've called off our engagement. It's over between us."

Mommy scoffs. "If there's one thing I know, you and Wiley are far from over. The two of you are just beginning."

"What do you mean?" I ask, turning to face her.

"Zaire, you are my favorite child, and I know you better than anyone. Wiley has a permanent place in your heart. I can feel how much you love him. You need to get out of your own way and put this foolishness about kids behind you."

"You don't think it's a big deal that I want kids, and he doesn't?" I ask, trying to stick to the story I'd told everyone.

"I think a man doesn't know what he wants until he's found a good woman that can help direct him to a better way," Mommy says with a smile. "He respects you and values your opinion. If you'd get over being upset, I think you'd find it won't take much effort to change his mind about children."

"Let's not talk about this right now. Making sure we can get Persia down the aisle is a big enough challenge for today," I say.

"Fine, but one last thing."

"What is it?"

"Promise me you'll have an honest conversation with Wiley about your relationship and your future. It's natural to rush to judgment and double down on choosing sides before you realize the consequences. Enough time has passed that you two can revisit the topic with calmer heads."

"And what if it still doesn't work out?"

"Do you want it to work out?" Mommy asks, tugging on my arm. "Be honest."

"More than anything."

"Good. Because I know my firstborn child is brilliant. There's nothing she's wanted that she hasn't gotten. Nothing!"

"Are you forgetting my history with Kei?"

"Honey, if I thought for one minute you had a tenth of the feelings for Kei that you have for Wiley, I would've stopped India in her tracks at Sydney's wedding. Should have stopped it anyway, but too late now," Mommy says, shaking her head. "When you introduced him to us, I could tell that you were going through the motions. Kei Yamamoto was not the man for you. He was convenient with a good resume, but that's not the same as love."

"It was that obvious to you?" I wonder how Mommy had recognized what had taken me years to figure out ... with Wiley's help.

"Like a neon sign, Honey."

"And you see something different with Wiley and me? You think Wiley is the man for me?" I ask, searching her face for confirmation or agreement.

Mommy shakes her head at me, feigning disappointment. "Follow your heart. Only you know what's in there. It could be a gigantic risk, but—"

"It can also be a big reward."

"Just like everything else you've conquered in life," Mommy says, then pulls me toward the door. "Now, let's get some liquor in your sister so she stops freaking out about walking down the aisle."

CHAPTER 44

Z AIRE

~

An hour later, I'm gazing at the guests seated in a semicircle within the winery as I pass down the center walkway toward the arches covered in dazzling flowers. I scan the crowd, hoping that Wiley came to the wedding. When I don't see him, it's hard to keep the smile plastered on my face.

It's been four days since our last conversation when we agreed to be … friends. But his friendship is the tip of the iceberg of what I want from him. I want all the things we pretended we had. The things developing between us, despite our insistence that our closeness was a charade. Wiley found his way into my heart, and I don't want to let that go.

As I take my place next to Sydney at the altar, I inhale a deep breath. I want to rush away from the wedding and find Wiley now. I want to tell him these feelings I have for him are so deep and pure and transcend the friendship we'd developed. I want him to know I'm falling in love with him and hope it's not too late for us to see what the future could be.

Pachelbel's Canon in D transitions into the wedding march. I turn to see Persia emerge from the foyer entrance of the winery. Her hand loops around our father's, who is beaming with pride. She looks stunning and every bit like the pampered princess she is. Tears spring to Yves's eyes as he watches her walk down the aisle. The love he has for my sister is etched on his face. I couldn't be happier for Persia to find her perfect mate, a man who loves every part of her.

Daddy gives Persia a kiss on both cheeks before turning to hug Yves. They exchange several words that none of us can hear but leave both men emotional. Moments later, Daddy sits next to Mommy in the front row.

Persia takes a trembling step toward Yves, then stops. She turns to hand me her bouquet. Her face is pale, and there's panic in her eyes. I give her hand a gentle squeeze.

"I'm so happy for you. I love you," I whisper to her.

She nods at me and takes a deep breath. I hope my words calm her, but I'm not sure they have the effect I hoped.

The minister begins the ceremony.

"On this day, Persia and Yves will transition as a couple by celebrating the love they share for each other. Their bond will also connect their families and closest friends, expanding the circle of love that will support them throughout their lifetime. With this abundance of love, today will be the most joyous of occasions," the minister says.

Yves looks lovingly at Persia, who is visibly shaking.

I shift, catching the frown on Sydney's face. I can almost read her mind. Our sister has been a nervous wreck for the past twenty-four hours, and looks like she is about two seconds away from a full-blown panic attack.

Sneaking a glance at Mommy does nothing to calm me. Her face is a mask of concern as she shifts towards the edge of her chair.

"Before we begin, I would be remiss to not inquire if there is anyone present who knows of any reason that this couple should not be joined in holy matrimony. If so, speak now or forever hold your peace."

Persia's face whips toward the minister, then back toward the crowd of a hundred guests seated in a semi-circle around the constructed altar. Her eyes are wild, like a trapped animal desperate for an escape. I take a step toward her, but Mommy raises a hand. I stop in my tracks. Maybe if we don't react, Persia will calm down.

Yves strokes Persia's hand, smiling at her. He seems oblivious to her stress. Persia swipes her other hand along her forehead, which beads with sweat.

The door bangs open.

A shriek escapes Persia's lips, and she jerks her hand from Yves's.

The rustling of movement fills the air as all the guests turn to see who has dared to enter the wedding at this most inopportune time.

I glance toward the foyer, and my heart catches in my throat.

Wiley stands in the arch doorway, impeccably dressed in a black tuxedo. He's immaculate, straight off the pages of GQ. Blond hair is meticulously styled, with a hint of a five o'clock shadow on his chiseled jaw. His aqua blue eyes sparkle as they scan the room.

An involuntary smile spreads across my lips, but it isn't returned.

He looks serious, with a hint of something that I can't read in his expression. My heart thunders in my chest, and I can't ignore the butterflies racing through my body. I know there's so much I need to say to Wiley, the man I'm falling in love with, but now is not the right time—

"Wiley? You came!" Persia steps away from Yves.

Her words are like a bomb detonating within me, obliterating all rational thought. Why would Wiley be here for … her?

"I'm sorry, Yves. I can't do this. I should've told you earlier." Persia rips her hands from Yves's.

"What are you saying?" Yves demands, reaching for Persia. She dodges his grasp. He looks crushed as the reality of what's happening in front of his friends and family crashes down on him.

"I can't marry you. I have to get out of here!" Persia screams.

Yves takes a step toward her, but his family holds him back. The anger wafting from them is palpable as they glare at Persia with hatred. A flurry of words in French fills the air as they converge around Yves, who looks stunned.

Persia races down the aisle, running out of her shoes as one hand lifts the edge of her dress. Her hair floats in the air as she dives into the waiting arms of … Wiley.

My arms fall to my sides, dropping Persia's wedding bouquet to the floor. I can't breathe. Dizziness overwhelms me as my vision blurs with unshed tears. How could she do this to me?

"This can't be happening." Sydney turns to me. "Not again." She grips my hand, giving me a lifeline when I need it most.

"Please, Wiley," Persia pleads as tears stream down her face. "Get me out of here."

The pure concern in his eyes is like a knife through my heart, plunging deep and twisting. It's like none of us are here. His full attention focused on my youngest sister.

His hands caress the sides of Persia's face as he says sweet words to her I can't hear. Persia clings to him as his arms encircle her.

My legs turn to jelly, and I feel faint.

Without a second glance toward me or any of us, he carries Persia out of the winery and out of our sight.

CHAPTER 45

Z AIRE

~

I WILL NOT CRY.

I will not let a single tear fall from my eyes.

Blinking, I take in the chaotic scene playing out within the winery. Harlow-Rose and her staff weave in and out of the crowd, trying to contain the frenzy. Yves is rushed out a side door to a waiting limousine that was supposed to take him and Persia to Austin for their flight to the Maldives after the reception. His mother and father anchor each side of him as they leave without a word to my parents. The rest of Yves's guests pour out of the building, desperate to put as much distance between themselves and the wedding that wasn't.

Mommy paces in front of the constructed altar, calling Persia's cell phone over and over and getting no answer. Daddy gets a description of Wiley's F-150, then barks orders to Matthieu to take the road to San

Antonio and Troy to take the road to Dallas, while he'll head toward Houston to search for the runaway bride and the man I love.

"Are you going to be okay?" A deep baritone shakes me out of my trance. Troy is standing before me, his face etched with genuine concern.

"She's fine, Troy. Now is not a good time." Sydney steps between him and me. "Can you try to find Persia?"

"Yes, I'm going to look for your sister. I wanted to see if there's anything Zaire needed before I left," Troy insists.

I look away as Sydney says, "You can help by finding Persia. That's what Zaire needs. It's what we all need."

"Do you know what Wiley was thinking? Why would he come here and take Persia away like that?" Troy persists, rubbing salt in the gaping wound of my broken heart.

My hero, Sydney, takes charge, so I don't have to. "There's a lot to process and not a lot of answers. Finding Persia and Wiley will clear all of this up. Can you get on the road before they get too far ahead?"

Troy inhales a deep breath, then nods. "Fine. Zaire, call me if you need anything."

I can't look at him.

Troy warned me this would happen, but I didn't listen. I didn't believe that I'd ever care this much for Wiley. I never thought Wiley would resurrect the most painful moment of my life with a fresh new twist—this time, it's not just the betrayal of a beloved sister.

I've lost the man I'm in love with.

The pain of that truth is gutting me to my core.

Sydney hugs me as I watch Troy leave the winery.

"We will get answers, Honey," Sydney says, releasing me from her grasp. "I promise you that."

"The answers are crystal clear," India says, waddling over to where we're standing near the altar.

My gaze flicks in her direction, and I can't contain my anger.

India continues, "I'm not the outcast sister anymore. Persia's little stunt beats mine by a mile. Another man decides your sister is too irresistible to pass up."

"Shut up!" Sydney screams at her. "You think this is helping? It isn't. You started this mess when you swooped in and lured Kei away from Zaire. How well did that work for you? How you got him is the same as how you lost him. Now you're knocked up and alone. I don't know what Persia thinks, but Wiley won't be with her for long. She'll end up in the same boat you're in."

"Sydney, don't." I pull her back from being in India's face.

"Honey, none of this is right. None of this is fair to you. I can't believe Wiley would be so cruel and evil to come here for … Persia." Sydney says, spitting our baby sister's name like it's something vile. "He was never good enough for you."

Harlow-Rose emerges from the aisle and wraps her arms around me. "I'm so sorry I encouraged you to be with him. To give him a place in your heart." She releases me, then caresses a hand down my face. "I never thought he could hurt you like this."

The barrage of words rifling between India, Sydney, and Harlow-Rose blur into chaotic noise, assaulting my ears. When I caught Kei with India at Sydney's wedding, I was livid that my sister would stoop so low to hurt me by stealing my boyfriend. I felt the loss of a sister. Losing Kei had been an afterthought. I was embarrassed that he picked India over me, but I wasn't heartbroken. It only took weeks, not months, to stop thinking about him and what I thought our future would be.

This moment, seeing Wiley swoop Persia away from the wedding, is different. The pain is visceral, like wild animals tearing at the carcass of my heart. It hurts because I'd found a man to love. Wiley respected and appreciated me in ways I didn't think were possible. He was the perfect blend of fun and seriousness I've always craved in a life partner. We could flow from discussing business plans and strategic goals to debating whether Transformers or Power Rangers were more iconic within hours. We had an unconditional acceptance of each other and enjoyed being together.

And all of that was snatched away from me in one devastating moment.

"They don't call him the Playboy of Kimbell for nothing," India says. "I believe he cared for you, but it wasn't enough to stop him from slipping into his old ways. I hate that Persia fell for him, too."

"Who's side are you on? Zaire is your sister, and you're trying to defend what Wiley has done? You are unbelievable!" Sydney screams at India.

"It's not Wiley's fault that Zaire has flaws. The common denominator in all of her failed relationships is her. Those are facts," India retorts.

"That's not fair or true," Harlow-Rose says.

"Wiley misled her into thinking he loved her when he was a player looking for a sugar mama! Then he sees Persia and trades in one Kincaid sister for another. He's disgusting!" Sydney says.

"Stop it! Stop saying these horrible things about Wiley that aren't true." I swipe at the stupid tears coursing down my face. The tears I swore I wouldn't let fall are like fountains pouring from my eyes. "He did nothing wrong. He didn't betray me. He's not a horrible person."

"Oh yes, he did, and yes, he is." Sydney looks at me like I've lost my mind. "Do not give that jerk a pass!"

"No, you don't understand. I made the mistake of falling in love with him. But that's on me. Not Wiley. He did nothing wrong by falling for … Persia." I can barely get the words out. "He didn't break any promises to me because we were never together."

"What are you talking about?" Sydney asks. "You and Wiley were engaged. He was going to be your husband."

"NO!" I scream. The room grows quiet as all attention settles on me. "It was all a lie. We weren't in a secret relationship for the past six months. We didn't spend Thanksgiving together in St. Barts. We pretended to be engaged. It wasn't real. We were acting."

Harlow-Rose rubs my back as she steps closer to me. "It's true," she says. "I knew about it this whole time. I knew the engagement was fake."

Mommy rushes to me, pushing Sydney and Harlow-Rose out of the way. "Talk to me. Why did you do this? Did he threaten you? Did he force you to go along with this? Does he have something on you?"

"No, Mommy," I shake my head as shame washes over me. "Y'all know Wiley's dating app was going to be featured on love guru Heather Grimley's vlog. She has fifty million followers. It was a tremendous opportunity. One he only got because he lied and told her he knew his app was the real deal since it's how he met his fiancée. Heather got so excited about the human interest side of the story with the dating app she gave him the feature on the spot. Wiley was forced to figure out how to conjure up a fiancée in less than three weeks."

"So he asked you?" Sydney presses her hands on her hips. "That doesn't make sense. What about the guy you told us about? The one you went to St. Barts with."

"He doesn't exist." Nausea washes over me. "He was a lie, just like the fake engagement was a lie. I went to St. Barts alone so I wouldn't have to suffer through Thanksgiving dinner with India and Kei."

India scoffs. "Looks like we aren't so different after all. I skipped the family gathering to avoid seeing you since Kei and I were going through a divorce. But making up a fake boyfriend is pretty pathetic, Zaire."

"You know what? You're not helping being so nasty when Zaire is hurting," Harlow-Rose says. "You should keep your opinions to yourself."

"Why did you go through all that trouble? Zaire, I don't understand," Sydney says, hurt clouding her eyes as she grabs my hand.

"I was so tired of the constant badgering about my love life. The questions were never-ending every time I talked to y'all. When was the last time I went on a date? When am I going to settle down? Hey, there's this great guy you should meet. I know y'all love me and your hearts were in the right place, but it got to be too much." I snatch my hand from hers and stalk over to the center bar to grab a glass of white wine. Chugging it until it's gone, I wipe my mouth, then place the glass on the counter. "No matter how happy I was and how much success I had with my businesses, that wasn't good enough. All of you kept asking when I was going to find a man. So, I made up one." I say, biting my bottom lip.

Mommy looks away. "Honey, I never meant to make you feel bad. I never wanted you to pretend to have a boyfriend when you didn't."

"The only way to get peace was to pretend I was in a relationship. The minute I told y'all I was dating someone, everything changed overnight. It was disappointing how quickly y'all felt better about me when you thought I had a man. I felt wretched for lying, but it made my life easier. So, I kept up the lie. Wiley's proposition was perfect timing after Persia moved her wedding to the Hill Country. I didn't have to figure out how to explain why my mystery man would miss the wedding. He was the perfect stand-in."

Sydney says, "You should've told me. I could've made everyone back off. You never need to lie to me, Zaire. I will always be there for you. I don't care if you have a man or not, as long as you're happy."

"Maybe so, but having Wiley on my arm was much better than enduring the looks of pity I'd get when I thought I'd be coming face to face with India and Kei for the first time in years."

"Nobody would look at you with pity, Honey," Mommy says, her brows knit in a frown.

"Really? Because you all are doing it right now. Poor Zaire got dumped again at the wedding of one of her sisters. She can't seem to keep a man or make a relationship work," I say, pulling away. "Only India has the guts to say that to my face. I know that's what everyone thinks, and I don't care anymore. I'm perfectly fine with who I am. I don't need a man to complete me or to make my life feel full."

"But you love Wiley," Mommy says, stepping toward me. "You can't hide that from any of us. We all can see it."

I can't force myself to admit what she's saying is true. Not in front of everyone, while my heart is an obliterated mess. "Wiley is a wonderful man. He's going to make some woman an amazing husband. But that person isn't me. We got close, but love was never part of our deal. The relationship and the engagement were fake. We planned out how it would end, and we would go our separate ways. That's all he's doing now. So, I don't want any of you trying to cast him as the bad guy because he isn't."

Sydney paces in front of me. "I don't care what kind of deal y'all made at the beginning. I saw the way Wiley looked at you. The way he treated you. The way y'all were together. That closeness and chemistry. You can't fake that."

"Stop it, Sydney, please. This isn't helping." I thought Wiley was developing the same feelings for me as I was for him, but I can't be sure. We kissed and shared special moments but never talked about what was happening between us. He refused to. I thought it was to wait until the lies were behind us, but maybe that was his way of letting me down easily. He didn't want to ruin the fake engagement by admitting that he wasn't falling for me like I was for him.

The time I spent with him over the past few weeks was the most genuine connection I've ever had with any man. It's killing me to face the stark realities that my feelings weren't reciprocated. Somehow, he made that connection with Persia, and I was clueless about it all.

Or maybe he didn't.

Maybe Brianna was right.

Wiley falls in and out of love so fast that no one woman can ever satisfy him. His interest in me had waned, and the best way to kill my feelings for him would be to subject me to the most horrible pain. I still can't believe that after everything he learned about me over the past few weeks, he humiliated me in the worst way possible.

"Can y'all call me when you hear anything about Persia?" I stumble away from my stunned family. "I need to get out of here."

CHAPTER 46

ILEY

HIGHWAY 290 IS CLOGGED WITH CARS ON CHRISTMAS
afternoon. I grip the steering wheel and wonder what I've gotten
myself into. The whole scene was like a nightmare. Persia crying and
screaming at me to take her away from the wedding while shock and
pain spread across Zaire's face. The beautiful love of my life was
confused and blindsided as I swooped Persia in my arms and carried
her out of the winery. I made a snap judgment call and can only hope I
chose right. Persia's frantic text had derailed all my plans.

PERSIA KINCAID

Wiley I need you. PLEASE come to the winery. I
can't do this. You're the only one who can
help me.

As I sped from Kimbell to Fredericksburg, I wasn't sure what to make of the text. Why Persia thought she needed my help had me stumped. But I had to help her for Zaire. No matter how much her spoiled brat of a sister annoys her, Zaire would want me to help Persia. Pulling over to the side of the road, I texted a quick message back.

on my way

Now Persia is stuffed in her poofy wedding dress in the passenger seat of my Ford F-150, crying her eyes out. She hasn't stopped crying since we left the winery. All my attempts to figure out what made her bail on marrying Yves were met with more wails and a rush of tears. I look at her face—puffy, bloodshot eyes, makeup a runny mess, hair disheveled. She keeps wiping her face with the fabric, leaving brown, red, and black smears on the expensive dress.

As her cries lessen to a whimper, I try one more time.

"What happened back there? Why did you leave Yves at the altar?"

She sniffs and grabs a tissue from the box in the center console. Blowing her nose, she tosses the snotty rag to the side and takes a deep breath.

"When did you know you loved Zaire?" Persia asks, staring at the side of my face.

I don't turn to look at her as my mind races through all the times I shared with Zaire. When was the first moment that it hit me? That I knew I was in love with her? The answer comes to me with crystal clarity.

"After our first date. I took Zaire to a drive-in to see the Princess Bride," I say, remembering how we cuddled in the back of my pickup truck. "I had promised her the best date of her life. At the end of the night, when she laid that stunning smile on me as I held her in my arms, I'd done what I'd set out to do. What I hadn't planned was falling head over heels in love with her at that exact moment."

"That is so romantic," Persia says, a wistfulness in her tone.

"Why did you ask me that?"

"I wanted to see if you could answer that question. Most people can, within reason, pinpoint that special moment when it hit them they were in love. Especially when the person is someone they want to spend the rest of their lives with like you do with Zaire."

"I take it you can't pinpoint that moment for yourself. You don't know when you fell in love with Yves?"

"Oh, I know when Yves stole my heart. The problem is that he doesn't know when he fell in love with me." A fresh set of tears flow from Persia's eyes. "I woke up this morning with so much anxiety and panic about marrying him. Mommy, Zaire, and Sydney were all trying to get me to calm down, but nothing was working. Until I realized only one person could help me relax."

"Yves. You wanted him to comfort you."

"I asked Mommy to get him so I could talk to him through the door. I didn't want to risk bad luck on my wedding day, but I needed him to calm me down. He came without hesitation, and I asked everyone to leave so we could talk alone."

"That's when you asked him to tell you the moment he fell in love with you," I say, feeling bad for Persia. "I'm guessing he couldn't tell you when and that ruined your day."

"I wish he couldn't remember. But he claimed he did. Then, he gave me this long, elaborate, wonderful, beautiful response, but it wasn't a moment he'd shared with me. He described something that he'd experienced with another woman. I listened to him and couldn't believe what I was hearing."

"Ouch, that's … terrible."

"I was too stunned to say anything to him, and then it was time for the wedding to start. I didn't know what to do. If I had told my family, they would've made an excuse for Yves and convinced me to go through with the wedding. So I texted you."

"Even though Zaire and I called off our engagement," I say, sticking to the lie we constructed to tell our families.

"You still love her, and you need to get back in her good graces," Persia says, squeezing my forearm. "What better way than to help her runaway bride sister?"

"Not too sure she's happy about this." A sickening feeling comes over me as I realize how this must've looked to Zaire. How it would remind her of what Kei did five years ago. The thought that she could suffer thinking the wrong thing about this situation makes my heart seize.

"Trust me, she will be once I'm through with you."

"What does that mean?"

"This disagreement over having kids is foolish. You would make a wonderful dad and should keep an open mind about all of this. Is it worth losing the woman you love because you can't imagine yourself being a father?"

"Absolutely ... not."

"I didn't think so." Persia smiles for the first time since we left the winery. "So, after you drop me off, you'll go back and convince Zaire to take you back, right? More than any of us, she deserves to have a man who adores and loves her."

"And where am I taking you—"

My cell phone rings again. Darren's number pops up on the screen in my truck.

"I need to take this one," I say.

Persia looks panicked but nods.

Tapping the talk button, I say, "What's up?"

"Where are you?" Darren demands.

"Better that you don't know."

"Persia is with you?"

"Yeah, she is."

"Fine, bring her to my place, and I'll take care of this. You need to go to Zaire while you still have a chance of salvaging your relationship," Darren says. His ominous tone has me on high alert.

"What happened?"

"The whole town is buzzing about what happened at the winery. Some think Zaire got dumped again for one of her sisters, but now the truth about you and Zaire faking your engagement is spreading like wildfire."

"Faking your engagement? What is he talking about?" Persia asks.

Darren continues, "Seems that there was some heavy Wiley bashing at the wedding after you left with Persia and Zaire stood up for you. She told all the guests that you weren't a bad person and had done nothing wrong because your engagement was fake from the beginning."

I slam on the brakes, then put my flashers on as I steer the truck to the next exit.

"This can't be happening. Why would she do that?" I mumble to myself. But I already know the answer, and I don't like it. By telling the town that our relationship was fake, that frees her up to go back to St. Barts guy—also known as Troy Renault. She can convince the town and herself that I don't have feelings for her, then go back to the man she wants, guilt-free.

"The whys don't matter right now. What does matter is you need to find her and set her straight. She needs to know that you fell in love with her and want to be with her more than anything," Darren says. "Trust me, Wiley. You don't want to let Zaire go. Going from being close to having it all, then losing it is much worse than never getting close in the first place."

"She doesn't want me," I shake my head. "She's still in love with the guy she went to St. Barts with. That's why she broke off our fake engagement and told everyone the truth. Gives her a chance to be with him."

"Are you crazy?" Darren and Persia say in unison.

Maybe.

"Look, I can't process why you and my sister would need to fake an engagement, and I don't need to know the details right now. All I know is that Zaire loves you. Whoever she went to St. Barts with can't compete with you," Persia says.

"I'm with Persia on this one. Sure, she had something with that guy, but whatever it was fizzled after Thanksgiving. That's why she went along with the fake relationship. There's a reason the whole town bought into y'all getting married. It's because we could see that the love between you, regardless of how it developed, is real."

"I don't know. After everything Zaire has been through, shouldn't I take the pressure off? Let her decide without forcing the issue?"

Persia says, "My sister is used to men walking away from her. She needs a man who will risk it all by staying and proving he wants to be with her."

Darren says, "Sounds like advice we both need to take. So, what are you going to do?"

"I'll take the chance if you do," I tell Darren, hoping he'll finally make his move with Jasmine.

"Let's do it. Good luck, my friend."

I end the call, then turn to look at Persia. "I don't know where to start."

"You don't need to know. That's why you have me," Persia says, bouncing in her seat. "I know how you can get Zaire back."

CHAPTER 47

Z AIRE

~

"THANKS FOR COMING," I SAY, LEANING AGAINST THE DOOR of my BMW. I'm shaking, and it has nothing to do with finding my front door ajar when I made it back to my house at Lake Lasso. Every time I think I'm past my disappointment and pain of watching Wiley carry Persia out of the winery, a fresh wave of sadness hits me.

"You were right to call me," Detective Jaxon Jones says, resting a hand on his police-issued gun. "How you feeling, Z? I heard about what happened at the wedding."

"Please don't say you're sorry about what happened to me. I can't take it," I say, glancing over at my old friend.

"Should I also not mention how insane I think it was for you and Wiley to lie about being engaged?" Jaxon asks, raising an eyebrow.

"Why don't you keep that part to yourself, too," I say, blowing a rush of air out of my mouth. "If I could go back in time—"

"You wouldn't change a thing, and you know it. You and Wiley were special. I'm not sure what's going on with this Persia situation, but I don't think it's what it seems. You need to talk to Wiley."

"Part of me agrees, but they've disappeared. Neither one of them is answering their phones. By the time they resurface, who knows if I'll care about the truth."

"Well, I, for one, am sick of your sisters screwing you over," Jaxon says, beckoning for me to follow him up the curving driveway to my lake house. "And that's all I'm going to say about that."

"Alright, Forrest," I say, chuckling. It's the first time I've felt a little lighter all day.

"What's the deal with the security app?" Jaxon asks as we stop at the edge of the portico leading to my front door.

"I couldn't log in. I'm not sure why the app is malfunctioning. Perfect timing, right?"

"And you only have exterior cameras. None on the inside?"

"That's right. The main panel is off to the left once you walk through the foyer. You can access any of the recordings from there."

"Wait here. I'll come get you once I check the place out." Jaxon eases out of his Kimbell Police Department jacket. He hands it to me. I realize I'm freezing for the first time, standing here on my lawn with the sleeveless bridesmaid dress on. The temperature has dipped into the high forties, with a blustery wind underneath the blanket of light gray clouds.

I wrap the jacket around my shoulders. The outdoor decorations flicker on as the clock strikes six, taunting me with holiday cheer when I'm feeling none of it.

Worst Christmas ever.

I shake my head, then kick at the inflatable Santa waving at me. He crumbles in on himself, then re-inflates as if I hadn't tried to give him a death blow.

Ten minutes later, Jaxon emerges.

"I got bad news and worse news. Which do you want to hear first, grinch?" Jaxon asks.

"With the way this day is going, why not pile on the worst you have?"

"While I was inside checking the house, it's clear by the way, I got a call from the forensic investigators pouring over the footage from the Lake Lasso Center parking lot. The video we've been scouring to get a trace of who slashed your tires—"

"You know who did it?"

Jaxon frowns. "Got a positive ID. Undeniable. Question is, will you want to press charges once you find out who it is?"

"I don't understand. Of course, I want to press charges. Whoever vandalized my car needs to pay for what they did."

"Even if that person is your estranged pregnant sister?"

"India?" I screech, unable to believe what I'm hearing. "You can't be serious."

"It was her." He hands me his cell phone, with still shots taken from the security footage and time stamps. The photos are undeniable. India, with a butcher knife in her hand, stabbing my car's tires.

"Why would she do that to me?"

"Come on, Z. She's been jealous of you since y'all were kids. Always trying to one-up you and failing miserably. I'm guessing she came to town divorced and found out you were engaged to the most sought-after dude in Kimbell. It set her off."

"I can't believe she hates me that much. I've always tried to be a good sister to her, but nothing I do can salvage the relationship."

"Some relationships you have to let go of. India is toxic. Until she can be happy with who she is, she won't ever be able to have a stable relationship with anyone—family, friends, or men."

"I can't press charges. She's pregnant, Jaxon. Mommy would be devastated."

"I'll make this disappear. You've dealt with enough, and I don't think you want this getting around town," Jaxon says.

I take a deep breath, realizing he has more bad news to drop on me. "What's the bad news?"

"Your intruder was Persia. Her wedding dress is in the middle of your living room, and it looks like she walked out wearing your clothes."

"Was Wiley with her?"

"Not that I could see on the footage. No sign of him or his truck."

"I wonder how she got here," I say, not expecting any answer. "How long ago was that?"

"About an hour ago. I'll give your folks a call and tell them. We can't divert resources since Persia is a grown woman who ran away because she wanted to, but the timeline should help with the folks out looking for her," Jaxon says, then wraps an arm around my shoulder. "The place is safe for you to go inside if you feel comfortable."

"All I want is a hot shower to wash this day away. Thanks for everything."

"Anytime. I'll have a black and white stationed nearby. If you get spooked, call, and an officer can be here in five minutes, okay?"

"Got it," I say, handing Jaxon his jacket back. He gives me a half-hug, then walks down the driveway to his police car.

Ignoring the dancing glittering lights on my house, I walk through the door and close it behind me. I lean against the wall and stare across the living room at the massive Christmas tree in the center. The sparkling white lights, silver and gold ribbons, ornaments, and bulbs shine beautifully in the darkened room. Persia's wedding dress is discarded in a heap to the left, next to the dozens of wrapped empty boxes underneath the tree.

The whole thing is for show, like my relationship with Wiley.

I never should've let myself fall for him.

As wonderful as the experience was, I can't see any joy in it now that I'm in so much pain. I stroll toward the tree, trying to remind myself that I've been through this before. I've had disappointments in love too many times to count, and each time, I pull myself together and find the strength to try again.

I will get over Wiley.

I'm not sure how long it will take, but a day will come when I will see him and not feel anything.

That day can't come soon enough.

Bending over, I pick up Persia's wedding dress and fold the massive fabric when a box catches my eye. It's small, wrapped in bright metallic red paper, standing out among the other gifts wrapped in silver and gold.

"What is this?" I drop the dress and lean over to pick up the box. Did Persia leave it behind for me? Maybe it's a note or something that will indicate where she's headed now that she's left her fiancé at the altar.

Kneeling on the floor, I untie the gorgeous sparkling red ribbon and tear off the paper. The blue box looks familiar. My heart pounds. I've seen this box before, and I know when. But how did it get here and why?

I take a deep breath and open the lid.

"Oh my God."

In the box is a thin platinum chain.

Dangling on the end is the stunning diamond ring Wiley placed on my finger weeks ago.

CHAPTER 48

ILEY

"HEY, BUTTERCUP."

My breath catches in my throat as she turns to face me. I take a moment to allow my gaze to roam along her body from head to toe and back again. Her elegance in the red sleeveless bridesmaid dress is undeniable. She takes my breath away. If what I felt for Zaire was only physical, this wouldn't be so hard. I wouldn't be scared out of my mind at how she will respond to what I need to say.

My heart sinks as I see the pure fury in her eyes, which are brimming with tears. She's holding her engagement ring dangling from the necklace in her right hand.

"You have some nerve coming here," Zaire says, clenching her fists.

I'm not sure what I expected, but her unbridled anger was not on the list. I take a deep breath, bracing myself to weather this storm.

"And this ..." She holds up the ring. "This is more cruel than watching you walk out of the winery with Persia in your arms."

Before I can duck, the ring comes hurling toward me, pelting me on the nose. It bounces off my face, and I catch it in my right hand.

"How could you do that to me? How could you be so cruel?" Zaire screams.

"I'm not the only one who was cruel," I say, unable to fight my frustration. I'm not sure Zaire and I will survive this conversation, but I'm certain it's one we need to have.

"You started the cruelty."

"Are you serious?" Zaire asks. "How? Enlighten me!"

"When you stood in the gazebo and took this ring off your finger and gave it back to me," I say, unable to stop my voice from choking with emotion. "You ripped my heart out."

Zaire's mouth falls open, but she doesn't say a word.

"We had gotten so close. You knew how important getting exposure from Heather's vlog was to me. Losing it felt like my world had imploded, and the only person I wanted by my side as I suffered through that loss was ... you." A sarcastic laugh slips from my mouth. "But when I needed you the most, you walked out on me. You abandoned me. You told me you didn't need me. How do you think I felt? I can tell you it was a lot worse than what you're feeling right now."

"So, was today some kind of payback? Is that why you left the wedding with Persia?"

"You think I'm capable of that?"

"I don't know what to think anymore!" Zaire yells. "None of this makes any sense to me. One minute we're getting closer, and your dating app has us as a ninety-eight percent love match, and the next, the app is wrong, and we can't seem to recapture the magic we had before."

"There was never any magic! What we felt for each other had nothing to do with algorithms and AI love match ratings. It was real and pure and existed between you and me. But you threw all of that away, and I know why." A sickening feeling spreads through my gut, killing all the hope I have about Zaire and me finding our way back to each other.

"You're trying to blame me for our relationship or whatever it was imploding. You're unbelievable."

"After we kissed, you wanted to talk about our future. I told you we should wait. Do you know why?"

"Because your feelings for me weren't strong enough. I was falling for you, and it reminded you of what you'd gone through with all those other girlfriends."

"That's crap, and you know it," I say, pointing my finger at her as I stomp across her living room.

"Really? If that's not why, then what is the reason? I'm tired of trying to guess what you're thinking and feeling. Be a man and tell me!" Zaire throws her hands in the air, closing the distance between us.

Her exasperation matches mine as we face off. If she comes any closer, I won't be able to stop myself from pulling her into my arms and kissing the breath out of her. But I need her to know what I feel for her is real. I'm not a heartless player she can sweep to the side and not take seriously. My feelings for her are strong. As strong as Troy's, and I'm going to force her to face that and deal with it.

"You're not available. Not completely. Someone else still has a hold of your heart."

A frown creases her face, and she shakes her head. "I don't know what you're talking about."

I squeeze the knot building at the base of my neck. She's protecting him. She has feelings for Troy. I don't know if I should fight for her if she won't tell me the truth about him. Resentment bursts out of me. "You don't know about St. Barts guy? The guy you cared so much about that you spent time away from your family to share the Thanksgiving holidays with him. You let everyone think I was the one by your side in paradise, but I wasn't. I'm not the man who made you blissfully happy that week. But I figured out who it is."

"St. Barts guy?" Zaire fumbles the words as her chest heaves with shaky breaths.

"Troy Renault," I say, spitting his name from my mouth. "All the pieces came together when Sydney and Matthieu told me about what you said when you were in St. Barts. Now it makes sense why the guy hated my guts. He'd spent an amazing week with you where y'all had fallen in love, then probably got into some stupid argument that he thought would blow over. But it didn't because I swooped in with the fake engagement. You used me as an excuse to not deal with your relationship with Troy. You love him. It was clear from what Sydney said about y'alls conversations when you were with him—"

Zaire bursts into laughter. The sound infectious and delightful. My anger melts into ... confusion.

"Damn it, Zaire. I'm being serious. Why are you laughing?"

She covers her mouth with her hands, then falls back onto the couch. Her body shakes as she tries to stop the giggles from escaping her lips. I yank at the buttons of my shirt, sending a couple skittering across the floor. Heat flames up my neck as I watch her writhing until she can gasp a few breaths and stop laughing. Slumping down on the ottoman across from her, I lean forward and wait for her to explain.

Her smile sends flutters through my heart, but I ignore the feeling. I forget everything she does to me because I need to know what is happening.

"Troy is not St. Barts guy ..."

CHAPTER 49

ILEY

"I CAN'T BELIEVE ALL THE TIME WE SPENT TOGETHER BEING fake engaged, you thought I was in love with Troy?" Zaire asks.

"Not the whole time. I didn't know who St. Barts Guy was until we talked to Sydney and Matthieu at Persia's wedding shower. I saw your face when they brought up everything you said and how they'd thought the man you'd gone to St. Barts with was Troy. You couldn't hide your panic at being exposed."

"Wiley! I told you before. I have no romantic feelings for Troy Renault," She says, unable to stop herself from laughing again. "Never have and never will. I don't care how many times he tries to force the issue. Yes, he showed up on the island and ambushed me. Trust me, I was not happy about the stunt he pulled, and I sent him packing. I was blunt, but it didn't seem to get through his thick skull. He still thought he had a chance with me until he found out about our engagement."

I throw up my hands. "Fine. If he's not St. Barts Guy, then who is? Who am I competing with for your heart?"

Zaire's smile fades. "You want to compete for *my* heart?"

"Buttercup, I wouldn't be here if I didn't. But only if you want me to. The last thing I want is to be like Troy, trying to be with you if you're not interested in a future with me." Saying the words stick in my throat, hurting more than I imagined they would. "The only thing I know about your relationship with St. Barts guy is what Sydney told me. You never ever talk about him." I shift from the ottoman over to the couch and sit down across from her, leaving a cushion between us. "We talked about all the relationships in our pasts that were significant. I told you about Izzie and Brianna. You told me about Kei. But it's like St. Barts guy was off limits. You wouldn't talk about him. I'm going crazy trying to piece together why. The only thing that makes sense is that you're still in love with him. Whatever you feel for me doesn't stop you from loving that guy. A guy whose name you won't tell me."

Standing, I walk over to the giant Christmas tree and focus on the glittery gold ribbons as I calm my pounding heart. This is too hard. I can't keep pouring out my heart to her and getting nothing in return. Maybe this is what I deserve. How many women have I done this to in the past? Five? Ten? More?

I can't complain when I'm getting a dose of my own medicine.

"St. Barts guy is you, Wiley," Zaire's voice interrupts my downward spiral.

I swivel around to look at her.

Her shoulders are slumped as she fidgets with her hands.

She won't look at me.

"I made him up," Zaire says, her voice shaking. "He was imaginary."

"He's not ... real?"

"No. Not exactly. He was supposed to be a culmination of all the positive experiences I'd had with men through the years, but the more I weaved lies about him, the more the stories sounded like … you. And the way he made me feel was how I felt spending all those weeks with you as you worked on the website for Kincaid Furnishings."

She still won't look at me. Walking back to the couch, I stand in front of her, gazing down at her stunning body as she stares at her feet in the crystal-encrusted stilettos.

"I don't understand." The words tumble from my mouth as I struggle to make sense of what I'm hearing.

"I think you do. You remember how much fun we had that month. How we were in sync and having a blast. I got to see firsthand what an amazing man you are. Not just handsome and charming, but deeper than that."

"I didn't think you noticed."

"I have a great poker face."

"Pretty one, too."

She looks up at me and smiles, causing my heart to leap.

"We got to know each other more than either of us realized. You are brilliant and passionate about your work. You care deeply for people and our community. You grab onto life and enjoy every moment, squeezing all the fun and excitement you can. While other people waste time focusing on what they don't have or their problems, you always find something that makes you laugh and others smile," Zaire says, her eyes never leaving mine. "I found you … fascinating. After the website was done, I kept thinking about you and how I wanted my next relationship to be with a man like you. I wanted someone with your qualities. I wanted that man to make me feel like you did."

I don't need to ask how I made her feel. Her eyes say it all. The look mends my broken heart, merging the pieces back together. For the first time since I got here, I'm hopeful again.

"How did that turn into me becoming your imaginary boyfriend without knowing it?" I ask.

"I realized no one knew what we'd been up to. Not my friends. Not your friends. No one. It was a secret that only you and I knew. It got me thinking that if we were sneaking around romantically, we would've kept it from the entire town." An adorable frown creases her brows as she sighs. "So, the next time Mommy called badgering me about neglecting my love life, I told her I had met a wonderful man and that we'd been seeing each other secretly."

"And that wonderful man was me?"

"Yes."

"But you had no plans of telling me you were interested?"

"No," Zaire shakes her head like the idea is preposterous. "Ninety percent of the women in this town are tripping all over themselves to get your attention. They all fantasize about dating you, and I had become one of them. It never crossed my mind that you were interested in me because you flirt with everybody."

"I used to. I don't notice other women anymore. That's your fault."

"Honestly, you were a means to an end. A way to get my family off my back. But real enough that when I talked about the secret boyfriend, I could think back to the time we were together and make the relationship sound authentic."

"Then the things Sydney told me you said about your secret man were about me?" I ask, sitting next to her. Our thighs and shoulders touch. I turn her face with my finger to look at me.

"Yes, Wiley. I said those things about you," Zaire says, fighting a smile.

"I was the one who made you deliriously happy?"

"Yes."

"And I was the one who was everything you didn't realize you wanted or needed in a man?"

She nods, biting her bottom lip in the sexiest way.

"You know what, Buttercup?"

"What?"

"You are the woman of my dreams. The woman I never thought I'd find but stumbled upon in the most jacked up of ways," I say.

Zaire's laughter fills the air.

"I'm going to put all my cards on the table right now." I push the sleeves of my shirt up higher on my arms, then take a deep breath. "I'm in love with you, Zaire. The seeds were planted months ago when we worked on your e-commerce website but blossomed the moment I took you on our first date. I don't need an algorithm to tell me you're my perfect love match. I know that right in here." I reach for her hand and press it against my heart.

Zaire stares at me. Her eyes roam over my face as if trying to memorize every detail. Nothing about her intense scrutiny makes me uncomfortable. It's impossible for me to feel anything but at ease with her. She's the only woman who has ever made me feel this way.

The anticipation of what she will say is killing me.

I'm about to break the silence when Zaire tilts her head to mine and places a sweet, delicate kiss on my lips. As she pulls away, her lips brush against mine, and she whispers, "I love you, Wiley."

Those four words are all I need to hear.

Scooping my arm around her waist, I pull Zaire onto my lap. She lets out a delightful squeal as I cover her mouth in a long, sensual, and passionate kiss.

CHAPTER 50

Z AIRE

~

"CAN I GET A HIGH FIVE FOR SAVING CHRISTMAS?" WILEY asks, holding up his hand. I roll my eyes and push past him, walking toward the back of his F-150. Lowering the tailgate, I feel a flutter of butterflies as Wiley steps behind me and effortlessly lifts me into the back cab. I'm not sure how he pulled off the basket of our favorite foods, plus the blankets and pillows, in a couple of hours, but he did. I turn toward him and hold my hand up.

"That's my Buttercup," Wiley says, slapping my hand.

"You know, I thought this would be the worst Christmas of my entire life. But you've made it the absolute best. Thank you for that," I say, grasping his hands. "Any word from Darren?"

I already know the answer, but I wait for him to confirm. Wiley filled my family and me in on his last moments with Persia. After she and Darren convinced him to find me, Wiley took Persia to Darren's house, where they switched to one of his cars and drove to my house. Persia used my security code to get in and change clothes, then disabled the camera over the garage so Wiley could sneak in undetected. Then, Persia accidentally left the door open, which stalled Wiley's plans to surprise me. He waited in a nook in the garage while Detective Jaxon Jones checked the house when I thought someone had broken in.

"Nothing new. He took her back to his house and gave her the keys to his Jeep. She insisted she needed some time alone and didn't tell him where she was headed. He hasn't heard from her since."

"I hope she's okay. At least we know what she's driving and the license plate. That will help us track her if we don't hear from her over the next few days," I say, still worried about my sister. Jaxon explained that because Persia left of her own free will, there's no reason for the cops to track her as a missing person. If she's gone for several days with no contact, that could be considered unusual behavior and allow them to start an official search. Until then, we have to wait and trust that Persia will reach out when she's ready.

"You sure you feel up to this?" Wiley asks, rubbing his hands over my goosebump-covered arms.

I look beyond him to the giant drive-in movie screen and nod.

"This is the distraction that I need," I say, pushing thoughts of Persia from my mind. "And this time, we get to watch one of my all-time favorite movies."

Wiley jumps up on the back of the truck and lands next to me. He slips an arm around my shoulder and pulls me into his arms, placing a sweet kiss on my forehead.

"Before we do that, there's one more thing I need to do for you while it's still Christmas," Wiley says.

"Trust me, you've already given me the best gift. I'm not sure you can top this." I wrap my arms around him. After everything we've been through, Wiley put his heart on the line and admitted he loves me when he was unsure that I felt the same way. His willingness to take that risk means the world to me, especially since I'd resigned myself to have another strike in the love column and move on. I'd gone through heartbreak many times in the past and knew I'd come out of it okay. Still, it's such a sweet feeling that I don't have to do that. This time, I was who Wiley wanted and needed. The man I'd fallen in love with was truly and completely in love with me, too.

"Will you let me try?" Wiley asks, a seriousness in his tone.

I lean against his muscular chest and kiss his neck. "Of course, Honey. What is it?"

"When you got back to your house, you found a small box wrapped in bright red Christmas paper. It's the gift that I want you to have," Wiley says, then leans over to reach into his pocket. He pulls out the platinum chain with the engagement ring looped onto the end and raises it in the air. "It's way too early for us to think about marriage. But this ring stopped being my grandmother's the minute I put it on your finger. I can't help but believe it's inevitable that we'll end up in the same place our fake relationship started."

"You proposing to me?" My words are breathy as I force them past the lump in my throat.

"With time, we're only going to grow closer and stronger. When the time is right, I will take this ring off the necklace and put it on your finger where it belongs," Wiley says, dangling the necklace as it swings through the air. "In the meantime, I want you to have it and wear it around your neck as a sign of our commitment to each other. It would mean the world to me. Will you do that?"

I swipe at the tears escaping my eyes as Wiley's aqua blue gaze settles on my face. "I'd love to." I dip my head as he places the necklace on me. My fingers grasp the ring, twirling it around. Light dances off the beautiful diamond, sparkling. "Best Christmas present ever," I say, then reach up to wrap my arms around Wiley's neck. Our lips find each other in a playful, silly kiss that grows more intense. The passion and sensuality overtake me as the full breadth of Wiley's love for me is unrestrained. I return it with the same intense fervor. Seconds turn to minutes as we lose ourselves in the decadent kiss, exploring and enjoying every single minute. Wiley breaks the kiss against my protests as we both heave deep breaths.

"Agreeing to be your fake fiancée was the best decision I ever made," I say, swiping my red lipstick off his lips. "Now we need to figure out how to explain to everyone that while we were faking being in love and engaged, we fell in love for real, but we're not engaged yet, though we expect to be in the future."

"Yeah, that's going to blow everybody's mind," Wiley says as he bursts into laughter. "Clear as mud, right? Or we can say nothing and let them wonder as we go around town as a couple. That might be a lot more fun."

"So, what should be the first thing we do as an official couple?"

Wiley frowns. "Isn't this it?"

"Technically, yes. Okay. Second thing, then." I amend my question.

"I have an idea, but I'm not sure I should say it," Wiley says.

"Now, I'm intrigued. What is it?"

"Hold on, let me consult my trusty magic eight ball. It's never steered me wrong." Wiley pulls his cell phone from his pocket and taps on an app. Shaking the phone in the air for a few seconds, he stops and reads the display. "Outlook not so good."

"I thought we were done letting algorithms control us," I say, playfully slapping the cell phone from his hands. "Your heart should tell you otherwise."

"Well, in that case, I think the real St. Barts guy," He says, pointing a finger at his face, then continues, "deserves a chance to go to St. Barts for real with the woman he loves. Maybe for New Years?"

"I love the way you think."

"And I love you, Buttercup."

"Right back at you," I say. "Shall we watch my favorite movie now?"

"As you wish," Wiley says.

A bright smile stretches across my face as Wiley lifts me and places me on the blankets and the pillows. We maneuver into a more comfortable position, with me resting in his arms as he covers our bodies with the throw blankets.

I reach into the picnic basket and grab a Fun Dip candy for Wiley and Buncha Crunch for me.

"So, will you tell me what we'll be watching tonight?" Wiley asks as he hands me his cell phone.

I launch the app that connects the streaming movies to the drive-in theater's projector and find the best movie for the end of the best Christmas Day.

"The best holiday movie ever ... Love Actually!"

CHAPTER 51

W

ILEY

One Week Later

"I DON'T KNOW WHY YOU WOULDN'T LET ME BOOK A charter," Zaire says, arms crossed over her chest and a sexy scowl on her face. "Standing in this line is ridiculous. We could be sipping champagne on the private jet right now."

Leaning forward, I kiss the scowl away and bask in Zaire, slipping her arms around my waist.

"Because Buttercup, as much as I enjoy letting the whole town of Kimbell believe that you're my sugar mama, I don't want you to be my sugar mama," I say, wrapping my arms around her. "But I did splurge to get us first class. I hope that makes up for you dealing with the masses."

Luckily, the first-class tickets didn't require me to empty my savings account, and Darren pulled some strings to help me rent a luxury villa in the mountains overlooking Gustavia Harbor in St. Barts.

A trip that I wasn't sure we'd take until Zaire and her family heard from Persia. The phone call came the day after Christmas, and despite not revealing where she was located, Persia explained to her family why she'd walked away from Yves at the altar. They were as supportive as I expected once they understood why Persia felt she and Yves weren't meant to be. Although Persia refused to tell them where she was, Zaire convinced her youngest sister to text and call them every other day so they wouldn't worry. So far, Persia was holding up her end of the agreement, and Zaire and I were free to escape to paradise without a cloud hovering over us.

Zaire chuckles against my chest. "I'm sorry. Please tell me I'm not turning into Persia! That sounds like something she'd say."

"Nothing wrong with enjoying the finer things in life," I say.

"And you are at the top of the list of the finer things, Wiley," Zaire says with a dreamy sigh. "I can't wait to ring in the New Year with you as my man tonight."

"Me too," I say, at ease with being in love with Zaire. She's everything I ever wanted in a woman, and I have zero doubts about my feelings for her.

We inch a few feet closer to the plane's door, squeezed between a large wedding party and two other couples probably headed to their honeymoon. Anyone looking at Zaire and me would guess that we were going on our honeymoon, too, instead of our second official date as a real couple. I'm setting the bar pretty high, but seeing that gorgeous smile on Zaire's face is worth it. I would do anything to make her happy.

"Do you know what I heard while grabbing snacks from Elevation Cupcake Shop this morning?" Zaire says, pulling away from me. I keep my arms around her so she can't get too far.

"What?"

"The whole town is convinced that my outburst at Persia's wedding was a lie and that we staged it so we could sneak off to St. Barts and elope. There's a wagering board at Baker Bros, and the pot is large," Zaire says, shaking her head.

"How large is large?" I wonder why Darren or Ronan didn't tell me about this.

"Almost ten thousand, with most people thinking we'll come back, Mr. and Mrs. Wiley Alexander."

"Ma still would prefer me to take your last name and become a Kincaid—wait, that's why she called me this morning to reiterate that. She must think we're sneaking off to elope, too," I say, laughing. I'm tempted to call the Baker Brothers and put a wager against it anonymously, of course, but I resist the urge.

Zaire pulls the platinum necklace from underneath her shirt and holds the engagement ring between her fingers. She looks at it wistfully. "You still think we'll end up where we started?"

"You mean me holed up in your house working on an e-commerce site in the middle of the night for days?"

"You got jokes now, Wiley? I'm trying to be serious."

"Serious is overrated."

"Tell me about it."

"To answer your question, yes, I will ask you to marry me for real. The question is, what will you answer?"

"Hmm, what will I answer?" Zaire says, a playful glint in her eyes. "I'm going to need some time to think about that. Might need to consult your magic eight ball."

I give her side a playful pinch, and she squeals.

"But I want to give you all the time you need to be certain about us. We both need that … for different reasons. We made the right decision to do this our way and ignore all the pressure and input from everyone else about our relationship."

"Despite what they like to think, they don't get a vote on what we do," Zaire says.

"I, for one, am going to enjoy doing all the things we would've done if we'd been honest with each other months ago about our mutual attraction and interest," I say, giving her all the seriousness she's requesting. "I don't want to rush anything. I love you too much to not give us the time to explore all the aspects of being in a relationship with each other. The ups and downs."

"You need to discover all the things about me that will drive you crazy."

"And you need to see me in the morning when I'm … ugly."

Zaire gives a mock gasp.

I hold her hand and pull her forward as she pretends to get away. A few more shuffling steps, and we're on the plane. Zaire settles into the seat by the window as I grab our laptops from our carry-on luggage and lift the bags into the overhead compartment. I turn to see the flight attendant, a petite woman with long brown hair, gaping at me as her face flushes.

"Can I get you something to drink?" The flight attendant asks.

"Yes, my girlfriend and I would love a couple of glasses of champagne," I say, then ease down into the seat next to Zaire. I place her laptop on the tray table in front of her.

"She looked so crushed when you called me your girlfriend," Zaire says, shaking her head.

"Did she? I didn't notice," I say, then lean over to kiss Zaire. "Now, here are the rules. You can work only while we're on the plane. The minute we touch down on the island, laptops go away, and you're all mine. Got it."

"I'm already all yours," Zaire says with a wink.

Her words go straight to my heart, and I feel like the luckiest man in the world. "Don't distract me with sweet talk. You wanted serious. This is me being serious."

"Fine!" Zaire says, booting up her laptop.

My cell phone rings as I lower the tray table and place my laptop on top. Reaching into my pocket, I pull it out and glance at the screen.

Even though I deleted her from my contacts, I still recognize the New York area code phone number.

"Is that your mom?" Zaire asks.

"No, but I need to take it," I say, hoping Zaire doesn't ask any more questions.

I turn away from her and lower my voice as I answer. "Hello."

"Wiley, this is Heather Grimley. I hope I caught you before you left the country."

My heart thuds in my throat. The last thing I need is to find out that Heather plans to switch the focus of her feature from dating apps of the future to hustlers using misleading marketing to sucker people looking for love into joining a fake AI dating app. That's the spin she'd try to put on things, even though it's not true.

"How did you know I was leaving the country?"

"Well, because I'm in Kimbell now with a friend of yours … Darren Manning."

"You're with Darren. Why?"

"I have great news. I was hoping to get his help to surprise you and your fiancée. As we worked on the feature, we realized the tests we ran on your dating app were flawed."

"Flawed?"

"Yes, your algorithm changes the order of the questions each time a new subscriber joins the dating app. We didn't consider that, so my experts weren't submitting identical submissions into your app."

"Which explains why the results were all different," I say, sneaking a glance at Zaire. She's focused, typing on the keyboard with earbuds in her ears.

"Once we realized our mistake, we reconstructed our tests, and your dating app passed with flying colors. It is the most accurate and sound of all the dating apps, using an impressive algorithm based on artificial intelligence—"

"Wait, so that means all the results the app has delivered since inception were … right. They weren't random but reflected real love match likelihood."

"By our estimation, yes. The app works as you designed and pulls from the research you used to formulate your love match methodology," Heather confirms.

I steal another look at Zaire. "So we are a ninety-eight percent love match."

"I'm sorry? I don't understand," Heather says.

"So, what does this mean?"

"It means I want to do my Valentine's Day feature on your dating app and how you used it to find the love of your life," Heather says. I can hear her excitement through the phone. "Mr. Manning told me you'd be away on vacation in the Caribbean for the next five days. I don't mind sticking around Kimbell until you get back so we can film the segment. This is the game-changer you need to catapult your dating app to national success. You could become a household name in the business of love. What do you say?"

Zaire looks over at me and removes an earbud from one ear. "Everything okay?"

I mute my cell phone. Zaire rests her hand on mine, squeezing it as a look of concern etches across her face.

"Everything is perfect, Buttercup."

She knocks me over with another one of those devastating smiles, then quickly kisses my lips.

Turning my attention back to the call with Heather, I unmute the line and say, "Thanks for the offer, but I'm not interested. Turns out I already have everything I need."

Want more of Wiley and Zaire? Get a bonus alternative ending to their love story delivered straight to your email inbox!
https://BookHip.com/QBQGJXK

Next up to find love in Kimbell, Texas is Wiley's friend Darren Manning. Ex-pro football player Darren Manning has had his fair share of women, but not the one he's loved since he was six years old—his best friend, Dr. Jasmine Jones. When Jasmine makes a New Year's resolution to find the man of her dreams, Darren is determined to be the one she finds …

Check out the next book in the Kimbell Texas Sweet Romances …
WANTING MORE!

ABOUT THE AUTHOR

Angel S. Vane never imagined she'd stumble into becoming an author. An avid fan of books her whole life combined with an active imagination were the right ingredients to embark on a single goal of completing one book.

Now she's written several books and has tapped into her love of Jane Austen novels by writing her own brand of satisfyingly sweet romances. Learn more at Angel's website.

ABOUT THE PUBLISHER

BONZAIMOON BOOKS

BonzaiMoon Books is a family-run, artisanal publishing company created in the summer of 2014. We publish works of fiction in various genres. Our passion and focus is working with authors who write the books you want to read, and giving those authors the opportunity to have more direct input in the publishing of their work.

For more information:
www.bonzaimoonbooks.com
info@bonzaimoonbooks.com

facebook.com/BonzaiMoonBooks